The Long Forgetting

R. P. Poe

Yesterday and tomorrow cross and mix on the skyline.
The two are lost in a purple haze. One forgets. One waits.

-Carl Sandburg

It is not enough for a man to know how to ride;
he must know how to fall.

-Mexican proverb

For Linda and Priscilla, their kind words,
their encouragement

Part One

Love is so short, forgetting is so long.

-Pablo Neruda

Chapter One

Past unhorsed present. Her faded image hovered within his sight, looking out at him from a frame tarnished by age and neglect, her gaze a perfect retribution, the payment made in years of days, hours, minutes, the shame familiar, wizened but tough, knowing where to prod, a constant reminder of his failings. He hunched up his shoulders against the thought, moving through a house once hers but now his by squatter's rights, a place of habitation without refuge, of value long forgotten.

Angling toward the front door with his one-sided limp, he stopped and stood idle, staring through the rusted screen at the bright of midday but seeing little, his mind's eye still caught in a place beyond reclaiming, loosed to the swirl of time like the coursing wind, capricious and changeable. A sudden cloud passing across the sun cast the room in indigo, pulling him back into the moment. Then a car door slammed shut. He took a breath and moved to the entryway, trying to prepare himself while his son's footsteps sounded on the gravel drive.

Webb looked up as his father stepped through the door and moved to the top stair, his hands in his back pockets, his good eye studying Webb the way it might a horse, sizing him up, looking for weakness, expecting it even. Horses he knew. He'd once had a stable full but gave them up sometime after Webb's mother left, instead retreating from the world like a spoken word lost to the wind, as closed to his son as a scar-sealed wound. He peered at Webb in his usual way, silent, ineffable.

To Webb's way of thinking his cloudy eye still seemed the wiser of the two, as if blindness was the price of understanding. In his father's case, he could believe it. He saw in his son only what he wished to see. He had lost use of the eye to a ricocheted bullet while surveying for

1

rabies down along the Nueces River, south of Crystal City. The authorities guessed he had spooked up some smugglers. Squinting at Webb, he again hunched up his bony shoulders, never taking his hands from his pockets.

"Well?"

"Well, yourself." Webb squinted back, in no mood to play his game.

"What do you have to say, then?"

"I got nothing. It was you that asked me all the way out here. Or don't you remember?"

"Sure I do."

"You know, not remembering is what happens when you get on in…"

He poked a gnarled finger into the space between them, glaring at his son.

"My memory works good as it always did, if that's what you're getting at."

"Then why am I here?"

"I'm not as old as you think," he continued. "You just believe that way because you're young and figure you know what's what. A man who starts thinking he knows it all stops seeing the world as it is."

"I never claimed that."

"You'll find out you're wrong soon enough."

"Did you ask me out here just to have someone to argue with, Maves?"

He had started calling his father by his first name after his mother was gone and it was just the two of them in the cramped house. Without her around to keep the peace, he slipped into the surly existence of a motherless teenager. He took care of himself and Maves did the same. Most everyone thought his father's full name was Maverick Van Horn but Webb knew his French grandmother had named her son Mavis, in that language meaning joy. A bitter smile crossed his lips at the thought. Maves looked at him askance.

"Did I miss something?"

"I don't know, did you?"

"You're grinning like a whipped dog."

Webb lost the smile, knowing his father had more than enough reason for his somber ways. He held up both hands, palms out.

"Let's start again, Maves. Why *did* you ask me down here?"

"I suppose the practice of having a visit before you get to your point is long gone. People in this day and age just want to get on with it, whatever *it* happens to be. Well, at my house I'm going to follow what I was taught, so come on in and let's get us something cold to drink before we set to the matter at hand."

He disappeared through the door. Webb mounted the top stair and hesitated, turning toward the rock-strewn hills, the land below him falling away, stretching southward, vast, formidable, cut by dry wash and arroyo, thick with mesquite and juniper. Further on, the tepid flow of the Rio Grande meandered between sand banks and cane breaks, the strangled river no match for the fuming heat. Further still, the saw tooth line of the Sierra Del Carmen range loomed above the torn horizon, their wildness beyond hope of understanding.

The land still held him even after so long, as if from his mother's blood some essence of dirt and wind had passed, a dark tincture flowing beneath his skin, restless and unquiet. His father had none of it, instead the cool of stone his sole nomenclature. That Webb's mother had left him at a young age, a boy not yet a man but expected by his father to be so, had always haunted him. The reasons never spoken, he was left to blame them both as the cause, or neither, finally settling on himself, the black bile in his veins then turning white hot, incandescent but for the tight hold of will and effort.

Passing through the doorway, he crossed the creaking floor of the front room before stepping into the small kitchen. The quiet air smelled of dust and camphor. Maves

3

set two bottles on the table, popping them open with a rusted church key and sliding one toward him. Beads of sweat trailed down the brown glass.

He lifted his beer, taking a long pull as he studied his son, wondering how he would take the news he was about to hear. The unsettling possibility Webb held no affection for him crossed his thoughts. He turned his gaze to the window and again considered the chasm between them, tracing the thread of time to where it began, recalling the moment his wife had walked out the door, disgust clear in her eyes, the sting of her ire known then and felt again now as if new. Regret swelled in his throat though the sentiment seemed almost pointless after so long. He turned back to face his son, doing his best to sound friendly.

"How is work?"

Webb stared at him, surprised by the question. Maves rarely asked anything personal.

"Why do you ask?"

"Are they treating you alright?"

Feeling his father's critical gaze, he searched for a way around answering.

"I'm between jobs."

"You change jobs," he groused, "like women change clothes."

"The truth is, the company was bought by a competitor," he lied.

"Whatever the reason, it looks bad to switch so much. Why can't you find something permanent?"

"I've already been approached about another position," he lied again, figuring another made little difference. "If it works out I'll probably even see a pay increase."

"You're going to be alright, then?"

"Do you have a reason for asking, Maves, or is this just us visiting?"

"I know we haven't done enough talking between us," he mumbled, ashamed to admit it, "or I haven't anyway. But we'll have time to catch up while we're on the road."

"Here it comes," Webb snorted. "What road is that, Maves?

"I asked you here because I'd like you to take a trip down south with me, west of the Devil's River, near Langtry."

"You want to take a vacation? If Langtry is your idea of fun, I can think of about a hundred better places to go."

Maves' expression turned grave.

"There'll be no fun to it, Webb. An old friend has asked for my help and I mean to do what I can. I'll go on my own if I have to but I could use a hand. Understand it could get dicey. We'll be crossing the border and you know the danger down there these days."

"Why go across, then?"

"My friend needs to get out from under trouble and can't exactly cross in the normal way."

"You're asking me to help sneak someone across the border?" he said, incredulous. "Do you know what they'll do if they catch us?"

Maves glared at him. "I spent twenty years patrolling those back roads, remember?"

"I'm just surprised you'd want to take the chance, knowing what you do."

"Then you know I wouldn't do it unless I had good reason, just like I wouldn't ask you to take the risk if I didn't need your help."

Realizing his father rarely asked for anyone's help, he decided he must go.

"Alright then, what's your plan?"

"A friend near there has a boat. We'll put in at the western edge of the park, near Seminole Canyon. There's a spot upriver from the lake that's fairly narrow but deep enough for a boat. At least, I believe it is. I guess we'll find out one way or the other when we get there. If it all works

5

out, we'll pick up my friend and hightail it back across before the Border Patrol gets wind of us."

"When is all this supposed to happen?"

"We're due to meet up this afternoon and cross a little after midnight."

Webb tilted his head back and drained his beer. Setting the bottle aside, he leaned toward his father, a smirk on his face.

"You're mighty sure of yourself, counting on me to just drop everything and get myself down here on the spur of the moment."

"I know it's sudden and all," he replied, slowly shaking his head, "but I had no choice in the matter. Time is running short."

"Why is that?"

"My friend needs to get out soon. That's all I know." He pointed to the window. "The truck is out back."

Webb stood and started for the door. "Then we best get on with it."

Maves ran a hand through his thinning hair, knowing his deceit, trying to remind himself of the necessity, hoping his son would forgive him of it and more when the time came. The tattered photograph of Webb's mother peered out at him from atop the mahogany bureau, the burn of judgment still in her eyes. He paused in the doorway, the past again stirring in him like an illness, recurring, malarial. Then he turned the frame on its face and stepped through.

Chapter Two

A dry wind swirled through the truck, rattling empty beer cans and stirring loose papers beneath the seat. Otherwise, they rode in silence. Beyond the windshield the two-lane road stretched into the distance, disappearing amid mercurial pools of reflected light. Though the unblinking sun of summer had yet to fill the sky with its white heat, the drought-plagued land already stood bleached to a hue almost free of color. Ivory streaks of cloud stretched above the horizon like dry-brushed paint, the blue behind them depthless and clear.

Maves stared into the midday glare, the weight of his past pressing in on him. Though he knew he must soon tell Webb the truth, he had little idea how he would go about it. For the moment, saying nothing seemed the easier course. He swallowed hard, despising himself for the deception.

Then out of habit he did what he always had, forcing the thought from his mind, instead imagining the friend he would soon see. Abel Ordaz had worked along the border his entire life, making a living in a dozen ways from short order cook to carpenter. Seeing his round face, wild hair and drooping mustache never failed to lift Maves' spirit. He hoped history would hold true once again.

They rounded a curve and the road fell away in a sudden shift from hill to plain, descending the face of a massive bluff that flanked the truck on both sides. Below them the open landscape reached toward Mexico, razor-straight and without feature. The sky loomed above the road, vast, wall-like, somehow altered in the moment, a white haze filling the air, thick and oppressive. Maves recalled the feeling, as if the truck, the highway, even the two of them shrank beneath its weight.

They followed the road for an hour more, passing acres of wilting corn and in and out of small towns, some no more than a post office and single blinking light. The flat plain stretched out before them. Abandoned farmhouses sun-bleached to a dull gray appeared along the roadside, their sagging roofs marking the passage of time. Needing no such reminders, Maves looked away.

The land changed yet again, regaining feature and form. Sharp hilltops capped with outcroppings of limestone and granite pierced the ragged horizon. Cottonwoods marked meandering creeks. Maves slowed the truck as the scattered buildings of a town came into view beyond a well-kept cemetery. Low-slung frame houses lined the street, their yards crowded with goats and chickens. Vegetable gardens shared space with broken-down cars.

Pulling into a short driveway, he parked next to a green, two-tone panel truck that could be mistaken for Border Patrol. He wondered what use his friend might have for such a vehicle. In front of him, a carport lined with crab traps and fishnets held a large freezer while a nearby barbeque pit poured smoke into the air.

He turned as Abel's round form appeared in the doorway. The lilting sound of accordion music drifted from an open window and he began dancing down the porch, humming a lively tune under his breath. Maves climbed from the truck and glanced at Webb, expecting his disapproval, but his son's face held no emotion. Stopping at the edge of the porch, Abel pointed to the smoking pit.

"I got the cojunto music on, a big brisket on the grill and some beer in the cooler. Sit yourselves down. It's a little hot out but not too bad in the shade and nothing like it will be later on. Enjoy the good life while you can is Abel's advice to the Van Horn muchachos."

He shook Maves' hand, nodding at Webb.

"This must be that son I always heard about. I was starting to think you just made him up. Good thing he didn't turn out ugly like his father."

Maves squinted at him. "Is that why you never had kids of your own?"

"No, I got kids scattered over five counties. I just don't know who they are and they're afraid to come tell me."

He shook Webb's hand and pointed him toward a chair before fishing several cans of beer out of the ice. Maves sat and leaned toward him.

"Save the Ordaz family tree for later. Tell us about your new vehicle. Funny choice of colors, don't you think?"

"What do you mean?" he said, feigning anger. "That is a quality paint job, Maves. My uncle, he did it for me."

"That truck doesn't make some folks around here a tad nervous when they see it coming?"

"It did a little at first," he said, chuckling, "but they got used to it. Besides, everybody knows that paint job is perfect if you want to do business down along the river.

"And what business would that be, Abel?"

"I started me up a fishing guide service, Maves. We finally got us some water in the lake and now you can *see* the fish you want to catch, pick him right out even if he's forty feet down. That damn lake is like bath water. And with all the brush that grew up during the drought, the fish are growing into monsters. People are coming from all over to fish here."

"Is that all you do down on the river?"

"Well, I do a little transporting from time to time."

"Transporting is an interesting choice of words." Maves winked at Webb. "Wouldn't you say so?"

"It depends on what gets transported." Webb tried to look thoughtful as he sipped his beer. "I suppose that word could include almost anything, legal or otherwise."

"I am just trying to encourage free trade between Mexico and Del Norte." Abel did his best to look offended. "What's wrong with that, young Van Horn?"

Webb shrugged. "I wouldn't know, Abel. Speaking of the river, can we talk about the plan for tonight?"

The smile vanished from his face. He turned to Maves.

"We have a change of plan for our cargo."

Maves stiffened at the word. "Is there a problem?"

"I don't know for sure." He ran a hand through his wild hair. "Things in Mexico change day to day. It's hard to know what to expect."

"How has the plan changed, then?"

"We don't cross to the other side."

"They're coming to us?"

"No, we meet in the middle. The hand off will happen there."

"But how will we find them in the middle of a river at night? We can't use any lights unless we want to bring the law down on us."

"It won't be easy, Maves. They also changed the time to just after dark. Not so bueno. The good news is a boat out on the water just after sunset is not so suspicious as one out after midnight."

"I don't like it, Abel. Why the changes?"

"The word from my cousin is the federales are on high alert after a new set of beheadings by one of the damn drug cartels."

"That's bad timing for us but I guess we don't have much say in the matter."

"We got no say in it. You sure you still want to do this, Maves?"

"I'm sure."

"This friend of yours must be important people."

Maves nodded, wondering at the wisdom of his plan but seeing no alternative.

"I suppose I owe them this much."

Abel stood and lifted the lid from the pit. A cloud of smoke swirled about him as he spoke.

"Well then, we got us some time to waste. Grab another beer, Maves. I want to hear what you've been doing with yourself."

"You know about all there is. Things haven't changed much."

"You never were much of a talker. But you got to do better than that for your old friend. What about that vet business of yours? Are you still spending the night with large animals?"

"When I have to, I am."

He lowered the lid and faced Webb.

"When we were working the survey together, Maves would go on and on about a horse that almost lost its foal or how some big bull just missed running him down. I wanted to talk about girls or football and all I could get from him was animal stories. Of course, he had a family and had to settle down a little. But we still had our share of wild times."

"Wild times involving Maves?" he scoffed. "That's hard to imagine."

"You mean he hasn't ever told you about them? I mean, when you were a kid I could understand but once you got grown I figured he would spill the frijoles."

"Like you said, Maves is not one for talking. Make that double when it comes to his family."

Abel chuckled, shaking a finger at Maves.

"You remember those girls we rescued down in Piedras Negras?"

Maves squinted at him, looking for a way to change the subject.

"I'm not much interested in reliving the past, Abel. Tell us about your guide business instead."

Abel turned to Webb, a grin on his face.

"You know how low-key your dad is, right? Nothing ever riles old Maves, I mean nothing. Well, we were in this bar and this bad dude starts harassing these two good-looking chicas. One was tall and glamorous, the other shorter but real cute, like the girl next door only better. I mean, these women looked like models or something. Anyway, pretty soon this guy slaps one of them, hits her hard, and before I knew what was happening Maves had the guy up against the bar with a broken bottle pressed to his face."

"Abel, are you sure you're not thinking of someone else?" He glanced at his father. "Maybe you'd had a few too many."

Abel took a long pull on his beer, waving his hand through the air.

"We had just gotten there, Webb. I'd had maybe half a beer. I'll never forget the look on that dude's face. He was so scared I thought he might piss himself."

"What happened then?"

"We got the hell out."

"What about the women?"

"They came with us."

Webb leaned back in his chair, surprised at the thought. "They left with a couple of strangers?"

"What the hell else were they going to do? They sure couldn't stay. Anyway, that was my lucky day. Me and Rosie, the tall one, had it hot and heavy for awhile. Those were some good times.

"Then she left me for a rich guy from San Antonio. I can't say I blame her. This is not exactly your beautiful model's dream home." He pointed his beer at Maves. "Didn't you stay in touch with the little one? What was her name?"

"It was a long time back, Abel. I prefer to live in the here and now."

Abel ignored him, instead turning to Webb."

"Don't get the wrong idea here, Webb. I don't mean no hanky-panky like with me and Rosie."

Webb peered at his father, sensing he was holding back.

"Well, Maves, what was her name?"

"I don't recall at the moment."

"And did you stay in touch with her?"

Maves squinted at him, looking for a way out but finding none.

"I did until I could be sure she was safe. Other than that, I don't remember much. Like I said, it happened a long time ago."

Abel grunted his agreement.

"Fifteen years is a long time, Maves, too long for old friends to see so little of each other. In all those years you've been down here maybe three or four times?"

He nodded, his regrets again crowding in. "Time has a way of slipping by, Abel."

"But we had ourselves some adventures back then, didn't we? You remember old Riley Banks? He had a wild streak and those strange blue eyes, like ice or something. I still wish I had been with you and him that day he got shot, Maves. Maybe things would've turned out different."

"I can't change the past, Abel." He shook his head, refusing to let the memory return. "So I don't allow myself to think about it."

Abel whistled through his teeth. "That's a hard line to take, Maves. There's still a good memory or two lying around back there."

Webb looked askance at his father.

"Are you sure that's all you remember?"

"Why wouldn't it be?"

"That scene in the bar sounded like a close call. I'd expect it to stay with you."

Maves glowered at him. "I've said what I have to say."

"Why don't you ever talk about those times?"

"I'm done talking about them," he barked. "The past is past, so leave it alone!"

He turned away, the untruth of the words catching in his throat.

Chapter Three

A gibbous moon sat low in the west as Abel angled the panel truck down a pothole-covered road ending at a marina tucked between sheer bluffs. Maves surveyed the towering cliffs, figuring the lower to reach at least two hundred feet above them. A narrow finger of water led from the marina to the main part of lake, at that point no more than a river channel, and on to the town of Langtry, a dozen miles upriver. The area had changed little from his days as a health department veterinarian.

Dusk had settled onto the canyon floor, although sunset still blazed on the open water despite the late hour. Abel pulled next to the gangway and hopped out, pulling several fishing rods from the rear of the truck and thrusting them into Webb's arms. Grabbing a tattered duffle bag, he headed down the floating walkway toward a low-slung boat moored at a middle slip. Webb staggered along behind him.

Maves peered up into the fading light, hoping his determination to follow through with the plan was not a mistake. He had little idea what to expect. Yet in spite of the risk he felt compelled to continue, the shame of his past forcing him along, leaving no room for turning back. He had let down too many people to quit now.

Webb looked back down the walkway at his father, wondering why he still stood next to the truck. Maves could be cool and distant, his analytical mind turning all he saw into problems and solutions, but he seemed changed, the usual calm detachment replaced by a grim restlessness. He passed the fishing rods to Abel and motioned him to join them.

Moments later they were passing beneath the cliffs, the limestone sides scattered with cactus and sage, the lower portions scrubbed by eons of moving water to a smooth sheen. Clouds of swallows swarmed about rock overhangs and shallow caves. Above the bluff, a turkey

14

vulture searching for an evening roost tilted against the amber sky.

Webb studied his father's sharp profile, the furrowed lines of his brow highlighted by the slanting light, and again puzzled over his mysterious past. What was he unwilling to face? Why the anger over his questions? Maves turned and stared at him with a familiar intensity, his good eye clear and intimidating. Webb returned his gaze, relieved to see the look still there.

The boat rounded the cliff, turning into the main channel of the lake and angling along the broken shoreline. Before them the moon perched on the horizon like a half-closed eye, red and misshapen. The wind-tossed lake pulsed with the somber hues of dusk.

Cutting the engine, Abel grabbed two fishing rods, handing one each to Webb and Maves. Then he lowered the trolling motor, flipping it on before busying himself about the boat. After a moment, he stopped and looked at the two of them.

"You hombres get to fishing," he snapped. "We need to look legit if we don't want to attract the wrong sort of attention. I'll keep an eye out for my contact."

Webb moved to where he stood amid the growing darkness. "Who is your contact?"

"We're meeting my cousin, Raul. But we could be in for a long wait. The man is late for every damn thing."

"And who is it that he's bringing across?"

"He didn't know and neither do I. You'll have to ask Maves but I'll bet he won't say."

Webb hated asking his father for anything but wanted to know why he needed their help.

"What about it, Maves? Who are we waiting on?"

"Like I've already told you, it's an old friend."

"Does this friend have a name?"

"You'll soon have a chance to ask them yourself."

"You see there, Webb?" Abel put a finger to his nose. "Abel, he sets you straight, unlike the old man over there."

He sat, leaning his back against the gunwale and yawning. "That dang sun goes down and I'm ready to hit the sack. Me, I must be getting old too."

Maves moved next to him. "I don't guess drinking all that beer has anything to do with it."

"Hell no, it doesn't," he said, yawning again. "I've just been working too hard these last few months."

"From what I remember, you've always done your best to avoid work."

"You're damn right I have. What man wants to work if he doesn't have to?"

Webb snorted. "You're sitting right next to him, Abel. As long as I can remember, Maves was always off working somewhere more often than not."

Abel nudged the troll motor with his foot, angling the boat into the main channel.

"Old Maves, he never was much good at having fun."

"He doesn't know the meaning of the word," Webb grumbled.

Maves sighed, dismayed with the conversation. He absently reached down, rubbing the side of his leg, the dime-sized scar beneath his jeans palpable even after so many years.

"I had to put bread on the table, son."

Webb felt the anger rising in his throat.

"You wanted to be away," he sneered. "Why won't you just admit it?"

Webb had always been a sensitive boy, he thought, impulsive but more often waylaid by indecision. He had struggled to accept his son's passive nature, fearing somehow he had caused the flaw. He peered at his profile in the near-darkness, hearing the resentment in his words, knowing his part in it, dreading that soon he would add to it.

"I have plenty to regret. I won't deny that."

"It's a little late, don't you think?"

"I don't claim to be faultless, Webb."

16

"You don't admit much of anything either."

"Maves and me," Abel said, leaning toward Webb, "we got plenty of regrets between us. The older you get, the more the damn mistakes pile up, no matter who you are, no matter what you do. No man who comes into this world leaves without his share."

Webb sensed the truth in Abel's words but his anger swept him along, the bitterness clear in his voice.

"Well then, Maves outdid himself on that score. I'll give him that much."

The heat of his words burned in Maves' gut. Realizing he could no longer keep the truth from his son, he leaned toward Webb's silhouette.

Webb, there's something I need to…

Abel raised his hand as the low rumble of an approaching boat sounded somewhere in the night. Moving to the bow, he pointed the trolling motor toward the sound. Moments later a yacht appeared out of the darkness, its cabin silhouetted by the gray horizon.

Maves used a paddle to steady the boat as Abel pulled alongside and two men climbed from the yacht in, one angular, the other thick-set and bald. Maves leaned against the gunwale, peering through the darkened windows but finding no sign of passengers. Abel sat and stared at the two men. Then he pointed a finger at the thinner of the two.

"Where is Raul Ordaz, my cousin? That is his boat."

An unspoken threat flashed in the man's eyes.

"I am Blas. You deal with me now."

Abel thrust his chin toward the bald one, making no attempt to hide his irritation.

"What do they call you, then?"

The man stared at him with unblinking eyes, saying nothing. A scorpion tattoo circled his neck.

"No habla Ingles, hombre?" Abel sneered.

"He is Mata," Blas answered for him. "The Zetas cut out his tongue for cursing them."

17

"You bring two men for one man's work." Abel looked from one to the other. "I think you are afraid."

"Enough of this gringo talk!" Blas sliced the air with his hand. "Who will pay for the cargo?"

Maves moved next to Abel, pulling a roll of bills from his pants pocket.

"I'll pay once I see my friend in this boat."

He returned the money to his pocket. Blas shook his head.

"I hope you brought plenty of cash. The price has gone up."

Maves squinted at him, the paddle still in his hands. He tapped it against the floor as he spoke.

"And why is that?"

"The cargo is more than we were told."

"What do you mean?"

"There are two women. You must pay for both."

Recognizing the latent anger hidden beneath his father's expression, Webb sat across from him, next to Mata, where he could watch him. Maves stared into the darkness, trying to make sense of what he had heard. Then he turned back to Blas.

"Why should I believe you? I see no one in your boat."

"You must pay first."

Maves gripped the paddle, his knuckles white against the handle, shame and frustration rising in his chest. His voice seemed to come from deep within.

"I will see them first if you want your money."

Blas stared at him then nodded to his partner. Mata stood, turning as if about to climb back into the yacht but instead reaching beneath his jacket and pulling out a small pistol. Without thinking Webb jumped at him, grabbing for the gun. A shot exploded into the night sky. In a flash, Maves swung the paddle through the air, the blade catching Mata on the temple. He and Webb went tumbling over the side.

18

Maves pivoted just as Blas pulled a revolver from his pocket, the paddle moving in a smooth arc, catching Blas on the forearm. The gun skittered across the floor. Abel leapt past him, grabbing the pistol and pointing it at him just as he lunged for the rail, catapulting himself over the side and into darkness.

Abel rushed to the gunwale and peered into the black water as Maves hurried to the stern. Webb appeared at the rear of the boat. Relieved to see him, Maves climbed onto the yacht and disappeared down the cabin steps. Moments later he emerged alone. Abel turned at the thump of his footsteps.

"Did you find anyone?"

"The cabin is empty. It was a set-up from the start."

"Yes, it looks very bad for my cousin." Abel shook his head, his expression grim. "I hope Raul is still alive."

Dragging a barely conscious Mata into the boat, Webb spoke between breaths.

"The bastard can talk after all."

"Good, I want to ask him some questions." Abel nodded as a bitter smile crossed his lips. "Then I will hogtie him and put him back on my cousin's boat. He can drift out here until the Border Patrol finds him. I have a friend there who will keep the boat for me. I wonder if this one can talk his way out of jail."

"He owes us some answers," Webb said, wiping the water from his eyes. "He would've drowned if I hadn't hauled his big ass back to the boat."

Abel lifted the man onto the seat, leaning close to his face.

"I will feed you to the fishes if you don't tell me what I want to know."

Mata groaned, his eyelids fluttering. Abel whispered into his ear.

"I know you can hear me and I know you can talk. Tell us what happened. Where are they, the cargo you were supposed to bring to us?"

His left eye nearly swollen shut, he opened the right with difficulty and spoke, his words slurred by his mangled tongue.

"The young woman, the white one, she runs when she hears her husband sends his man to find her. The other, the dark-haired one, she helps her."

"How did you get my cousin's boat?"

"Blas, he knew of the plan to bring the women across. After they ran he stole the boat. He said we could still get the payment."

Maves knelt and leaned close to Mata's battered face.

"We expected only one woman, the dark-haired one. Who is the other?"

"The pale one is not of Mexico. The dark one, she helps her and when she must run finds another boat to cross them. That is all I know."

He winced as Abel pressed the pistol to his temple.

"Where did they run to?"

"I do not know but they say the husband, he sends his man to Del Norte."

"Not good enough, fish bait. *Where* in Del Norte?"

"They say first he goes to Quintero, and then to the town of Rock Springs. I do not know of this place."

"This man, who is he?"

"They call him Muntz."

"He doesn't sound Mexican."

"He is of Argentina not Mexico."

Maves leaned in again.

"Why does the dark-haired woman help the other?"

"I do not know."

Abel waved the pistol in his face.

"Try harder, amigo."

Mata winced and spit into the water.

"They say the young woman, the light-skinned one, her husband is of a gang. They say she gave him to the federales and he is in prison but still he is of the gang. They will have her dead. The dark one helps women, women who fear for their life. That is all I know. "

Maves fell back against the console, trying to make sense of the man's words. Who was the light-skinned woman and why was he only now becoming aware of her? Whoever she was, he had little idea how he would ever explain her to Webb, much less the other.

Chapter Four

He reached out to her, taking her hand in his and lifting her onto the floating walkway in one motion before stepping away, trapped in his own awkward silence. Her ebony-hued eyes studied him, her gaze friendly yet hesitant, searching his face as if reaching for a memory long absent. That she would have grown more beautiful in the passing years had never occurred to him, his recollection somehow lessening what he knew he could never have.

At last she smiled before turning toward the boat. He followed her gaze as a young woman looking to be in her teens emerged from the cabin. She seemed a younger image of the woman except for the clear blue of her eyes, eyes not unlike his. She, too, smiled at him. Then she reached into her purse, lifting out a black pistol, raising it to eye-level and pointing it at him. She smiled once again, and then she squeezed the trigger.

He awoke with a start. Climbing out of bed, he made his way through the house, looking for a clock as he went but finding none. He paused in the kitchen doorway. Webb and Abel sat at the table drinking coffee, a plate of greasy bacon between them. He again scanned the room for a clock. Nothing. Abel held up his cup.

"You look like hell, Maves. Have some coffee."

"What time is it?"

Abel glanced toward the dark window.

"Let's see, the rooster just crowed for the second time so it's about ten after five."

"You don't believe in clocks?"

"Hell no. Time, it goes by too fast. I don't want a damn clock reminding me my days are numbered."

Webb rubbed the bruise beneath his left eye and studied his father's face, wondering about the women and what connection they had to him. Rather than ask, he set aside the question, putting another in its place.

"What's the plan now that your friend is in the country?"

Maves poured himself a cup and sat.

"We go find her."

Remembering the mention of Quintero, Webb eyed him skeptically.

"We're going to go snooping around some border town?"

"I gave a promise and I intend to keep it."

"But she made it across. What else is there to do?"

"We don't know her circumstances or what she plans to do next. I won't stop until I have the whole story."

Abel leaned toward him. "Maves, who is this friend?"

He ignored the question. "First, we have to go see a man over in Langtry."

Abel pointed a finger at him.

"Okay, if you're not going to tell us about your friend, at least tell us who you need to see in Langtry."

"His name is Ray Rob Bean."

Webb slapped the table. "Don't tell me he's related to Roy Bean, the famous judge."

"The man is his great grandson."

"I don't believe it."

"Well, you can ask him yourself soon enough."

"Why on earth would you want to talk to Judge Roy Bean's great grandson?"

"He was in communication with my friend and she asked him to contact me. Drink up, we leave in five minutes."

A treeless plain emerged from the darkness, framing the road as fingers of light crept above the horizon, signaling the approach of dawn. Maves followed the winding blacktop, crossing over arroyos and washes, their striated walls rubbed smooth by eons of moving wind and water. To the south the Rio Grande flowed just out of sight.

A bridge spanning a deep canyon came into view down a scrub-strewn slope, the dirt streets of Langtry a quarter mile beyond. Moments later Maves angled the truck next to a sagging frame building. The once-red siding stood coated white with dust. A hand-painted sign above the door read 'Cold Beer'.

He pushed through into an open room lighted by two windows and a scattering of neon signs. Several mismatched tables crowded one wall. Filling the opposite wall, an ornate but battered bar stood below a faded image of a reclining nude. A man with his back to them sat reading a newspaper. Webb nudged his father.

"That's bound to be him."

"I suppose it is, though I've never seen the man in the flesh."

The seated figure turned toward them, smoothing his thick beard before stepping off the stool. Thinning hair rose from the top of his head like a forest of burnt toothpicks. He blinked several times and then eyed them for a moment.

"You gents want beer for breakfast or are you just sightseeing?"

Maves shook his head. "I take it you're Ray Rob?"

"And you would be?"

"I'm Maves Van Horn and this here is my son, Webb."

He walked to where they stood, squeezing his eyes shut twice before shaking their hands with an iron grip. Webb whistled through his teeth.

"That's some grip you have, Ray Rob," he said, massaging his palm.

He blinked again and nodded across the room to a cast iron stove, an odd sight in the morning heat.

"I spend most mornings splitting firewood, so the hands get some serious work in. Believe it or not, in winter we can get a raw cold down here that'll turn your privates twelve shades of blue."

24

Webb squinted through the open door. "That's hard to imagine on a day like this."

"Today is downright cool compared to what we'll see come August. So, what brings you Van Horns to Langtry? I figured you'd pick up Blanca and make tracks north."

"We had a change in plans." Maves took a breath, silently hoping the man would know something of use. "How well do you know her, Ray Rob?"

"I knew Blanca's father before the goddamn cartels murdered him. He was a good man and a good friend. I don't know her as well but I'd do anything for that family. That's why she asked me to find you. Is she alright?"

"We don't know. She came across early, before we had a chance to meet up."

"I'm surprised to hear it." He blinked again. "She was real strong about it being you and no one else. Where is she now?"

"That's why we're here. Did she say anything about who she might bring with her or where she might go?"

"I don't know about her bringing anyone," he answered, tugging at his beard as he considered the question. He blinked twice, his eyebrows jumping, and then pointed into the air. "I do recall her to say something about a place she planned to see again. I believe Quintero was the name. She may have said something about Bandera too. I wish I could remember better. Some drunk feller crashed his pickup through that side wall over there and knocked me clear across the room. Ever since I woke up from that headache, I don't recall so well."

"You remember well enough. At least now we have something to go on."

"It sounds like she's headed for your place." Webb turned to Maves, trying to make sense of the news. "Why would she do that?"

"I can't say."

"You can't or you won't?"

Ignoring him, Maves nodded his thanks to Ray Rob and started for the door. Stepping into the blinding sunlight, he weighed Ray Robb's words against what Mata had told them. If Blanca had gone to Quintero, Muntz would likely catch up with her and the woman. He could only hope he and Webb would find them first.

A white monolith of sky stretched along the horizon, reaching above them as if the fuming heat of summer had appeared overnight, bringing with it swirling clouds of dust laced with dried corn husks that drifted over the landscape like strange birds. Paralleling the river, the highway soon crossed the lake in a long causeway that traced the border in concrete. The rich smell of fresh water filled the truck.

Hearing Blanca's name spoken had stirred Maves' memory. Why had she asked for his help after so many years? Could she want to see him again? He would not let himself think it possible. Searching his past for clues to what she might look like now, he could find only the unfocused image of a young woman.

In the distance a steeple appeared above the flat horizon, the gold cross atop it glittering beneath the cloudless sky. Acres of pecan orchards flanked by irrigation canals stretched away from the highway in broad rows. Moments later the whitewashed buildings of Quintero appeared, rising above the scrub-filled plain like freshly-baked bread. Webb stirred in the passenger seat.

"There's something that doesn't add up about this friend of yours, Maves. If she could get across the border on her own, why ask for your help in the first place?"

"They're running from this man, Muntz. That may be the reason."

"You don't sound so sure."

"There's little I can be sure of," he admitted. "I do know they'll be in a fix if we don't find them before he does."

"What do you think he'll do if he locates them?"

26

"I won't waste time thinking about what might happen," he replied, biting off the words.

He gripped the steering wheel waiting for Webb to ask about his connection to Blanca but instead he turned to the window without another word. Maves decided to let the matter play out in its own way. If Webb could wait, then he could too.

The two-columned bell tower fronting Our Lady of Guadalupe Church stood white beneath the noonday light, its bronze bell shining a muted orange. Next to the entrance a priest bent over a bed of flowers. Maves slowed the truck and pulled next to the sidewalk, leaving the engine running as he climbed out. He leaned through the window.

"The priest may know something useful. Take the truck and check the cafes in town. Since it's close to noon, they might be getting some lunch."

"What does this friend look like?"

"I don't know, exactly, at least not anymore.

"I need something to go on, Maves.

"She's small, with dark hair," he answered, again trying to imagine her after so many years. "And… and her eyes are brown, almost black."

Webb followed the highway for a half-mile before turning onto a main thoroughfare. Resale stores and antique shops lined the broad street. Spotting a yellow brick building in the distance, the vacant lot next to it crowded with cars, he angled the truck next to the curb and cut the engine. Halfway down the block a sign read 'Paula's Café'.

He followed the wide sidewalk, ambling along a row of tall windows fronting the cafe. Painted ads for lunch specials crowded the glass. He stopped before a posted menu and stood as if reading it while trying to peer inside but the reflected street obscured his view.

He had almost decided to step through the door when a flash caught his eye. He peered into the reflection,

27

surveying the street behind him. A stray dog loped along the curb, its tongue lagging. Otherwise, the sun-drenched scene stood empty.

Then a lone figure emerged from the shadow of a boarded-up doorway opposite him. Webb studied his image. Angular and thin with close-cropped blonde hair, he seemed to take a particular interest in the cafe. Webb felt the hair on the back of his neck rise.

An instant later a cloud passed across the sun and the scene vanished, the inside of the café suddenly standing clear before him. At a booth beside the door an attractive woman with ivory-hued skin sat opposite a woman with dark hair. He hesitated then pivoted, scanning the street but finding nothing. The sidewalk opposite him stood empty, the man in the reflection gone.

He turned back to the cafe. Doubting his luck, he stepped inside and found an empty table with a clear view, though all he could see of the dark-haired woman was the back of her head. The woman facing him had thick auburn hair that shone satin-like beneath the fluorescent lights. He had trouble taking his eyes off her.

She glanced at him, looked away and then back, her eyes locking with his. Confusion mixed with fear crossed her face. Webb knew then he must move quickly or she would bolt. He stood, stepping toward the table while trying to appear friendly.

As he came even with the booth, the woman looked up at him with an expression both questioning and fearful. She seemed young, probably in her mid-thirties, and even more beautiful up close. With difficulty, he shifted his gaze to the woman opposite her. A mass of curling hair framed eyes so dark they appeared black against her clay-colored skin. Though older, she was no less beautiful than her companion.

He again wondered what connection she could have to Maves. Was he, like Ray Rob, an old friend of her father? But if true, why had he never said so? How else might he know her? He stood before them unable to move, to speak, looking from one to the other, trying to find some foothold of explanation.

Chapter Five

Maves faced the chapel, its whitewashed brick blinding beneath the relentless light of midday. He tried to recall the last time he had entered the dim confines of a church. The years had slipped by without notice. A part of him wanted to walk past the priest and into the quiet sanctuary, to breathe in the musty air, feel the smooth coolness of polished wood, allow the weight of his thoughts to drift away.

Shaking off the notion as the foolishness of age, he started up the walkway. The man turned at the sound of his footsteps. Standing upright, he set aside the hoe, wiping the sweat from his brow with a threadbare handkerchief before stuffing it back into his pants pocket. A head shorter than Maves, he seemed imposing in spite of his stature, his hands too large, eyes too hard for those of a priest. He peered at Maves with those deep-set eyes, running a hand along his square jaw, the dark stubble scratching like sandpaper beneath his touch. Maves nodded and held out a hand.

"I suppose summer is here for good."

The priest shook his hand.

"I do not know how these cursed weeds can grow without rain. God must provide for them somehow. There are times I wish God would be a little less attentive, or else give us rain along with the undesired plants. But enough talk of weeds. I am Father Palamedes Zakros. Most of the congregants call me Father Zak. The rest is too much."

"The name is Maves Van Horn. I don't mean to impose, but I'd like to talk if you can spare a moment."

He studied Maves before answering.

"You strike me as an independent man, Mr. Van Horn, one unused to asking for something. We will go to my office."

"It's just Maves, Father."

"I believe I can find us something cold to drink, Maves. That is, if after all my complaining God is still willing to provide."

Maves tried to place his accent as he followed him to a brick building set adjacent to the church. They passed through the entrance into a wide foyer. The smell of fresh-baked bread surrounded them. At the end of a long hallway, nuns in gray and white habits scurried about a large kitchen, speaking one to another in hushed tones.

Leaving the hallway, they climbed a stairway to a cluster of rooms serving as his living quarters. A large crucifix hung on the far wall. He motioned Maves to a wooden table flanked by two chairs before he disappeared through an open doorway. Despite his friendliness, Maves found the nearly bare walls and sparse furnishings of the apartment unsettling. Moments later, he returned with two cans of beer.

"I hope beer is acceptable. It is all I have cold. I can give you water but the tap tends toward the warm side."

Maves popped open a can.

"This'll be fine."

"You have visited a priest's rooms before, Maves?"

"I can't say that I have."

"You are not Catholic, then?"

"I was raised Baptist but you'd be more likely to find me in jail than church these days."

"You have misplaced your belief?"

"My wife was the church-goer of the family. I went along to please her. After she left, I had a hard time seeing the point."

"Then you have found God a little, let us say, unresponsive?"

"You could say that, Father."

"For an unbeliever such as yourself," he said, the hint of a smile crossing his lips, "a simple Zak will do. So, what has happened to make you visit this place of God, Maves?"

31

"I'm looking for a friend, a woman. There also is another woman, younger than my friend. I believe they may have come this way. It is likely they're in considerable danger."

Maves saw in his eyes a flicker of recognition.

"I see." The priest nodded his understanding. "And what does this friend look like?"

"I've not seen her in many years but she is small, with dark eyes and hair."

"Why are you searching for her?"

"She's had some sort of trouble and asked for my help."

"And what will you do should you find her?"

Maves noticed with surprise that he had no interest in the trouble.

"I'll do what I can to help."

"Why should you bother if you have not seen her in so long?"

He took a breath, searching for a way around the truth. "I owe her."

"You owe her?"

"I owe her what help I can provide. That's as much as I can say about it. Have you seen her?"

Drumming the tabletop with his thick fingers, Zak considered the question.

"My family came to this country from Greece," he finally said. "My parents expected that I would always be in the Greek Church but in my adolescent rebellion I instead went to the Roman Church, what you know as the Catholic Church, and on top of that I became a priest. Needless to say, they were not happy."

"Religion is a sore point in many families."

"Not that I regret my decision. I did what I had to. I felt called to be a priest, a Catholic priest. In fact, I'm not sure I had any decision in the matter. God called and I answered."

Maves nodded gravely, trying to guess at his point. Zak locked eyes with him.

"You're probably wondering why I'm telling you all this. What I'm saying is that at some point or other we all do what we must. But though my parents are long dead, I still feel that I let them down."

Maves turned his eyes as the priest's real message became clear. Then he faced him again.

"You know them, don't you?"

He gave his round head a nod of consent.

"Blanca came to me asking for help so I promised to assist her in gaining asylum for the woman. I once had a parish in Mexico and Blanca's family attended church there. After her father was murdered by the cartel, I dedicated myself to fighting that evil. Blanca is only one example."

"Did she tell you about me?"

"Not in name but otherwise, yes. I guessed who you might be when I first saw you. I didn't know for certain until you described her."

"Can you tell me where she is?"

Zak eyed him as if trying to decide whether or not to trust him.

"The young woman, Maves, what do you know of her?"

"I know almost nothing. I understand she's in some sort of trouble. Is she the reason Blanca asked for my help?"

He stood and stepped around his chair, leaning toward Maves.

"Did you know that Blanca has a daughter?"

Maves stared at him, unable to imagine her with a child.

"She has a girl?"

"I would think a friend would know of this."

"I haven't seen Blanca in some time." He wiped the sweat from his lip, searching for a way to explain away his negligence. "There's a lot I don't know."

"Then you don't know what the girl looks like."

"How could I?"

"She is beautiful like Blanca but with blue eyes."

Maves said nothing, unsure of his point. Zak leaned toward him.

"How many years since you last saw Blanca?"

"Fifteen or so, give or take."

"The girl just turned fourteen."

Maves stared at him, his mind resisting the implication.

"What are you saying, Zak?"

He placed a thick hand on Maves' shoulder.

"To have an answer, Maves, you must ask Blanca."

A waitress drifted by for a second time. Webb watched her move past and pivot, eyeing him from a safe distance as he stood before the booth. He looked past her into the daylight beyond the windows, again trying to find an explanation for Maves' connection to the older woman.

He turned back to the table. The pale-skinned woman held his gaze for a moment and then took a breath.

"What do you want?" she asked. Beneath the fear, her voice carried a note of defiance.

"I mean you no harm." He raised his hands, searching for the right words. "It's just that I'm looking for someone, two people, but I don't know what they look like."

The older woman peered up at him.

"Why do you search for these people?"

"They're in trouble and may need help."

She looked at him askance.

"How will you find someone you never have seen?"

"I'm looking for two women. One of them is light-skinned and the other has dark hair."

"Then you do know them."

34

"I know only a vague description."

"There are many women in the world. Some must have pale skin or dark hair. Some also must be in trouble. Why should you care?"

He decided he would need to push harder. "A man called Muntz is also trying to find them."

The younger woman gasped and reached across the table, grabbing the other's hand. She nodded to her before turning back to Webb.

"You have seen him?"

He stared at her, mesmerized by her dark eyes and luminous skin, again thinking how Maves had failed to mention the beauty of his friend.

"No, at least I don't think I have."

"Then how do you know this?"

"A man named Ray Rob told us."

"Who do you mean, this 'us'?"

"My father and me."

A hint of relief crossed her face.

"He did come for me after all," she said to herself. "And you must be Webb. I am Blanca and this is Frida."

Webb nodded to the younger woman, again reluctant to take his eyes from her. Blanca's voice drew his attention.

"Where is he? Where is Maves?"

"Then you are his friend?"

Disappointment drifted across her face. "Is that what he called me, his friend?"

"You were more than that?"

"We were once lovers."

Frida looked up in surprise. He peered into her green eyes and tried to ignore the questions dogging his thoughts, questions only his father could answer.

Chapter Six

Maves faced the dark tabletop, the priest's words settling onto his consciousness piecemeal. Zak paced behind him humming bits of church hymns under his breath. Maves felt his hovering presence like a pall over his self-deception, bringing to reality the shame he had long tried to avoid.

Zak rounded the table, his hands behind his back, his deep-set eyes intense but not unfriendly, his round head bobbing. He faced Maves without a word, pausing in the way a teacher awaits an answer. Maves took a breath, part of him looking for a way out, the other part relieved finally to face what was to come. He peered into the priest's broad face.

"So you think the girl is mine?"

Zak held his scarred hands before his chest, pressing them palm to palm as if in prayer.

"What I think counts for little. As I said, it is Blanca you should be asking."

"It may sound strange but I never imagined her with a child."

"I am not surprised."

"The truth is I was married when I met Blanca."

"I guessed as much even before she told me."

"I never strayed before or after, although the after didn't last long so I suppose it counts for little."

"Everything we do counts for something in the eyes of God."

Maves winced at the thought.

"I have enough anger directed at me without adding God to the mix, Zak."

"Perhaps God has something other than anger in mind, something more like understanding or forgiveness."

"I don't expect to be forgiven." A dark mood passed over him as he squinted at the priest. "And I don't need confession."

"I'm here to listen, Maves, not judge."

"Of course, Zak, you're right." Maves ran a hand through his hair, the shame again rising up. "I spoke out of turn."

"Then please continue."

"Blanca was young and scared, involved with a violent man, a man who hit her and worse. Something about her made me want to protect her. I can't say why."

Zak nodded his understanding.

"Blanca needed the kindness of strangers. After her father was murdered, she and her mother were alone in a difficult world, a place that would become ever more dangerous. Perhaps that's the reason God sent her to you."

"God has a strange sense of humor."

"God has a way of giving us what we least expect."

"I've had enough in the way of surprises."

"Fate or divine providence - take your pick - sweeps us along, Maves. What happened after you and Blanca met?"

"I kept in touch with her. Like I said, I needed to be sure she was alright and over time we became friends. Then one night she called, upset and tearful. Her ex-boyfriend had found her and was threatening to turn her in to the authorities. Because she had come across illegally with my help, I felt responsible.

"I went to her hiding place intending only to offer comfort. Our involvement happened so fast I never saw it coming. Or maybe my pride wouldn't allow me to admit it could ever happen to me. I don't know which is true."

"Life is rarely clear cut, Maves. Perhaps both are true."

"Almost from the start I promised myself I would break it off. But I was working as a veterinarian monitoring animal disease along the border. The situation made seeing her too easy. There's no telling how long it might've gone on, but the funding got cut."

"So, you no longer had an excuse."

37

"I should have ended it then but I didn't. Instead, I made up a story about taking a fishing trip down here with an old friend. As shameful as that sounds now, I didn't hesitate."

"But something happened."

"My wife packed a change of clothes with my tackle. She sensed something amiss. That was my undoing. I never even opened the box. Within minutes of my return she caught me in the lie. She walked out an hour later. I thought that was the low point of my life, knowing what I had done to her and my son."

"But God had other plans?"

"He did if those plans meant to punish me."

"Something happened you didn't expect?"

Maves nodded, his throat filling with remorse. "I fooled myself into believing she and I would get through the mess I had made of our marriage and she would come back. I would have done whatever it took."

"But she refused to consider it?"

"Not exactly." He slowly shook his head. "Less than six months later she hit a curve too fast and flipped the car. She was two miles from the house. They said she might've lived if someone had come along in time."

"You must not second guess these things, Maves."

"I should have been with her. If I had been…"

He turned away, unable to finish the thought.

"And you never saw Blanca again?"

After a moment, he looked up, compelled to continue.

"About three months after my wife left they sent me on a last survey along the Nueces River along with another vet, Riley Banks, a local down there and as good a man as I've ever known. We had worked together so long people often confused us with each other. We did look like we could've been brothers.

"On that day I kept telling myself I should go to Blanca and explain why I had stopped coming to see her but I kept making excuses not to go. I'm ashamed to say I didn't trust myself. In any event, I never got to find out what I might've done."

Zak laid a scarred hand on his shoulder.

"Your life again took a turn."

He nodded.

"We were in a narrow box canyon when we rounded a corner and came on two men with backpacks. I just took them for a couple of hikers but within seconds they pulled out pistols and started shooting. Riley went down ten yards in front of me. I ducked behind a rock, knowing I should try to reach him but unable to make myself move. In that narrow space, the sound of gunfire was deafening.

"I had a rifle but I couldn't stop my hands from shaking long enough to use it. I was finally able to get off two rounds before I took a ricocheted bullet in the leg. A fragment of stone caught my left eye. I suppose getting off those shots kept me alive but they did nothing to help my partner.

"I've gone over what happened a hundred times or more, trying to see what I could've done different but I always end up back where I started. Instead of paying attention to where I was, I was preoccupied with Blanca. If I'd been doing my job things might've turned out different. In any case, I'm still here and he's not. Why is that, Zak? The world would be a better place if we'd traded places."

"I'm going to tell you something, Maves," he said, raising his thick fingers to his chin, "but you must promise never tell anyone else, even Blanca."

He looked up, surprised at the request.

"For what it's worth, Zak, you have my word."

"Before I had any idea of becoming a priest, I had dreams of becoming a professional boxer. I had been undefeated in the junior program, and you know how the young can delude themselves. My third match was against a veteran fighter from Mexico, a boxer who had his own dreams of fame but could never move out of journeyman status. At that point, he was only trying to finish out his career. I saw him as a way to advance mine.

"In the fourth round, I knew I had him beaten. He knew it too and would have given me the fight but I wanted to make a statement, impress the boxing world, so I went after him relentlessly. Just before the bell, I caught him on the left cheek. He went down and never got up."

Maves stared at him.

"You killed a man?"

He nodded. "It makes no difference that it was in a boxing ring, you know. God makes no such distinctions."

"Is that why you became a priest?"

He smiled and gave his round head a slight shake.

"That would be the worst possible reason to enter the priesthood, Maves. But as inadequate as it sounds, I have tried ever since to make up for my selfishness."

"Even a priest has to atone for his past?"

"The past is beyond changing, Maves. What matters is what we do from this day forward."

"Webb's mother is dead. I don't see that I can ever make up for what I did to her."

"You have come here for a reason, have you not?"

"You know I have. What are you getting at?"

"Blanca needs your help, Maves. I fear she is in a great danger that has only just begun. That she is not your late wife does nothing to lessen the good you can do."

"Are you trying to give me penance, Father?"

A smile moved across his round face. "Would I ask such a thing of a skeptic like you?"

"You're a sly one, Zak. But I…"

The priest looked up as footsteps sounded in the stairwell behind them. His gaze held an odd mixture of hope and fear. Maves turned to find Blanca standing in the doorway. He rose from the chair and blinked, trying to shake off his disbelief. Webb waited on the landing behind her, a young woman next to him. Blanca turned to him.

"Please take Frida downstairs. I must talk with your father alone."

He glanced at Maves before starting down the stairs. Zak approached Blanca and took her hands in his.

"It's time I prepared the liturgy for this week. I'll be nearby if you need anything."

He disappeared and she again faced Maves. He gestured toward the chairs.

"You'd be more comfortable if you sat."

"Is it my comfort or yours you worry for?"

He took a breath, knowing the truth of her words.

"I admit I'm having trouble believing my eyes, but I suppose we'll both feel less awkward if we sit."

"I too have trouble, Maves. Are you truly here with me?"

She moved into the room and stood before him. Peering into her dark eyes, he tried to decipher her intent.

"We were lucky to find you, Blanca."

"Your eyes," she said, studying his face, "they are still blue like the sky, just as I remember."

"The rest of me is a good bit older. You haven't changed a bit though."

She reached out, lightly touching his sleeve. "Thank you for coming, Maves."

She seemed even more beautiful than he remembered. A sudden awareness of his cloudy eye gripped him. He would not allow himself to believe she still might have feelings for him, yet a part of him hoped for it despite his effort. He reminded himself that he had abandoned her.

"What made you get in touch after all this time, Blanca?"

"I need your help, Maves. *We* need your help."

"She's in trouble?"

She nodded. "Frida is a refugee. Guatemala, it is a dangerous place for a beautiful young woman. Mexico is no better."

"She is a friend of yours?"

41

"No, I only just met her. There is a group that helps women escape the danger in Guatemala and other such countries. The gangs, they do what they want, take what they want. They work with the cartels. I have known much violence in my life. That is why I help. I want better for young women like Frida. Perhaps I help because she is someone's daughter and I have a daughter."

He studied her, looking for any clue to her meaning.

"I was surprised to hear it. Zak said she has blue eyes."

"Estela's eyes are the blue of topaz."

"I understand she's a teenager."

"She is only fourteen, a tender age to be without a father."

"Zak wouldn't say who the father is."

"Would you refuse to help us if Estela was yours?"

Maves flinched at the boldness of her question. "Are you saying she is?"

"If someone else was the father, what then?"

He stared at her, unable to answer.

"You will help us, won't you, Maves?"

"What have you told Webb?"

"I told him we were once lovers."

He sighed, realizing he had been wrong in waiting. "Did he believe you?"

"Why would he not?"

"He doesn't know about you, about us, about that time."

Seeing pity in her eyes he looked away, unwilling to accept the sentiment. She studied him a moment.

"You are still so private, Maves, even with your son?"

"I planned to tell him but somehow the time never seemed right. And now I've waited too long."

"Did you forget me so easily?"

He winced at the thought. "No, Blanca, I never did."

"But you put me from your thoughts just as you put me out of your life, did you not, Maves?"

"Webb's mother found us out, Blanca. I had no choice."

"I waited for you, Maves. I waited and waited until I could wait no more."

"I'm not proud of what I did."

"After the sisters helped me with Estela's birth, I had to go back to Mexico and live with my mother until a man was willing to marry me. To return with a baby was to endure much shame. At least my father was spared the humiliation."

"You managed to find a husband anyway."

"You don't know what Mexico is like for a young woman. I too had no choice. Did you not wonder what became of me?"

"I did, Blanca."

"But you returned to your wife."

"No, she left me."

She stared at him in disbelief. "And still you did not try to find me?"

"Webb's mother died, Blanca."

"I do not understand."

"I had a motherless son to care for."

"A man and a woman can get past this if they wish to."

"I couldn't move past it, Blanca. I had wronged the two people who counted on me most. From then on I was determined to do right by Webb. But look at me. Even now I can't get it straight."

Seeing the pain in his face, she took his hand in hers.

"It is not too late to talk to him, Maves."

He shook his head, guessing at the thoughts running through his son's head.

"I suppose it is, Blanca. Webb and I don't exactly get along. Now that we're done here, he'll head home and things will go back to the way they've always been."

She gasped, letting go of his hand. "You will not help us after all? Are you angry with me for what I have said?"

"I have no right to be angry, Blanca."

"Then why will you not help us?"

"Zak told me he promised to help the woman gain asylum. Isn't that what you want?"

"You do not understand, Maves. It will take much time to obtain asylum. It may never be granted. Such things are impossible to know. But Frida is in much danger now, today."

"The authorities will protect her."

"If they find her they can deport her. It would mean her death. Her words sent four gang members to prison, Maves, and one of them was her husband. He wants her life for what she did. He has sent a man to kill her, so she must go to a place he will not find her, a place that is safe."

He took a step back, the realization of her request hitting him.

"Aren't there organizations that take in refugees?"

"That is the first place he will look for her. Without our help, she will be caught and sent to detention. He will look there also. She must go a place he will not know."

He studied her face, deciding he would agree to nothing until she told him about her daughter.

"I want the truth, Blanca. Who does Estela belong to?"

"She belongs to me, Maves."

"You know what I mean. Who is her father?"

"Please do not ask me this, Maves," she pleaded with him. "You will not help us if I tell you."

"I won't help unless I know."

"Did you listen to me, Maves?" She sighed as a look of resignation filled her face. "Did you hear how I described her eyes? If you did, you would know."

"That's not an answer, Blanca. What about her eyes?"

"They are not blue like the sky, Maves. Her eyes are of the lightest blue, the blue of topaz."

He stared at her, his mind refusing to believe her words.

44

"You're saying... you're saying it was Riley? Riley Banks was her father?"

"I was so lonely and afraid after you stopped coming, Maves. I was terrified my ex-boyfriend would again find me. I needed someone and Riley was there."

"I never knew."

"He was just a friend, Maves, someone who helped me through a difficult time. We were not lovers like you and I. Estela was an accident. Riley also did not know."

Maves turned away. The room seemed to float about him, nothing about it real. Then an image of the canyon flooded his mind, the deafening gunshots, the burn in his leg, the blinding flash, the shame. He looked into Blanca's dark eyes, realizing what he must do.

"Tell me how I can help."

She stepped toward him, touching his cheek.

"You are a good man, Maves. You need only to take Frida to my sister's home in Rockport. It is all arranged. She will be safe there."

"You aren't coming with her?"

"My mother is old and very ill. I must stay so I can care for her."

"You staying here seems wrong, Blanca. This Muntz, the man Frida's husband sent, he might come after you to get to her."

"I have no choice, Maves." Her eyes seemed to grow even darker. "I will not leave my mother to die alone."

"I don't like it, Blanca. There must be a way you can bring her north. Perhaps Zak can help her gain entry."

"She would never leave her home, Maves. I must let her die in peace. You can understand this, I think."

He nodded reluctantly, knowing he would do the same. She again took his hand in hers.

"Then you will help us?"

He peered into her depthless eyes, the hope of gaining her favor again pulling him along.

"Yes, Blanca, I'll take Frida to your sister."

Chapter Seven

A hot wind blew through the truck, swirling about Frida's head, tugging at her hair, the silken ends tapping Webb's shoulder like the hand of a child. He turned and studied her profile. Squeezed between him and his father, she seemed younger than her age, as if the woman had somehow returned to adolescence. A hint of worry flashed across her green eyes.

Webb wondered what must be going through her mind, riding with two men she scarcely knew on her way to see a woman she had never met. Hailing her attention, he pointed out the windshield as a seagull sailed over the road. Though mesquite and cactus still crowded the narrow blacktop, the shorebird signaled a coastline somewhere beyond the featureless horizon. She watched it disappear before settling back into the seat.

Though he had not seen the broad bay and mudflats of Rockport in years, Webb could almost smell the rich fragrance of the coastline, organic and alive. As a boy, he had spent summers at his grandmother's bayside house. For a short while the town had almost become a second home. His mother loved the area and had hoped he would come to know it as she did.

Her memory weighed on his thoughts as he stared out the window, his resentment toward Maves again stirring in his chest. Yet Frida's presence somehow lessened his anger, as if she offered a buffer between them. He again turned his gaze on her. She glanced at him once then twice before he realized he was staring at her. She turned away, clearly embarrassed by the attention.

A moment later, a scattering of buildings appeared along the highway. Maves slowed the truck, turning onto a side street of crushed oyster shell. Angling to the edge of the road, he pulled a crumpled sheet of paper from the dashboard and studied it before surveying the view before them. Compact frame houses lined the street, their low-slung silhouettes framed by palms and oleanders. The leaves vibrated before a restless breeze. Setting aside the paper, he pointed toward the corner.

"That place on the end belongs to Blanca's sister. Are you ready to go meet her?"

Without speaking, she nodded a response. Maves eased the truck down the street, pulling into the short driveway. Moments later they stood before the door. Webb moved next to her, trying to gauge her reaction.

"You know she's expecting you, don't you?"

She gave no response. He gestured at the house.

"Go ahead and let her know you're here."

She stood frozen in place.

"Go ahead and knock." He waved at the door again. "She knows you're coming."

She gave her head a slight shake, nearly imperceptible. He took a breath, trying to hide his impatience. The woman and the entire trip reminded him of a past he wanted to forget. He stepped toward the door, ready to be rid of it all.

"I'll do the knocking for you, then."

"No, Maves," Webb said, grabbing his arm, "she's not ready. Can't you see that?"

He frowned, looking from her to Webb, no longer hiding his frustration.

"We can't stand around like we have nothing better to do."

Webb pulled him down the sidewalk and leaned in, speaking in low tones.

"Why can't we? We're still getting to know her."

"I agreed to bring her here, not have a tea party."

"Treat her with some consideration, Maves. She's scared and without a place to call home."

"Well, not for long." He waved off the idea, in no mood to argue. "There's a woman here that's about to take her off our hands."

48

"How can you be so sure? Maybe the woman doesn't want her. Maybe Blanca talked her into it."

"You don't know that and I don't know that."

"Maybe she's not even Blanca's sister."

"Where do you come up with these cockamamie ideas?" Maves squinted at him. "You must be mad that I never told you about Blanca."

"This isn't about what you did or didn't do fifteen years ago," he hissed, angered that he was right. "It's about that woman over there. She's counting on us, Maves. We've promised to get her somewhere safe and until we do we're all she has."

"This woman here is about to take her off our hands!" He chopped the air with his hand. "As far as I'm concerned we're done."

"How'd you get to be so hard-hearted?"

"I'm just practical, is all."

"How would you like to move in with someone you'd never seen? The woman is a stranger to her, Maves."

"Then it's high time they got to know each other."

"I know how you are, Maves." He pointed a finger in his face, his resentment again taking control. "You live in your little world where everything is all neat and tidy, seeing only what you want to see, hearing only what you want to hear."

"What I hear now is a lot of nonsense."

Frida appeared between them, looking from one to the other.

"Do you know how immature you sound?"

Her voice held a slight accent, difficult to place. Maves took a breath and faced her, trying to hide his annoyance.

"We're just talking. This is how men talk."

"You're arguing back and forth like children."

He tried to soften his tone. "We need to get you situated is all."

"That won't be easy."

49

"Why's that?"

"There's nobody home."

He squinted at her.

"How can you know that?"

"While you two were wasting time talking about me, I rang the doorbell."

"They're at home." He turned to the house. "Doorbells hardly ever work right."

"I also knocked twice, tried the door and peeked in the window. There's a half-eaten pizza on the kitchen table. They left in a hurry by the look of it."

"I don't believe it." Maves approached the house and peeked inside. "Why would they leave when they're supposed to be expecting you?"

"Maybe that's why," she said, smirking at him.

"Now don't get smart with me."

"I'm serious, Mr. Van Horn. Look at the facts. Blanca has abandoned me. Her sister has skipped town. I figure it's only a matter of time before you ditch me too."

He eyed her a moment.

"How come you live in Guatemala but talk like you come from someplace else?"

"My father was Greek and my mother Irish. They owned a coffee plantation in Guatemala. He died before I was born but my mother kept the farm going so I attended the American school there."

"Along with reading and writing, did they teach you how to disrespect your elders?"

Webb winked at her. "At least when she talks, you listen."

"Well," Maves said, glaring at him, "I've had my fill of listening."

"What comes next then?"

He turned his gaze to the street, looking first one way then the other. The feeling they were being watched had dogged his thoughts since the moment they arrived in town.

"We'll check back later. Maybe there'll be someone home by then. In the meantime, my mother's cousin lives here in Rockport, if you'll remember. I believe it's time we paid her a visit. That is, if the old bird is still alive."

Minutes later they rounded a dense stand of acacia trees and a yellow, two-story house appeared through the windshield. Squat palms framing the entrance squirmed before the ceaseless wind.

Easing the truck down the drive, he parked near a set of stairs that spilled from the broad porch in a sweeping arc. A tower topped with a cone-shaped shale roof stood at one corner. Though once grand, the home carried the threadbare look of a well-used quilt, the paint worn thin, the moss-covered roof sagging. A single lamp shone from the bay window. Frida looked at him askance.

"Do you really know who lives here?"

He studied her face before answering, aware of her scrutiny.

"You think I would lie to you?"

"Everyone lies," she snorted. "Don't you know that?"

"I don't share that view of humankind."

"Well you should."

He waved a finger at her. "You're too young to be so cynical."

"I have my reasons."

"You do, do you? And what would those be?"

"My mother said she'd never send me away but she did. She said my father died of malaria when the truth is he was murdered. Then there's the question of Blanca's daughter and who the real father is. Do you know anything about that?"

Maves jumped from the truck without answering, hoping to avoid any more questions. She and Webb followed him up the steps. He rapped his knuckles against the cracked paint of the door.

"Alright, let's see if Lucille is still among the living."

Frida turned to Webb. "See how easily we avoid the truth?"

Maves frowned at her. "I'm not avoiding…

He stopped in mid-sentence as the heavy metal of a lock clicked inside the house. An instant later, the door swung open and a woman with orange hair peered out, squinting into the sunlight. She pursed her over-red lips, studying each of them in turn.

"Whatever you're selling, I don't need it and I don't want it. You people best go swindle somebody else. There are plenty of fools to choose from in this town."

She stepped back into the house but Maves pressed his palm against the door, keeping it open as he leaned toward her.

"Lucille, it's Maves."

Her eyes grew wide. "That's not a name you come across every day."

"We happened to be in town and…"

"Do you mean Mavis Van Horn, Cousin Colette's son?" She thrust her face past the opening, her eyes darting around the porch. "Where is he? I don't see him."

Maves pointed to his chest. "I'm right here, Lucille."

"You're too old to be Colette's youngest."

"Well, it has been a long while since mother and I stopped in for a visit."

She raised a pair of glasses before her face, scrutinizing him through the thick lenses.

"I'll admit I don't recall when I saw her last. It seemed her son was not much more than a boy at the time. You're a grown man. I'm not so old I can't see that. But I suppose you could be him. There is a resemblance."

He nodded toward Webb.

"This is my son."

"Why," she said, squinting through the lenses, "he does resemble the young Mavis I remember. And who is the young lady?"

"I'm a homeless orphan." Frida reached out, taking her hand. "They picked me up down near the border."

She cast Maves a glance as Lucille pulled her through the doorway.

"Oh, you poor girl. You must come tell me all about it. I was just about to have my afternoon tea."

She took Frida by the arm and led her to a coffee table stacked with cups, teapot and a squat bottle of brown liquid. She pointed Frida to the overstuffed couch.

"Now, you are to call me Lucille. I must say you have the most beautiful eyes, like matching emeralds. What shall I call you, dear?"

"I'm not sure of my last name since my father's identity is still somewhat of a mystery, although I've heard several theories."

She glanced at Maves again, a gleam in her eye. Lucille took her hand.

"Oh, you poor darling."

"But I don't believe any of them," she continued. "You'd better just call me Frida."

Lucille reached over the coffee table and lifted the bottle.

"That sort of news calls for a drink. Will you have tea or something stronger? This time of day I find brandy with my tea a perfect pick-me-up."

"Frida has an important meeting," Maves said, pointing to the teapot. "She'll have the tea."

"Careful, Maves," Webb snorted, "you're sounding like a parent."

Frida shook her head. "It'll take more than that to convince me he's my father."

Lucille flinched, nearly dropping the bottle.

"My, my, Mavis, are you in the running too?"

He glared at Frida, ignoring the question.

"We've brought Frida here because of some trouble down in Mexico." He shifted his gaze to Lucille. "She was supposed to stay not far from here, with the sister of a friend. The trouble is the woman is nowhere to be found. In fact, it looks like she left in a hurry."

Lucille tilted the bottle, filling her cup to the brim.

"Well, that might explain my visit from the sheriff's office. It seems one of my neighbors, a woman I have never met, was threatened by some strange man. The deputy was checking the area to see if anyone else had seen him. I'm sorry to say I had no such excitement. I could use a good scare. Apparently, the woman was so unnerved she left town."

"What did this stranger look like, Lucille?"

"The deputy said he was blonde, with a foreign accent."

"Muntz," Frida gasped.

Webb recalled the man in the reflection. With all that had happened, he had never thought to mention it. He turned to Maves.

"I think I saw him back in Quintero when I was searching for Blanca."

"You think or you know?"

"I can't be certain. I was standing at a window when I saw a man in the reflection. He was in the shadow of a doorway across the street but I'm sure he had blonde hair."

Maves tapped the table with his finger, considering the options. Then he stood and nodded to Lucille.

"We appreciate your hospitality, Lucille, but we need to get moving."

Frida jumped from the couch. "Where are you taking me?"

"There's no point in staying here. I need to return you to Quintero."

"You can't!"

"I have no choice."

"But there's nothing for me back there."

"You're wrong." He pointed her toward the door. "Blanca is there and she'll make other arrangements for you."

"She has way bigger concerns than me, like her mother and her daughter. Don't you know that?"

"Of course I know it," he growled.

"Then don't take me back," she said, blinking back tears.

Seeing her, Maves softened his tone.

"There's nowhere else for you to go, Frida."

"I heard what you told Webb." She made no effort to hide her anger, wiping away the tears with the back of her hand. "You just want to be rid of me."

"This is not up to me. The decision belongs with Blanca. I'm only doing her a favor."

"You're no different from any other man. Men are pigs. They have no feelings."

Maves turned his gaze, unable to face her. "I've made my decision."

"You can't mean that, Maves." Webb pointed a finger at him. "You know it's not safe in Quintero."

"Blanca will ask the Father to arrange something. Maybe he can hurry up the asylum."

"Why don't you just stay here, sweetheart?" Lucille took her hand. "We'll get along famously."

She turned to Webb with a terrified look. He gave her a knowing wink.

"Your kind to offer, Lucille, but with this Muntz character around she's no safer here. She'll have to go home with us."

Maves glared at him.

"Don't give the girl false hope."

"There's nothing false about it, Maves. As I see it, we're the only hope she has."

Maves cut the air with his hand, his patience gone.

"That's enough talk! I've made up my mind. We're going back to Quintero."

Chapter Eight

A tense silence filled the cab, mixing with the fuming heat of late afternoon. Threads of dust swirled above the highway. Maves glanced at where Frida sat staring through the windshield, anger still clear in her face. As much as he hated abandoning the plan, knowing it would disappoint Blanca, he could see no alternative. They must return to Quintero.

The church's gold-topped steeple rose above the shimmering blacktop like a beacon marking their destination. Moments later the low buildings and dust-covered streets of Quintero came into view. He slowed as a stray dog hobbled across the highway, its three legs a reminder to stay vigilant.

To his left the border bridge emerged from the sloping plain. Half a dozen police cars, their lights flashing, sat scattered across the center section. Men in uniform milled about, some on phones, others scribbling onto clipboards. He pulled his eyes away with difficulty as the church appeared midway down the block.

Zak stepped through the doorway, frowning as Maves climbed from the truck and started up the sidewalk. Frida remained in the cab, her face set. Unsure what to do, Webb loitered nearby.

He had spent the entire return trip trying to figure a way to convince Maves she needed to come home with them. Knowing his father's stubbornness, he was nevertheless determined to keep his temper in check and win him over with the logic of the plan. Frida's safety was paramount. That meant going somewhere no one would expect.

He watched the priest shake Maves' hand, looking past him toward the truck. Webb glanced again at Frida. Her eyes remained without expression. He poked his head through the passenger window. After a moment, she blinked, her face softening.

"I know it's not your fault, Webb. It's no one's fault... or everyone's. I can't see what difference it makes if I end up getting jerked around again. Nobody cares what happens to a refugee from Guatemala."

"Lucille offered to help."

"Webb, don't even kid about that." She winced. "I mean, Lucille seemed nice but staying with her would be like getting stuck in a real-life Dickens novel. I'd end up wearing dresses made of old curtains and reading to her by candlelight."

She nodded toward the church.

"Does he really think Blanca will keep helping me?"

"Why wouldn't she? She's gotten you this far."

"You don't know the whole story, Webb. Blanca is up to something."

"What sort of something?"

"I don't know."

"What makes you think so?"

"I've seen things, heard things, nothing I can put my finger on but I'm pretty sure she wants me out of the way."

"Could it be that she just wants you safe?"

"Maybe, but it feels like something else."

"Regardless, it's no safer for you in Quintero now than when we left."

"Where else can I go?"

"We have to convince Maves to take you with us."

"But you heard what he said about false hope. He'll never agree to it... will he?"

He had no answer. He turned his gaze to the church entrance where Maves stood before the priest, his eyes to the ground. Zak glanced at the truck again and stepped closer.

"You can't truly mean to leave her here, Maves," he said, "knowing what you do. Yes, the nuns will take her in and, yes, they will do their best to protect her. But what sort of life is that for a young woman? And she will not be completely safe in this lawless place despite our efforts. You must know this."

Maves locked eyes with him. "You're sure Blanca will be away for a good while?"

"Yes, and I have no way to reach her. She was determined to keep her plans to herself in spite of my questions. I fear she is taking risks she should not. But that is her way. Once she makes a decision she becomes very single-minded in seeing it through."

He laid a hand on Maves' shoulder.

"I believe in your heart you know what must be done."

Maves said nothing, wishing he had such certainty. They turned as a police cruiser sped past, lights flashing. He gestured toward the car.

"We passed all sorts of commotion on the bridge. What happened?"

"Shots from a cartel gun battle crossed the river," he sighed, "striking a young girl in the leg. They grow bold, Maves. I fear worse is to come."

He took Maves' hand and peered into his face.

"I must return to my duties. If you are determined to leave her, the nuns will assist. Travel with God, my friend."

He disappeared through the door. Returning to the truck, Maves motioned Webb to climb in. Instead, he stayed put.

"I'm not leaving here until I know the plan."

Maves squinted at him, in no mood to argue.

"Blanca is unreachable for the time being. We have no choice but to take her back with us."

"Well, I'm glad you finally came to your senses." Webb gave Frida a quick glance. "We've been dancing around this for too…"

Maves raised a hand to stop him.

"I admit we can't leave the girl here." He moved to where Webb stood. "Father Zak said as much just now."

"Like I've been trying to tell you."

"But this is a short-term solution," he added, leaning close, "nothing more."

"What makes you so cold?" Webb sneered at him. "The last thing she needs is to hear that. She needs stability, reassurance."

"She'll be with us only until Blanca returns."

"But what about…"

"She's the one that has to figure out what to do with the girl!" he barked.

Frida jumped from the cab, her eyes flashing.

"Don't talk about me like I'm somebody's pet! I'm a real person and I'm right here in front of you."

Impressed by her boldness, Maves pointed her back to the truck.

"You're no one's pet, that's for sure. Now will you give me a moment's privacy to talk with my son?"

She stomped back to the truck and climbed into the cab, slamming the door behind her. Maves moved down the street. Webb hesitated and then followed, expecting an argument.

"You think I should just take in a young woman without giving it a second thought?" he said under his breath.

"She's all alone, Maves. She has no one."

"I've already said she's coming with us."

"Why are you so afraid to commit? You keep everything, everyone at arm's length. You always have."

Maves winced at the truth of his words.

"If you're so concerned," he hissed, "why don't *you* take her in?"

"I live in a one bedroom apartment, Maves. You know I don't have room enough. Besides, in a small town you know what people would say."

Maves took a breath, trying to corral his emotions. Suddenly, a solution came to him.

"Alright, she can stay as long as necessary, at least until Blanca gets in a position to take her someplace safe."

"Finally, you're talking sense."

Maves thrust a finger at him.

"But you have to share the responsibility."

"Sure, I'll look in on her when I can."

"You're not getting my drift, son," he said, shaking his head. "What it will take is you moving into my old office back of the house and sharing the duties with me, *all* of them, the housework, the cooking, the driving."

"How am I supposed to do all that and work?"

"You forget I have a business to run."

"But it's just you, no employees to keep busy, no payroll to meet. Besides, you're half-retired."

"It's that or I hand her over to Father Zak and the nuns."

Webb glanced at Frida, seeing no way around his father's terms. He gave his head a tentative nod. With that Maves stepped past him.

"I figured that's what you'd say," he called over his shoulder as he moved toward the truck. "So, we'll consider the matter settled."

Hours later he turned onto the familiar gravel drive, winding up the slope and past the stone outcroppings and clumps of cacti. His modest frame house rose briefly before the headlights. He cut the engine and slipped out of the door, the warm night air surrounding him, dense and formless.

A veil of stars slowly emerged above the roofline, silhouetting the house in a blaze of pinpoints, smoke-like and undulating. He traced the constellations with his gaze, naming each to himself one by one. The porch-side trees rattled before the shifting wind. In the satin-like darkness he stood idle, grateful for the momentary peace.

Webb's words echoed through his thoughts, unsettling in their truth. His inability to face his failings, to put words to his mistakes, had kept Webb from seeing him as

60

anything more than a shadow, a specter without form or substance, as untouchable as the air itself. Regrets were of no consequence now.

He mounted the porch steps and flipped a switch beside the door. The lights flickered and then came on. Below the stairs Webb still lingered beside the truck, a dazed expression on his face.

"I forgot how dark it is out here," he said, half to himself.

Frida moved next to him. He gestured beyond the pool of light.

"I have night blindness and once the headlights dimmed I was stuck."

"You can't see the stars?" she said, looking skyward.

He followed her gaze.

"I see some haze. That's about it."

Frida watched him squint into the darkness and then she suddenly turned away, blinking back tears.

"What's happened?" he said, leaning toward her. "Did I say something wrong?"

"I feel so sad," she gasped.

"But why?"

"You can't see."

"It's only night blindness, Frida. I'm not *going* blind."

"But the stars are so beautiful. It makes me sad to think you'll never see them."

"You're tired, is all." Webb took her arm and started for the house. "Let's go get you something to eat."

She pulled away, wiping her eyes as she gestured toward the porch.

"You talked him into letting me stay here, didn't you?"

For a moment, he was tempted to claim credit. Maves had been his ornery self throughout. But looking at her, he realized it would do neither of them any good to exclude him.

61

"No, Frida, we came to a decision together. He may not act like it but Maves wants you safe. You'll stay here until Blanca has a chance to work things out. I'm going to move into his old office and give him a hand."

"You're moving here?"

"I am, at least for a while."

"But you don't really want to live with your father, do you?"

"I won't lie to you. Living this close to Maves is not my idea of a good time."

"Then why are you doing it?"

"Maves and I have a deal."

"I don't want you moving back here just because of me."

"It's more complicated than that, Frida."

"But I'll feel like it's my fault you have to do something you don't want to do."

"Then let's just say I'm doing it for both of us."

He pointed her toward the door, unable to imagine the three of them sharing the cramped quarters. But Frida's tears had touched him in a way he had no words for. Despite his misgivings, he vowed to get along with Maves whatever it took.

Part Two

I am not dead yet, though in years,
And the world's way is yet long to go,
And I love the world even in my anger,
And love is a hard thing to outgrow.

-Robert Penn Warren

Maves slid the last box onto the bed of his truck, wedging it in among the others. He surveyed the garage for anything else he might give away. Making room for Webb and Frida had forced him into the long-overdue project of sorting through the mess of his spare rooms. The result sat in the boxes before him. Once started, he had felt he could empty the entire house without regret.

He pushed a candlestick that had belonged to his wife further into the nearest box, refusing to let his eyes rest on the tarnished brass, instead rubbing his fingers on his pants as if the metal held her memory in its touch. Returning to the border had filled his mind with long-avoided memories of her. He slammed the tailgate shut, forcing her image from his thoughts.

A branch snapped behind him and he turned to find Frida silhouetted by the morning sunlight. She gripped the doorjamb as if unsure whether to stay or run. Her eyes drifted to the truck.

"Have you had enough of me already?"

"Now why would you say that?"

"You look like you're moving out."

"I'm getting rid of some old things so we have more room in the house."

"Where's Webb?" She glanced around the room.

"He's probably out looking for work."

"He doesn't work?"

"He's always changing jobs," he grumbled. "I don't know why he can't settle on something."

"What kind of work do you do?"

"I'm a large animal vet. My office is right through there." He pointed to the back wall where a door stood half-open.

"Can I see it?"

He hesitated and then motioned her through the doorway, following her inside. Posters detailing sheep

64

anatomy and horse breeds filled the far wall. In the middle of the room a metal examining table sat across from a counter stacked with boxes of medications, sterile dressings and disposable syringes. A collection of sweat-stained caps hung from a corner hat rack.

"This is where I see the smaller animals." He gestured around the room, "Through that door is where I examine the large animals if they're brought in. Mostly I go see them where they live."

"Did Webb ever want to be a veterinarian?"

"He did once," he said, recalling a time long past. "He'd been around it all his life but I admit he surprised me when he decided on vet school. He and I didn't exactly get along during his growing up years, or even after. I figured he'd want to be as different from me as possible."

"What happened?"

"He dropped out after two semesters, said he didn't want to spend his life wading around in mud and manure. Turned out I was right after all." Hoping to change the subject, he pointed to a rear door. "The rest is through here."

He led her into a covered arena open on three sides. Wind hummed through the rafters. A weathered building sat twenty yards beyond, adjacent to a corral overtaken by weeds.

"Is that a stable?" Frida pointed toward the building.

"It used to be."

"You had horses?"

"A long time ago." He turned toward the office, hoping to shortcut the conversation.

"You don't keep them anymore?"

"No," he called over his shoulder.

"But why not?" she said, following after him.

"No reason."

"You're a vet and you don't like horses?"

He faced her, his mind again filling with the past.

"I've spent twenty years taking care of horses, other folks' horses. You don't do that if you don't like the animal."

"But why don't you have any of your own," she said, sweeping her arm in an arc, "when you have a place like this?"

He sighed, seeing no way around the question. "I quit keeping horses after my wife died. She was the one who…"

He stopped, unwilling to finish the thought. A look of understanding slowly crossed her face.

"Oh… I didn't mean to… I only wanted…" she murmured.

"It was a long time ago."

She glanced at the stable. "It's just that I always dreamed of having a horse."

"There's nothing wrong with dreaming."

She turned to him, the wind whipping her auburn hair. She grabbed a handful and held it to her neck.

"Having them around reminded you of her?"

"I just got too busy to tend them properly," he lied.

"She loved horses then?"

"Like I said, it was a long time back."

"When did she die?"

He squinted at her, making no effort to hide his annoyance. "Do you make a habit of asking questions?"

"I'm trying to get to know you."

"You know enough already."

"What makes you so private?"

"That's enough getting to know conversation for now. It's time for me to…"

An overhead speaker rattled with an earsplitting buzz. He started for the door as the speaker buzzed again. She hurried after him.

"What is that terrible sound?" She clapped her hands over her ears.

"The phone," he called back to her. "I need it loud so I can hear when I'm out back."

He vanished through the doorway. Moments later he reappeared, a leather satchel over his shoulder.

"You don't own a cell phone?" she asked in astonishment.

He stood glaring at her. "You think I'm just a clueless old geezer living out in the boonies, don't you? Go ahead and admit it."

"No, I…"

"The truth is that old office phone still works plenty good, so I don't see any reason to be rid of it. Being old is not the same as being useless."

"I didn't mean…"

"I have to get moving. Make yourself at home."

"You're leaving me?" she gasped.

"Like I said, I have a call."

"Take me with you."

"You'd be bored stiff."

"I can help."

"I work alone."

"Please don't leave me here," she pleaded.

"The house is safe enough."

"Maves, you don't understand. I have seen things, bad things. Being alone terrifies me."

All at once he realized she had never before called him by his given name. He peered into her face, touched by the gesture yet unable to get past the unease he felt in her presence, her youth and beauty a reminder of how time had passed him by. He sighed, handed her the leather case and started for the door. She hurried after him. Once outside he turned to face her.

"You'll have to work." He nodded toward a van parked beyond the arena. "Go ahead and get in. Maybe keeping you busy will stop you from asking so many questions."

67

Moments later they pulled away from the house, bouncing down the drive and across a cattle guard before turning southwest onto a two-lane blacktop. Tree-covered hills stretched away from them in all directions, layers of green-gray and ochre diminishing to blue. Dense shadows splattered the narrow highway.

He slowed as the road crested a boulder-covered ridgeline and began a gradual descent into a broad valley split by a winding ribbon of quicksilver, the meanderings of the shallow, tree-lined Medina River. Towering cypress and cottonwood trees edged the banks in a phalanx of massive trunks.

The caller had said a number of his sheep were down and others were showing signs of illness, and he had asked that Maves come out as soon as possible. He filed through a list of possible causes as they crossed the low bridge, the fast-moving water below it threading between roots and boulders, swirling into green pools and eddies.

In spite of his efforts, his mind kept returning to Frida's questions. She had meant no offence in asking them. He could see that for himself. Though a part of him wanted to answer, to put into words the thoughts that had dogged him for years, he could find no way.

Blanca's return had loosed the memories he had long kept at bay, memories he could only face in part, and dimly at best. After his wife's death, he had retreated into his work, a coward's way out he now admitted with reluctance. Having betrayed her trust, he had doubled his wrong by neglecting Webb, avoiding his guilt by cutting out his son in all ways save his physical presence. He winced at the unsettling realization.

Turning back on itself again and again, the road wound up a limestone bluff thick with underbrush and stunted trees. Tiny birds darted between their branches. Beards of maidenhair fern drooped over rock ledges and outcroppings, marking hidden springs.

They topped the bluff and the road opened onto a rock-strewn expanse of fenced grassland dotted with scrub oak and scattered with large stretches of barren soil. Here and there clumps of thin grass poked from the dirt like a bad haircut. Maves pointed out the window.

"That's what overgrazing does in this country," he yelled above the swirling wind, "even with a normal amount of rainfall."

She peered out the windshield. "Why would someone make their land so ugly?"

"Most of the time greed is the cause," he continued, grateful to discuss something he understood. "In any case the owner will ruin the place if he keeps it up."

"Maybe he doesn't mean to do it."

"I've never met the man so I can't say. Sometimes ignorance is the problem. But he bought the ranch from an old man who went broke due to the drought. The word is he paid far less than the place is worth. The old man was in such a state he barely noticed. That sounds a lot like greed."

He slowed the van, turning off the highway and onto a rutted drive that disappeared over a rise. A metal sign on the gatepost read 'Gitby'. Below it a wooden slat with 'No Damn Trespassing' scrawled across it in red paint hung from a length of baling wire. The track wound between groves of scrub oak crowded together like green bouquets, and past granite boulders, their rough sides splattered with orange and turquoise lichen. Yellow dust rose behind the van in swirling clouds.

Topping the rise, they followed a gradual slope to a dry creek. Maves stopped the truck and climbed out, leaving the engine running. He surveyed the roadside, moving along the edge until he spotted the plant he hoped to find. Pulling a folding knife from his pocket, he cut several clumps before returning to the truck. Frida watched with interest as he tossed the plants on the floorboard, climbed in and started again without a word of explanation.

Minutes later they came upon a cluster of gray-sided buildings and fenced pens scattered around a shallow swale. Sheep milled about behind the wire mesh. Thirty yards beyond, a weathered barn stood tucked beneath a massive cottonwood tree, its leaves shaking before a light breeze. There seemed to be no one about.

Maves pulled to a stop in front of the nearest pen. Grabbing his bag and the plants he had collected, he climbed out and motioned Frida to follow. The sheep seemed oblivious of them, staggering about the pen and coughing in a hoarse croak. Maves leaned over the top rail and surveyed the group before turning to Frida. He raised the plants to eyelevel.

"Try not to be too obvious about it but see if you can spot any plants that look like this."

She ambled along the fence line, casting an occasional glance at the ground. Returning to where he stood, she nodded toward the pen.

"There are plenty of those weeds outside the fence," she whispered, "but none on the inside. Does that mean the sheep have been eating them?"

"Sheep will eat whatever doesn't taste too bad if they can't find anything else." He pushed his chin toward them. "What else do you notice?"

She studied the animals as they stumbled about, their heads hanging.

"They look stiff and unsteady, like they might fall over at any moment."

"That's right. What else?"

"They're making a strange sound, a sort of a cough."

"Frida, you're a born detective."

She frowned at him. "I'm a detective?"

"A detective finds the clues and makes sense of them, and that's what you've just done. A lot of animal care amounts to no more than detective work."

"I get that the weeds are making them sick. But will they get better?"

"That all depends on whether…"

He paused at the ominous rumble of an approaching engine. Frida slipped behind him. He tried to imagine her fear as he watched a four-door pickup top the rise and race down the washboard drive, rattling to a stop in a cloud of choking dust.

The doors flew open and a man in jeans and a red shirt clambered out of the driver's seat, his face the color of his shirt. Maves studied his approach. He looked to be in his mid-fifties, lean and hard-featured, his thin-lipped mouth like torn paper. A sprout of hair rose from the top of his head in a puff of gray. A younger man in a straw hat crawled out of the passenger door and ambled after him.

"What the hell makes you think you can just waltz onto private property and go poking around wherever you want?" the older man called out from across the drive. "That no trespass sign is up there for a reason."

He spit into the dirt, wiping his mouth with the back of his shirt sleeve. Maves felt Frida move closer. Making no effort to hide his annoyance, he pointed at the two men.

"Which one of you is Gitby?"

"Who's asking?" the older man answered as he drew near.

"You called my emergency line and asked me to come out here straightaway."

"You're the vet?" he said, the surprise clear in his voice.

"You could've guessed if you'd bothered to stop and think about it."

"I saw a couple of people snooping around." He gestured behind Maves. "I had no way of knowing there'd be two of you."

"I bring my assistant along," he said, pulling Frida to his side, "when I decide it's necessary."

"And you'll be charging extra for bringing her, won't you?" He spit again. "I might've known. Most vets are prone to overcharge when they think they can get away

71

with it. And you don't even have a clue what the problem is, do you?"

"The only problem I see," Maves growled, "is you jumping to conclusions. People from around here don't appreciate…"

"Mr. Gitby," Frida interrupted, pointing to the pen, "we had a chance to look over your livestock and you've got a serious problem."

"That's why I'm not about to waste any more time talking nonsense," he barked, glaring at her before turning back to Maves. "Those damn sheep are more trouble than they're worth. What's wrong with them now?"

"They're sick," he answered, a faint smile crossing his lips.

"You think I don't already know that?" he snapped. "What's *making* them sick?"

"Yeah," the younger man leaned in, his eyebrows jumping as he ogled Frida, "what's making them poor little sheep all sick?"

"I'll let the expert answer that," she mumbled, turning her eyes to the ground.

"You're awful good-looking to be working with farm animals." The man looked her up and down. "You must like it all rough and dirty."

Snuff dotted his grin. Maves stepped between him and Frida, pointing a finger in his face.

"I never have been one to tolerate disrespect toward women. I don't intend to start now."

The man glared at him. He returned the stare before facing the older man.

"If you want my help, Gitby, you'll put junior back in his crib."

The man started toward Maves and then jerked backward as Gitby took hold of his neck and shoved him to one side.

"I didn't ask you out here to tussle, Van Horn. Do what you came to do."

"You asked me what's making your sheep sick." He pulled the cut weeds from his pocket. "Well, there are two causes. The animals have been feeding on milkweed just like this, which is poisonous."

"They've been poisoned?" he said, startled. "Can you cure them?"

"I'm going to send you some medication to put in their feed. Keep them in the pen until there is no more staggering or coughing. Based on how they look now, I don't believe you'll lose many."

"You said there were two causes."

"You've overgrazed to the point the sheep are exposed to the weed without much in the way of alternatives. They're hungry and they eat whatever they can find."

"Are you saying I've made these sheep sick?"

"I'm telling you what I see."

"Don't tell me how to run my ranch, Van Horn," he shouted. "This is a business and I aim to maximize my profits."

"Then you're likely to spend your profits on medicated feed." He pointed toward the scattered buildings. "But this place is yours. You're free to make all the mistakes you want."

Just then a border collie ambled through the barn door and limped toward them. As the dog drew near, the younger man kicked at it, narrowly missing. The collie cowered behind a fencepost. Gitby gestured at the dog.

"Since you're here, see if you can tell me what's wrong with that worthless bitch."

Frida knelt beside the collie, gradually coaxing her from beneath the fence with an open palm. Maves set his bag on the ground and moved next to her. The dog flinched at the sight of him. Keeping a distance, he held out his hand, giving her time to become familiar with his smell. Then he reached out to scratch behind her ears, gradually moving his hand down to her shoulders and along her spine, lifting her legs one by one.

"What do you think?" he asked her.

Frida glanced at the men standing over her and then ran her fingers along the collie's legs, lost in thought.

"When you examined her shoulders and hips I could see the pain in her eyes. It's unlikely she would have injured all her legs at once, so she must have some inflammation."

Maves peered into her face, trying to hide his surprise. Then he grabbed his bag and stood.

"Your collie has arthritis," he said, locking eyes with Gitby. "She needs to go easy on those joints."

"I don't need a pet," he grumbled, "I need a working dog. When can she do her job again?"

"I'll give you some medication to ease the pain but she's had enough of sheep work."

"Are you telling me she won't get better?"

"I'm telling you there are ways to manage arthritis so the pain is lessened and a dog can have a reasonably normal life, but a life without herding sheep all day, every day."

"That's all I needed to know."

He turned without a word and disappeared inside the barn. Maves glanced down at Frida, spotting the worry in her eyes. Moments later Gitby stepped through the door with a hunting rifle in one hand and a spade in the other. Frida drew the dog to her.

"Maves, you can't let him shoot her," she whispered.

"Hold on, Gitby." He raised a hand. "This dog is not lame. She has a lot of good years left if she's cared for right."

"Years to do what, lie around and cost me feed and vet bills?" He spit into the dirt. "You'd like that, wouldn't you?"

"I might have known you're one of them bleeding hearts," the young man said, spitting the words. "Any vet

74

worth his salt would know to put down a useless mutt like that one."

"Shut the hell up, Nestor," Gitby barked. "I don't pay you to talk. Get back to the stable and unload the feed."

"This isn't about me or my business," Maves continued, "it's about what's right and wrong. It's wrong to put down a dog for no reason."

"In my book a dog that can't work is money down the drain. That's worse than wrong."

Maves moved within inches of his face. "You have a damn poor view of this world, Gitby. And you don't deserve a dog as gentle and good-natured as that one."

"If you're so keen on the bitch, then you can take her off my hands."

"Say yes to him, Maves," Frida said, jumping to her feet. "Let's get her away from this place."

He took her arm and walked down the fence line. The dog followed at his heels.

"Frida, listen to me," he said under his breath. "A vet can't take home every unwanted animal that comes along."

"Please let me take her, Maves," she pleaded. "I'll care for her. I'll buy her food and medicine. Please let me."

"You can't take on that kind of responsibility right now," he said, shaking his head. "You know that better than I do."

"But what alternative do we have? If we leave her here, the bastard will shoot her."

"Maybe I can talk him out of it."

"But how can you? You heard what he said."

"I'll think of something. Just give me a..."

A muted ring stopped him. Turning away, he pulled the phone from his pocket and moved along the fence line. Gil Shannon's usually calm voice echoed in his ear, asking for him to come as soon as possible. Two of his horses were sick and three others appeared to be showing similar symptoms. Maves had never heard him sound so grim.

He turned back to the fence but Frida was nowhere in sight. Gitby stood beside the barn doorway, the rifle still in his hands.

"Don't forget to send out the sheep medication, Van Horn," he yelled. "And don't even think about charging me for that damned dog."

He vanished through the doorway. Before Maves could decipher his meaning, a bark caught his attention. He turned toward the sound, spotting Frida in the van, the collie next to her. He ambled over to the passenger window, knowing she had outfoxed him. By the look on her face, she knew it too.

"She looks right at home in here," she ventured. "Don't you agree?"

"I'm impressed," he admitted. "That took some quick maneuvering."

She avoided his gaze. "I don't know what you mean."

"Sure you do. If you got the dog in here, you figured Gitby would call it quits and I'd have no choice but to take her."

He leaned on the door waiting for an answer.

"Well, it worked, didn't it?" she said, finally turning to face him.

Her tone told him she was still unsure what he would do. He leaned in to make his point.

"You'll have to find a home for her."

"But I can keep her until then?"

"You'll need to take care of her feeding, bathing, medications, whatever she needs."

"More than anything, she needs a name."

"Giving her a name may seem like a good idea but it isn't," he replied, his voice solemn. "Better to leave it impersonal so you don't get attached."

"But everyone deserves a name," she countered. "Can't we talk about it?"

"Not now, I need time to think. That phone call was from an old friend of mine, a rancher who has some sick horses. He's not one to fret but he sounded worried, real worried."

He pushed away from the window and rounded the van. Minutes later they passed back through the gate and onto the highway, turning west toward the small town of Camp Wood. Gil Shannon's ranch sat ten miles beyond, along the banks of the Nueces River.

Though he had travelled the area for years, Maves had never tired of the rugged hills rimming the river canyon, the tops Salmon Peak and Black Mountain poking above them like the ears of a pony. Further west the Anacacho Mountains stretched south toward the Mexican border, a place where, he knew better than most, life can change in an instant.

Chapter Ten

Maves glanced at the collie on Frida's lap. Riley Banks had one like it when they made their last rabies survey along the Nueces. The upper reaches of the river flowed a mile to the west. He knew if he followed it far enough, he would find himself south of Crystal City near where Riley had died, the canyon where he lost his eye and his friend. A jolt of pain shot through his leg, real or imagined he did not know. Even after so many years the memories spilled from his mind like water breaching a dam.

With effort, he turned his thoughts to Gil Shannon's phone call. Gil had described the horses as excitable and restless, which could have many explanations. But horses wandering in circles, unsteady and heads drooping, sounded like sleeping sickness. He would know more after an examination. In case he had guessed right, he advised Gil to make a quart of coffee for each horse and get it into them as fast as possible. And under no circumstances should he allow them to lie down.

An hour later the van crested a ridge and the narrow oasis of Gil's ranch appeared in the valley below them like an emerald set in pink granite. Within minutes they were rattling across the cattle guard spanning the ranch entrance. A metal sign over the gate read 'Circle 6'.

Maves followed the road along the valley floor, passing through thickets of walnut and hickory, their branches heavy with ripening nuts. Further on, stone bluffs rising above the treetops flanked a meandering creek surrounded by hay fields and open pasture. The tall grass moved before the shifting wind in undulating waves. A two-story house appeared around a sharp bend, a barn and corral to one side.

Maves angled the van beside the barn and cut the engine, nodding Frida out the door without a word. The dog followed, circling her expectantly. As he watched her move toward the corral, he realized he had said almost nothing since leaving Gitby's ranch. She had assisted him without complaint and, he realized, deserved his gratitude, not his silence.

What she made of his quietude he could not guess. If asked, he would call it flaw though in truth silence was his nature. He climbed from behind the steering wheel, vowing to talk more.

"What do you think of this country?" he said awkwardly, gesturing to the surrounding cliffs. "There aren't many that get this far up into the Nueces watershed."

She glanced around, a confused look on her face. "What?"

"I've always found the Circle 6 a handsome ranch."

"Maybe we should talk about these horses," she said, nodding to the corral. "They don't look so good."

Coming to his senses, he turned his attention to the small herd. Several well-groomed horses wandered about aimlessly, their heads down. A sorrel mare stood next to the nearest fencepost. Maves turned a circle, checking for Gil before stepping up to the fence. He placed his palm on the horse's jaw. The mare leaned into him, nearly falling onto the rail. He grabbed the halter and pulled up her head, walking her along the fence line.

"Tell me what you see," he called to Frida, gesturing to the other horses as he kept the sorrel moving.

"They look unsteady. Have they eaten milkweed?"

"Keep looking."

She stepped onto the bottom rail and peered over the fence. "I don't think milkweed is the problem. They aren't coughing like the sheep. They look tired, like they want to sleep, but they're restless too."

"Anything else?"

She turned to him. "That horse almost fell over when you put your hand to him."

"You're right on all counts except that he is a she," he answered before handing her the halter. "Keep her moving, and no matter what, don't let her lie down."

"What's wrong with her?" She pulled the mare in a tight circle. "What's wrong with all of them?"

Before he could answer the door to the house flew open and a man in a wide-brimmed hat emerged, hurrying down the steps with his head down, a bucket of brown liquid in his hand. He had almost reached the corral when he looked up and spotted Frida. He jerked to a stop. The brown fluid sloshed over the rim, throwing up tiny clouds of dust.

His gaze drifted to where Maves stood watching and a look of relief moved over his face like a cloud crossing the sun. He lowered the bucket.

"I've been dousing these horses with enough coffee to keep an army awake." He wiped his hands on his pants and shook Maves' hand. "I sure hope it does some good."

"You're supposed to get the coffee in them, not on them, Gil," he quipped, nodding to the coffee-soaked ground.

"She just startled me is all," he said, cutting his eyes at Frida.

"This is Frida. She's here to assist."

"Now there's a surprise." He pushed back his hat and gave Maves a conspiratorial wink. "Long as I've known you, you've never done anything but work alone. What could possibly have made you change your mind and hire a young woman as an assistant?"

"Well, I just… I thought… I mean I figured…" he stammered, flustered by the implication. "Damn it, Gil, things change."

Frida met his gaze for an instant then turned her eyes back to the mare. Gil grinned and gave him another wink.

"No need to get all perturbed, Maves. I know you work long hours. Having an assistant, a good-looking one at that, should make the time…"

"I'm not getting any younger, you know," he barked, annoyed by Gil's ribbing. "Some days I just need an extra pair of hands."

"Sure you do, Maves."

"And I like doing a job right," he grumbled, "so we'd best get on with it. Tell me about these horses."

He gestured toward the corral. Gil's grin vanished.

"I've done what you said, coffee and all, although I had a hell of a time keeping that sorrel mare from going to ground."

"That's where she wants to be right now."

"What do you think, Maves," he asked, his tone anxious, "now that you've seen them up close?"

Grateful for a change of subject, he took his time studying the mares. Gil paced the fence, giving him an occasional glance. Suddenly he threw his hands into the air.

"Are you going to give me an answer," he shouted, "or not?"

"You haven't had these horses for long," Maves said without looking at him, "have you, Gil?"

"I bought them down near Del Rio just last week. Got them for a song too."

"How many head did you come back with?"

"There are about sixty in the pasture out back of the barn. You're thinking I got scalped, aren't you?"

"Well, yes and no. These are some fine-looking horses. But as you can see, they're real sick."

"Don't keep me in suspense, Maves," he said, leaning in. "What are they sick *with*?"

"How do the others look?" He kept his eyes on the mares.

"So far, so good."

"Did this man say they'd had their shots?"

"He guaranteed me they were all up to date."

"Well, he missed one."

"Damn it, Maves, *which* one did he miss?"

81

"Can't you guess?"

"They've got the sleeping sickness?" he whispered.

"They do."

"Can you save them, Maves?" He peered at him, his ruddy face lined with worry. "Please tell me you can."

He studied Gil's gray eyes. "Don't tell me you've you grown attached to these horses *already*?"

"Well, I…"

"Gil, you take to horses quicker than a ten-year-old girl."

"Don't rub it in, Maves," he spoke under his breath, glancing at Frida. "A rancher should be more impersonal about his livestock, I know. But ever since I was a kid I always did like horses."

"That's an understatement, Gil."

"More than anything, I hate to see a horse suffer, any horse."

"Try not to worry yourself just now." He laid a hand on Gil's shoulder. "It'll be dicey getting these sick ones through the illness, but we'll give it our best. The others need to be vaccinated right away. Since they're showing no symptoms, I'm hopeful you'll keep them all. Who knows, maybe the man just missed vaccinating these four."

"He'll miss more than that if I ever see him again," he grumbled as he pushed through the gate, grabbing the halter from Frida.

Maves started for the van, motioning her to follow. The collie limped between their feet. Opening the rear doors, he leaned into a small rectangle filled with cabinets and supplies, lifting out a box of vials and several large syringes and passing them to her. Then he slipped a syringe into his shirt pocket and grabbed the leather case from the shelf, starting for the corral.

Moments later they stepped through the gate and into the circular arena. He took the syringe from his pocket and lifted a vial from the box Frida held, inserting the needle and drawing out the serum. The mare stumbled as Gil moved her into position. After he had passed the rope to Frida, Maves pointed him toward the barn.

"Start bringing the rest of the herd up this way. We'll need to check if any others are showing symptoms."

He disappeared through the barn door. Maves motioned Frida to raise the mare's head.

"When you're treating a horse in this condition," he said, slipping a hand under the horse's neck and readying the syringe, "you have to be careful how you handle her. She will lean on anything she can find to steady herself. That's because the encephalitis is disrupting her balance. If I try to give her this serum like I normally would, she'll lean into the pressure of the needle and fall on me. You don't want an animal this size landing on you."

"How will you keep her from falling?"

"I'm going to press my palm on the opposite side of her jaw while I insert the needle into her jugular vein. She should lean into my hand. But even though she's sick, she may get jumpy. Horses don't like needles any more than we do."

"What should I do?"

"Keep her head up and gently move her forward if she starts to stumble. I'll keep up with her."

Maves pressed the needle to the mare's neck. She flinched but remained steady at Frida's direction.

"What are you giving her?" she said, looking over his shoulder.

"First, I'll give the serum to combat the virus, along with a stimulant to keep her awake and upright, although she may have had enough coffee to make do. Then I'll add a dose of vaccination under the skin. Together, they may give her a fighting chance."

"She's beautiful, Maves," Frida said, studying the mare. "We must save her."

He glanced at her, surprised by her ease with the mare. In truth, he found her entire life, as foreigner or refugee hard to believe. Her marriage to a gang member seemed an improbable mistake, a fact with no connection to the woman standing before him. He could make no sense of it.

Hours later they released the last of the herd. A crescent moon stood high in the night sky, casting dim shadows across the paddock. Frida lingered in the doorway, watching the horses amble away from the barn and slowly blend with the darkness. To the east, the sky had begun to lighten. Maves turned back to the yellow light of the stalls, collecting the remaining vials of vaccine and dropping them into his case.

Moving to a nearby bench, he sat hard and pressed a thumb into his stiff back, trying to ease the ache. Though he had claimed age as a way to explain away Frida's presence, perhaps the lie held more truth than he wanted to admit. He watched her turn from the doorway and wander along the stalls. The thought came to him that he would turn fifty in a year and a half. Fifty must seem ancient to a woman her age, he admitted reluctantly.

Gil appeared with two mugs and a grease-stained paper bag, handing a mug to Maves and setting the bag on the bench. Spotting Frida, he waved her over.

"It's nearly five so there's no point in trying to sleep. Come have some of Greta's coffee." He motioned to the paper bag. "She sent me with sausage and biscuits too."

"That's very thoughtful of her," she said, taking the mug.

"We'd ask you to stay for a real breakfast but in all the years I've known Maves, he never once agreed to join us. He always has to be on the move. And he gets ornery if you press him on it."

Maves glanced at her, wondering what she must think of him, a man unwilling to accept even the kindness of an old friend. Had he become what he most wished to avoid, he ruminated, a younger version of his father? An image of the old man, frail and bitter, rose in his thoughts like plume of smoke, blocking out all else.

Moments later the drone of a voice brought him back into the barn and he blinked, raising his gaze to find Gil standing over him. He pointed to a smoke-gray horse standing in the opposite stall, the only horse left in the barn. Maves stared at him for a moment, trying to fathom his meaning. Gil shook his finger at the horse.

"What do you have to say then, Maves?"

"We accept," he said, surprising himself with the answer.

Gil stared at him, his mouth half open.

"You do?"

"Sure we do," he said, grabbing his case, "as long as we don't have to hobnob all morning."

"I can't see that there's anything more to hobnob about."

"You can't?" He looked up in surprise. "Gil, I've never known you to run out of subjects to hobnob on."

"Well, I've got nothing more to say as long as you'll do your part."

"What do you want me to do?"

"Well, nothing special other than the usual."

"I can make a sausage casserole."

"Maves," he said, grimacing, "don't even kid about such a thing."

"What makes you think I'm kidding?"

"You would never even consider it, being a vet and all."

"Sure I would. I make a mean sausage casserole, if I do say so. But I don't see what being a vet has to do with it."

"I never heard anything so disgusting, making sausage from a... wait a minute." Gil squinted at him. "Are we talking about horse or breakfast?"

Maves blinked and peered up at him, exhausted by the conversation. "I must be more tired than I realized. I thought you just said we're having horse for breakfast. I'm hungry enough to eat a horse but that doesn't mean...."

"You mean to stay for breakfast?" he interrupted.

"Yes, we'll stay." He glanced at Frida. "How many ways do I have to say it, casserole and all?"

"Maves, we're talking about Marley!" he bellowed, his voice shaking.

"What's got you so worked up, Gil?" he asked, baffled.

"I thought you meant to make sausage out of *him*!"

"Who the devil are you talking about?" He looked around the barn, confounded by Gil's reaction. "The only Marley I know of is a ghost in the Dickens story."

"I'm talking about my favorite ranch horse, *Marley.*" He jabbed a finger at the opposite stall. "You're sure to remember him."

"What about your favorite ranch horse?" he said, eyeing him with considerable suspicion.

"The old boy has gotten me through many a rough spot but his ranching days are over, Maves," he answered, his voice a bit calmer. "In spite of your sick attempt at humor, I know you'll give him a good home."

Maves dropped his case and jumped up, looking from Gil to the horse and back. Then he turned his gaze on Frida.

"Oh, no you don't. One animal adoption a day is enough."

"But it's already tomorrow, Maves," she said with a wry grin.

"She's got you there, Maves," Gil snorted, pointing to the eastern horizon. "The sun will be up any minute."

"Why don't you keep old Marley," he grumbled, "if he's been such a good horse?"

"The younger stallions are harassing him and he won't give in. Still thinks he's in charge, I suppose. He even goes looking for trouble and he's gotten roughed up several times pretty bad. He's bound to get hurt beyond fixing sooner or later. Now, what sort of life is that for a horse that gave years of loyalty and good service?"

"Did she put you up to this?" he barked, thrusting his chin at Frida.

"The idea was Greta's. She said if there's anyone who cares about horses it would be Maves Van Horn."

"I'm not so sure I like being Van Horn's home for orphan dogs and horses."

As if understanding, the collie rushed to his side. Gil motioned at her and waved a finger in Maves' face.

"You got yourself a good dog and a good assistant so don't be complaining. Frida even figured out Marley's problem without me telling her."

"Those hoof-shaped bruises on his hip might have had something to do with it, Gil," she said, waving off the compliment.

Knowing he was beaten, Maves grunted a reply. Gil took him by the shoulder.

"There is one more favor I need to ask before we go to breakfast. I can't talk about it in front of Greta or she gets all broken up. There's an old Mexican feller, Cruz Guzman, with a small goat ranch about three miles south of here. After I fell off the roof and broke my leg, he spent weeks coming up here nearly every day. He did whatever needed doing and pretty much kept the ranch going until I got on my feet. That was some years back and he's well up in age now, eighty or more, but I have never found a way to return the favor.

"Well, Cruz has a pregnant mare that's down. He spent all his savings and nearly lost his ranch taking care of his sick wife, so he can't afford a vet. They had been married for over sixty years, Maves." He pulled two hundred dollar bills from his wallet and stuffed them into Maves' shirt pocket. "I can never repay what I owe him but I want you to stop in and see what you can do for that mare."

87

"Keep your money, Gil," Maves said, pulling out the bills. "I'll see to the mare just because you asked me to."

"This needs to be my favor to him, Maves, not yours. He's as independent as they come so just tell him it's my way of saying thanks for all he did." He motioned Frida toward the door. "Now, let's go introduce the new assistant to Greta. She'll be glad to have some female company at breakfast for once."

"I'll be right along," Maves called after him.

He watched them move into the early light, his mind filling with thoughts of his past, of Riley's death, of Blanca's lonely pregnancy, of how, unlike Gil and Cruz Guzman, he had failed at marriage. Peering into the blue-gray dawn, he pondered the likelihood of ending like his father, alienated from family, alone and angry at the world. Then, dismayed by the thought, he lifted the case and started for the house.

Chapter Eleven

The pitted and winding road to Cruz Guzman's house topped a rock-strewn ridge and dropped into a narrow canyon thick with Spanish oak and juniper. A dry creek scattered with limestone boulders paralleled the road, the huge stones glowing phosphorescent-like beneath the morning haze. Twisted lines of cloud drifted overhead.

All at once the canyon opened onto a wide valley. Lines of blue-gray hills rippled into the distance, sloping toward the horizon. Frida peered through the windshield at the angular forms of Spanish goats dotting the broad vale like spilled salt.

At the edge of the valley a house came into view. The once-red siding had faded to a dull pink. Set at the base of Kelly Peak, the tallest in the area, the sagging home overlooked a low-slung barn. Maves pulled alongside a flatbed truck parked just outside the building. A yellow-eyed dog stood before the barn door, watching them.

Hoping someone might appear, Maves made no effort to climb out. He knew from experience that arriving unexpectedly at such a remote location could prove risky, especially with a huge animal blocking their way. Seeing the dog, the collie yipped twice before Frida could silence her.

"Hush, Pilar," she whispered into the collie's ear.

Maves squinted at her. "I thought we agreed you wouldn't name the dog, seeing as how she won't be staying long."

"Oh, Maves, it's cruel to leave her nameless. Besides, we should have a way to get her attention if we need to."

"The only name Gitby used was bitch," he grumbled. "Maybe we should stick with that."

"Don't be such a typical man," she said, glaring at him. "I named her for the character in Hemingway's *For Whom the Bell Tolls*."

"I know the story."

"Then you know Pilar is a strong woman, and loyal." She stroked the collie's neck. "This one would need to be loyal and strong to have survived in such a dismal place. Pilar is a fine name for her."

Seeing her determination, he let the matter drop.

"Better keep her in here." Without looking, he nodded toward the barn. "Strong as she is, she doesn't want to get too near that big guy."

"I think it's a little late for that," she whispered.

He turned to find the dog below the window, peering up at them complacently. In one motion, he stood, draping his paws over the door.

"He looks friendly enough," she said.

"You're not face to face with him," he whispered.

"What do we do?"

"I'm open to suggestions."

A voice called from the barn and the dog slipped off the door, ambling away before disappearing around the corner. Seconds later, a man stepped through the doorway. Short and bow-legged, he had a broad, coffee-colored face split by a white mustache that drooped well below his bottom lip. Sheaves of hair poked from beneath his cap like snow-covered wheat. He motioned Maves inside with two quick waves before hurrying back through the door.

Moments later they stepped into the dim confines of the low-ceilinged barn. A row stalls lined one wall, all but one empty. Paralleling the stalls, a narrow aisle led to an open area crowded with hay bales and sacks of feed. In the middle of the room a horse lay stretched out on a bed of fresh straw, its breathing labored and shallow. The man bent over the mare, stroking its neck with a damp sponge. He glanced at Maves and then dipped his hand into a bucket, sponging the horse as he spoke.

"Please forgive my poor manners but the horse, she is very sick," he said in the hoarse tenor of an old man. "I must bring her fever down or she will lose the foal."

Maves moved next to him and knelt, running his hand along the mare's flank and udder. Then he rolled up his sleeve, inserting his hand to palpate the foal. Relieved to find it alive, he turned to the man.

"Mr. Guzman, my name is Maves Van Horn. I'm a vet. First, let me tell you the foal is big, which could present a problem, but seems to be alright otherwise. Gil Shannon asked me to come out and help with the mare if I can. Tell me about her."

"Please call me Cruz." He continued stroking the horse. "She had not been eating, and she had milk leaking more than a little. I know this is wrong but I hoped she would get better. Then the fever came."

"The fever started recently?"

"In the last two days only." He gave Maves a solemn nod. "I saw her milk three days before this happened, but until then she was on her feed and had no fever."

"Is she due to deliver soon?"

"It is past her time already. This foal I did not plan. A stallion from the next ranch got loose and..." he glanced at Frida before leaning toward Maves, "well, the stallion, he was big."

"Then we can hurry the foal if we have to, but I'd like the mare stronger before she delivers."

"Mr. Van Horn, I have no money but I ask you to save her if you can. She belonged to my late wife and, well... I will find a way to pay you."

"I'll do my best, Cruz. You can call me Maves. This is my assistant, Frida."

"I am honored to meet you, senora" he said, giving his head a slight bow. He looked up at Maves. "The mare, what is wrong with her?"

"I believe she has a problem with her placenta, most likely caused by an infection. I'm going to give her one medication to fight the infection and another for the inflammation. Then we wait. It would be best if the foal came on its own."

"I'll need my case," he said, motioning Frida toward the door, "a syringe and the other box of vials, the one with the red label."

She hurried out the door. He moved to a nearby bench, his legs aching. He could feel the lack of sleep in every muscle. He leaned his back against a support beam and studied the old man.

On his knees, both hands to the sponge, Cruz bent over the mare as if praying to the god of horses. Watching him stroke her neck, he tried to fathom losing a wife after sixty years but could find no foothold for such thoughts. The image seemed from another world, a place unknown to him. Etched by years of ranch work, Cruz's wizened face was completely absorbed in the task, as if caring for the horse was in fact a sacred act.

For a moment Maves imagined what he might ask the old man about those sixty years when all at once his voice sounded above the mare's labored breaths as if he had lost control of his own mouth. Cruz turned to him, nodding slowly as he listened, his gaze lost to another time. Then he sat back on the straw and gestured toward the morning light.

"When we were boys my father would take me and my brother to the coast south of Riviera, near the King Ranch, to catch the big redfish. Sometimes in the mornings the reds would move between us and the sunrise, and we would squint into that bright light trying to spot the tails of those redfish.

"Looking into the sun for so long took the color from our eyes so that all things, the clouds, the laguna, the mangrove trees, even the blue sky all turned to gray. My brother would say how sad he felt to have a world of no color, of only black and white and gray.

"I tell you this because that was my life after my wife, she died of the cancer. Without her I felt I walked in a desert, a desert of no color. I did not wish to see the world anymore. Then one day my eyes, they came open.

"My wife, she had prayed and prayed for children but God never gave them to her. The horses she came to love like her own blood, like her children. That is why I decide to keep this one." He patted the mare's flank. "I feel my wife in the soul of this mare. She is the last of her horses. When I am with her I feel my wife is close. That is why I let her have the unwanted foal, so I might keep my wife close until my time is finished. This, I think a man can understand."

Maves nodded as if he did. Suddenly, his thoughts turned to Blanca. He wanted her there with him, to hear her voice, feel her touch. He glanced at the doorway, imagining her at the threshold looking as she had when he last saw her. After a moment, he blinked, unable to escape the foolishness of such a wish.

He turned at the sound of Frida's footsteps. Dragging a bench next to the mare, she set the case and box of vials on the seat. Then she lifted out a single bottle and handed him the syringe.

He pulled a second vial from the case and filled the syringe from both bottles before kneeling beside the mare and motioning Cruz to hold her while he slipped the needle under her hide. She flinched but stayed in place, her breath still labored and shallow. She seemed to tolerate the medication with little difficulty.

All at once he realized he was exhausted, barely able to keep his head up. Frida stood with her back against a nearby stall, her eyes half-closed. He stood with a groan and surveyed the barn. A dilapidated couch sat in the far corner.

"Cruz, I'm going to ask a favor," he said, motioning toward the corner. "We need to get some sleep. I'll use the couch. Can you spare a bed for Frida?"

She looked up at the sound of her name. Rising stiffly to his feet, Cruz gave her a quick nod.

"You are welcome to my home." He turned to Maves. "There is room for you both, if you wish."

"Thank you, Cruz," he said, "but I prefer to stay here."

"As I do." He gestured toward the door. "After you, senora."

"But I should stay too," she protested.

Maves nixed the idea with a shake of his head. "I may need you to drive so I want you rested."

Nodding her understanding, she started for the door. Maves watched her fade into the mid-morning light. Then he moved to the couch and at once fell into a restless slumber, his dreams filled with visions of Blanca, her depthless eyes, her sand-hued skin. She seemed to be everywhere and nowhere.

In a flash, he found himself at the edge of a river. Below him a black torrent sped past in eddies and pools, tearing at the bank with an ominous roar. To his right a rope bridge stretched from bank to bank. The cables swayed before a coursing wind.

Blanca appeared on the opposite shore. She pointed to the bridge, motioning him across. He started but then hesitated, doubtful the frayed rope and weathered slats would hold. She waved him forward again.

Suddenly, he was halfway across. The wooden slats groaned beneath his weight. He gripped the rope sides and glanced at the far bank. She waved him onward with an impatient frown.

He started again just as a familiar voice sounded at his back. He pivoted, spotting Webb at the river's edge, a look of panic on his face. Pointing to the cables, he frantically motioned his return.

Maves stood unable to move, caught between the two of them, the water racing by inches below his feet. He knew he had to choose, go forward or back. But he stood frozen, unable to move.

Without warning the gunshot pop of a snapping cable echoed overhead. The bridge groaned and jerked to one side, quivering for an instant. He felt himself suspended in air, weightless, the slats fallen, the rope slack beneath his grip.

A surprising sense of relief moved over him, of a moment arrived, a choice made, the black water holding a welcome finality. He puzzled over the feeling. He had never been one to give up. Yet here he was.

He peered into the dark torrent, seeing his weakness, his wish for escape, his fear of being known, and a fierce anger swept through him. His hands again gripped the rope, pulling upward, unwilling to let go, as if they alone knew his true nature. Then the black water swallowed him.

He jerked upright. A shaft of afternoon sunlight angled through the door, casting the room in yellow. He stood and surveyed the barn. Nothing moved. Then the mare stirred and sat upright, tracing her flank with her muzzle. He knew at once she was about to deliver.

Jumping from the couch, he hurried to where Cruz lay slumped on a pile of blankets. Giving his shoulder a shake, he moved alongside the horse. Cruz scrambled next to him. Maves saw in an instant the mare was in distress.

"She has trouble, I think," Cruz said, leaning over him.

Frida appeared at his shoulder, case in hand.

"I had a feeling…" she said in a whisper.

He motioned her closer. "We have to hurry."

"What's wrong with her?"

"The placenta has come loose. Instead of breaking, it's blocking the foal's progress." He opened his hand. "I need a scalpel right away. Look on the right side… quickly or the foal will suffocate."

She rifled through the bag, pulling out the knife and passing it to him. Bending close to the mare, he ran the blade along the crimson outer lining of the placenta, careful to avoid the bulges marking the foal. A small hoof popped through. He tossed aside the scalpel and felt for the other leg, finding it turned under, blocking the delivery.

95

The mare raised her head and eyed Maves, straining to push. He ran his fingers along the foal's other leg, unable to reach the hoof and turn it. Using his free hand, he nudged the nose backwards and again felt for the turned leg. The mare pawed at the straw impatiently.

He motioned Frida to take the foal's free leg and then shifted his hand. A small hoof grazed his knuckles. Turning his arm, he grabbed the leg and pulled it alongside the other. The mare pushed again. Suddenly the foal moved, slipping free and nearly dropping into his lap. He grabbed the back legs and stood, lifting it free of the placenta.

Finding no sign of breath, he set the foal back on the floor and wiped its nostrils clean. Still no breath. He lifted the back legs and cleared its nose again. No change. Fighting a growing panic, he grabbed a piece of straw and held it to the foal's nose, tickling a nostril. It gasped, once then twice, finally taking its first breaths.

"Isn't there something we should be doing?" Frida paced a tight circle. "I mean, it's still attached to her."

She hovered over the foal like a nervous mother. Maves moved next to her.

"Both the mare and foal need to rest awhile. Leaving the placenta in place allows the foal maximum benefit. When she's ready, the mare will stand and the umbilical cord will break."

"It's going to be alright?"

"It's too soon to tell. But…" he tried to sound reassuring, "try not to worry."

On impulse, he reached out, touching her forearm, surprised by the heat of her skin, the soft down of her hair. She looked up at him, startled, and he jerked his hand back, feeling the blood rush to his face. An instant later Cruz appeared next to him.

"The mare, she will live, I think." He grabbed his hand. "I thank you, my friend."

"We'll need to watch them both for awhile," he replied, grateful for the distraction.

"What do you think of the colt?"

"He's had a close call."

"I told you his father was big."

"We're lucky his size didn't cause more problems," he mused, studying the foal. "You're going to have quite a feed bill once he starts eating."

"Yes but I always wanted a big horse to chase down the damn coyotes. Now I will have one."

He turned and vanished through the door. Moments later he returned with a plate of sausage and egg-stuffed flour tortillas.

"These I made this morning but they are still good, I think."

Maves grabbed a taco and cast a furtive glance at Frida, puzzling over his reaction and hers. What had he seen in her eyes, a reflection of his own awkwardness, of pity for his inept attempt to comfort her? Or was there something more, something he could scarcely let himself consider, that she might find him attractive in spite of his age? He refused to believe it possible. He absently reached for his bad eye, suddenly conscious of its cloudy hue.

An unbidden image of Blanca came to him followed by a tinge of guilt. He wondered where she might be at that moment and for an instant again wished he could see her. Then he turned his gaze back to the barn, to what he knew, what he could count on, hoping his troublesome past would leave him be.

Chapter Twelve

Webb paused in the kitchen of the spare, unadorned house, the house where he grew up, the house where he had last seen his mother. Even now her memory seemed to fill the room, the finger-worn cabinets, the faded countertops, her presence weighing on him. Suddenly the room felt claustrophobic, the air stifling.

He hurried across the living room and through the door, stepping into the fading sunlight. A shifting breeze whistled among the porch rafters. Closing his eyes, he breathed in the warm air, feeling the wind move across his face like the touch of a hand.

An image of Frida flashed through his thoughts. Standing before him, her pale skin glowing, her hair like fire, she studied the horizon in silence. Shadows cast by the setting sun outlined her in silhouette. He pondered why Maves had taken her with him and why he had returned none of his calls. A sudden wave of jealousy moved through him before he caught himself. The idea was ludicrous.

The roar of an approaching car pulled him from his thoughts. A battered blue truck appeared over the rise and slowed, turning at the gate and rattling up the drive. He reached the bottom step as the pickup rolled to a stop. A figure climbed out of the cab. In the dying light his face was unrecognizable.

Seconds later, the priest he recognized as Father Zak emerged from the shadows. Webb peered at him, trying to guess at what might bring the man so far. Do priests have no phones, he wondered. With the troubled look of a man unused to confession, the priest brought his oversized hands together before his chest, giving his head a slight bow.

"I am sorry to trouble you but it is urgent that I find Maves Van Horn. You are his son, Webb, are you not?"

He nodded. "What brings you here, Father? Has something happened?"

"First, I must ask." A mixture of hope and fear crossed his face. "The young woman, she is safe?"

"She seems to be."

"She is happy here?"

"I'm not sure if happy is the word I'd use," he answered, puzzled by his questions. "Considering her circumstances, she seems alright."

"I'm relieved to hear it."

"Is that what you want to see Maves about?"

"Uh... no, I... I must speak with Maves," he stammered. "Is he not here?"

Webb noted the worry in his voice. "He's out on a call."

"He is soon to return?"

"I think it likely but I can't be sure. I haven't been able to reach him. Phone service is iffy here," he said, gesturing down the hill, "and even more so to the west and south."

The priest ran a thick finger along his jaw, his gaze distant. Then he refocused, locking eyes with him.

"I fear I have made an error, an error of great importance. I must return to Quintero at once. Please tell Maves to come. I must speak with him. Most important, tell him do not attempt to call."

"That's why you drove all this way, to avoid using the phone?"

"He must not call."

"But why? What's happened?"

"I can only say that Blanca needs his assistance."

"I know him, Father. He'll want more if he's to help."

He sighed and nodded his understanding, his eyes growing dark with anger.

"I am much involved in fighting the cartels and their evil. As you might expect, the cartels do not like this meddling, this turning the people against them. There are threats, of course. That I accept. They are men only and I will not live in fear of them. But I do fear what might become of others who fight them, others who know me, others such as Blanca.

"Yesterday she contacted me and asked that I find Maves. She gave me the details of where she was staying and that she again needed his help. I agreed to pass the message to him. But now I fear I have exposed her to a new danger."

"How so?"

"Soon afterward a policeman came to the church," he continued, running a hand across his brow, "and he told me the cartel has tapped the rectory phone line."

"You think they'll go after her?"

"I cannot say with certainty. But, as I said, they resent those who work against them."

"What sort of help is she asking for?"

"I am sorry. That is all I can say. Now I must return."

He climbed back into the battered truck and the engine sputtered to life in a cloud of blue smoke. He leaned out the window, calling over the noise.

"A priest who owns no car takes what God offers, and he does so with gratitude, even when it is borrowed from an old farmer, even when a tire goes flat. Still, I hope God will take mercy on an old priest and return him to Quintero with no more such trials."

Webb watched the truck bump down the slope, gravel crunching beneath the worn tires like iced-over snow. Reluctant to leave the porch, his mother's lingering presence still palpable, he sat and puzzled over the hold Blanca had on Maves even after so many years. No doubt her beauty had much to do with it. But he sensed something more, something that escaped even the cold rationality of his father, something like a spell, an incantation.

Why had she suddenly reappeared after so many years? And what of Frida's belief that she was not all she appeared to be, that she was hiding something? If she did have ulterior motives Maves would be blind to them, of that he was certain. The way he looked at her told him so.

The low rumble of his approaching van drifted over the treetops. He again considered the priest's enigmatic words, and all he had left unsaid. Maves would no doubt want to leave straightaway despite the uncertainties. He could find little of substance to argue against his going. Yet he felt uneasy about the request, his thoughts dogged by a nagging sense his father was a pawn in someone else's game.

The next morning a haze-filled sky loomed over the eastern horizon, the morning sun spread across it like a smear of blood. Webb gulped the last of his coffee and set the cup on the porch rail. Climbing into his car, he cranked the engine and then paused, his thoughts again turning to his father.

Maves had said little after hearing of the priest's request, leaving for Quintero before dawn despite Webb's attempts to talk him out of it. Recalling the conversation, he wondered why he had made the effort. Maves rarely heeded his advice.

He forced the matter out of mind and put the car into gear. He had problems of his own. Having been out of work for almost a month, his bank account was nearing empty. A job interview in a nearby town had been his only good news in weeks.

He started down the drive when a voice called over the engine, Frida's voice. Seconds later she appeared at his window in a satin nightgown that clung to her like cellophane. With her auburn hair and ivory skin, she seemed the image of a Celtic goddess. He forced himself to look away.

"Where are you going?" she said, her breath hot on his cheek. She held a bundle under her arm.

"I have to be somewhere," he answered as the car continued rolling. "I'll be back in a few hours."

"You can't leave me here alone," she gasped, hurrying alongside.

"I'm in a hurry," he called over the engine.

He pressed his foot to the accelerator. Jerking open the rear door, she threw the bundle onto the back seat and scrambled after it. He stomped on the brake.

"What are you doing?" he yelled.

"I'm going with you."

He frowned into the rearview mirror. "You can't go dressed like that, and I need to leave now."

"Then get moving… and keep your eyes to the road."

She unrolled a pair of jeans, slipping them on under the nightdress before lifting the gown over her head and tossing it aside. Webb glanced over his shoulder. Pointing him to the windshield, she pulled on a tee shirt and then climbed into the passenger seat.

"Now that wasn't so hard, was it?" she said with a smirk. "Where are we going?"

"I don't know about you," he said, turning onto the highway, "but I have a job interview."

"You don't sound too happy about it."

"It's only temporary."

"Maves told me you lost your job."

"Did he enjoy saying it?"

"Why would you say that?"

"Never mind."

"Tell me why."

"Forget I said it."

"He's not like that."

"Yes he is."

"Tell me then."

He glanced at her, Maves' unspoken disapproval, the vague comments, the insinuations all coming back to him in a rush. Anger swelled in his throat.

"I'm a disappointment to him," he said, making no effort to hide his resentment. "In his view of the world, I haven't amounted to anything worthwhile."

"You mean because you dropped out of vet school?"

"He told you the whole sad story? I'm not surprised. That's just one in a long list of not living up to the Van Horn expectations."

"What about *your* expectations? Don't you have dreams of your own?"

He stared through the windshield, taken aback by the question. He had no answer for her. A wave of self-disgust passed over him.

"I thought you wanted to know where we're going," he grumbled.

"I do but… you don't have any?"

"Any what?" he barked.

"Dreams."

"No."

"You must, Webb."

"Did I say we're headed to Hondo?"

"Don't you want something more," she continued, "a good job, a trip to someplace you've never been, a life other than the one you have now?"

A bitter smile crossed his lips at the thought. To her he must seem a complete failure, unemployed, broke, a disgrace to himself and his father. How had he given up so easily?

"Not much of a life, is it?"

"You're not the only one to get it wrong the first try, Webb," she said softly. "We can still dream."

He turned to face her, the concern in her eyes catching in his throat as a wave of conflicting thoughts moved over him.

"It's, it's not that I… I don't…" he stammered, suddenly compelled to answer. "When I first started college I took an elective class, an architecture class. I

103

found I had a knack for it. Looking back, it's not that surprising. I'm good with my hands.

"As a kid I was always building something, picture frames, furniture, bird houses, all sorts of things out of whatever I could find. When I got a little older, I filled a sketchbook with drawings of courthouses, banks, Masonic lodges, all the old, empty buildings in towns Maves passed through on his rounds. I loved those old buildings. I thought they were beautiful. But they also had a touch of sadness about them. No one seemed to care enough to save them.

"But Maves had no use for architecture. He never said so outright but I could tell. So, I switched my major to biology and eventually got into vet school. I'd always been a good student. But early on I realized I was just going through the motions. I didn't want to be a vet. Finally, I gave up on school."

"But what about architecture?"

"I was done with that childish dream."

"You gave up what you loved just because of your father?"

"Nothing is ever good enough for him. He'll never change, so what was the point?"

"The point is your happiness."

He had a sudden urge to end the conversation.

"Happiness is overrated," he said, trying to sound flippant.

"You don't believe that."

"Why wouldn't I?"

"Do you want to know what I think?"

"Actually, no," he answered, a hint of anger entering his voice.

"I think you let Maves have too much say in your life."

"I don't recall ask…"

They topped a rise and a clutch of green and white trucks appeared in the shallow swale below them, their lights flashing. He slammed the brake pedal to the floor. The car screeched to a stop, sending up a plume of blue smoke that swirled around them in a choking cloud.

"Border patrol!" he shouted.

Jamming the car into reverse, he wheeled a half circle. A trio of sirens erupted behind them. Speeding back up the slope and over the top, the engine straining, he squinted at the roadside hoping to spot a side road or trail that might offer escape. He glanced at the rearview mirror, knowing the green and white trucks would top the hill in seconds.

A brush-choked road blocked by a metal gate appeared to his right. Aiming for the narrow opening, he jerked hard on the steering wheel, swerving onto the shoulder and jumping the drive. The car skidded past the gate, bursting through the barbed wire fence in a clatter of screeching metal before rejoining the drive thirty yards beyond. An instant later the thicket swallowed them.

He cut the engine. The sirens neared and then wailed past, slowly fading into the distance. He took a breath. The tight curves of the narrow highway had allowed their escape, at least for the moment.

He started again and a disturbing rattle drifted from beneath the hood. He wondered for a moment how they would manage on foot. The road rounded a bend and a small house appeared briefly between the trees. Frida glanced at him without a word.

Further on the underbrush thinned and then gave way to an open pasture, the small house again coming into view. Smoke drifted from a soot-stained chimney, an odd sight in the still heat of summer. Beyond the house the road continued, disappearing behind a dilapidated barn. Off to one side, a nondescript delivery truck sat parked beneath a gnarled mesquite tree, a rusted pickup next to it.

He stopped the car and sat wondering how the owners would react to intruders. Maves had often described the hazards of entering a gated ranch unexpectedly. But they needed to keep moving if they were to elude the authorities. He had little doubt the agents would soon notice the hole in the fence.

Deciding he had no choice, he restarted the engine and angled toward a dense cedar break, intending to hide the car. They would watch the house for awhile before approaching by foot. It seemed the safer course.

The engine rattle returned, louder than before. Suddenly a gunshot pop erupted from under the hood and the car jerked to a stop. Smoke streamed past the windshield, smelling of burnt oil and gasoline. He turned the key. Nothing. Again. Nothing.

Climbing out, he put his head to the ground. Oil dripped from the engine in a steady stream, pooling in the dirt. The oil pan had been punctured, overheating the engine. The car would go no further.

He moved to the rear bumper and pushed the smoking hulk deep into the cedars, repositioning a matt of lower branches to cover the trunk. Frida's hand lightly touched his shoulder. Without a word, she knelt next to him, putting a finger to her lips. Then she pointed to the house.

A man appeared on the porch, the butt of an unlit cigarette in his hand. His shaved head glistened in the morning haze. Squinting into the sunlight, he turned a half circle, raising the butt to his lips and then lowering it as his gaze reached the cedars. He leaned on the rail and peered in their direction. Then he jerked upright, dropping the cigarette and running back inside.

"He's seen us," she gasped.

"We need to explain before he calls the sheriff," he said, standing.

He started toward the house, Frida following close behind. Without warning the rear door burst open and a small crowd of half-dressed men, women and children clamored down the steps and toward the tree line. She grabbed his arm.

"Webb," she shouted, "stop!"

"What the hell..." he mumbled, watching the commotion. "What are they doing?"

"You're frightening them."

"Frightening who...?" he said, turning to her. "I don't understand."

"Look at them." She pointed him back to the trees. "Can't you see they're running too?"

She brushed past him before he could answer. He hurried after. As she neared the stoop, the bald man stepped back out the door, a fresh cigarette between his fingers, still unlit. A crude tattoo of a snake stretched across his knuckles. He looked past them to the road, glancing in both directions as Frida spoke a few words in Spanish.

"Speak English," he barked, "not the other."

"You don't have to worry." She moved closer, her voice calm. "This is not our house. We are..."

"Hold on," Webb said, grabbing her arm. "Before you start telling him all about yourself, maybe you should get a better idea who *he* is."

"We are hiding also," she continued, pulling free. She motioned toward the thicket. "There's no need for them to be afraid."

"They are always afraid, like sheep," he muttered. "That is all they know to be."

"They're people, not livestock."

"How about you, senora?" He stepped off the porch and leaned toward her. "Are you afraid?"

"Why, should I be?"

A hint of defiance had entered her voice. Webb glanced at her but kept his eyes on the man, reminded of the scene in Abel's boat.

"What about you, hombre?" The man squinted at him. "Are you afraid?"

Webb locked eyes with him, saying nothing as anger stirred in his chest like a caged animal. The man turned back to her.

"You look too good to be the law, chica." He sucked the air between his teeth, ogling her. "How about I give you a free ride up north?"

"What are you, a coyote?"

"I'm a businessman," he said, feigning offense, "taking those sheep to a new home in Del Norte."

"You don't have a name?"

"I am Fidel," he said, grinning. "You want my phone number too?"

"So, you don't own this house?"

"What I own is not your business," he grumbled.

She motioned toward the tree line. "You think you own those people?"

"Until I get paid," he nodded, "they belong to me."

"You broke in here to hide from the border patrol, didn't you?"

"You ask too many questions," he muttered, sticking the cigarette between his lips. "But maybe I will take you with me anyway."

He reached out, taking a strand of her hair in his fingers. She slapped his hand away. In a flash, he grabbed a handful, jerking her toward him. Without thinking, Webb was on him, twisting his arm back on itself. He cried out, dropping to his knees.

The glint of a knife flashed through the air, sliding past Webb's chest in a blur of silver and black. He jammed his heel into Fidel's kneecap. He stumbled and then lunged at Webb, the blade again barely missing. Frida grabbed Webb's wrist and jerked him backwards onto the turf, tumbling beside him.

Fidel stood and, wincing in pain, again started toward them but stopped at the unmistakable grind of car wheels on gravel. The green and white of the Border Patrol flickered through the underbrush. He pivoted and scrambled up the stairs.

Webb pulled Frida to her feet and they hurried toward the barn, hoping to slip out of sight before the trucks made the final turn. They ducked behind the delivery truck and paused to listen. Voices shouted from the thicket, some in English, some in Spanish. The agents had discovered the group.

They started again and then stopped at the sight of the smaller truck. Webb stuck his head through the driver's window. A ring of keys dangled from the ignition. Doubting his luck, he motioned Frida nearer, pointing her behind the wheel while he moved to the rear bumper and began pushing the truck toward the far end of the barn. From there the road sloped downhill before vanishing over a ridgeline.

Within seconds they were bouncing quietly down the rutted path. A sudden pop of gunfire sounded behind them. Webb peered out the back window straining to see if they were followed but the house and barn had already slipped behind the hill.

Thick clumps of grass crowded the road, slowing the truck as the slope eased and then leveled out. They came to a stop at the bottom of a broad swale and sat listening for sign of the agents. A hot wind rattled the treetops but no other sound came within hearing.

Webb climbed from the cab without a word. Somehow, silence had become their reality. He could see Frida felt it too, as if speaking might again bring the world down upon them. He trotted up to a sharp bend in the way ahead, checking to be sure the road continued as he hoped it would.

Returning to the truck, he searched the distant tree line. Nothing moved. He leaned into Frida's window and pointed to the keys, motioning her to try them. She gazed at him for a brief moment, her eyes like spring-fed lakes, each different from the other, each flecked with gold.

Then she turned the ignition. The engine sputtered and came to life, sending up a cloud of blue smoke before dying. She tried again. The truck shuddered and died again. Glancing at him, she turned the key a third time. The motor

coughed with a metallic grind and then caught, finally
settling into a low rumble.

He hurried into the passenger seat and they started
again, bumping along in a steady rattle. He stole a look at
her, taken by her beauty but equally by her courage. She
had faced down the man with the shaved head, in her eyes
a fierce determination to stand up for the group of travelers
at his mercy. She understood their plight and meant to help
them if she could.

He tried to imagine her and Maves spending all night
together and could not. What on earth would they talk
about? A tinge of jealousy moved through him, again
running up against the absurdity of the idea. He could only
guess at her age but she had to be at least fifteen years
younger than him.

He sat back and wondered where his father was at that
moment, and whether the priest's concerns were fact or
fear. The unease he had felt earlier returned and he found
himself wishing he had argued with more conviction
against making the trip. But, he admitted reluctantly,
wishing was of no help now.

Chapter Thirteen

Maves stepped into the foyer of the small church and the odor of polished wood and musty hymnals enveloped him, compelling and familiar, as if he had stepped back in time. He breathed in the cool air. A memory of another church rose before him, Webb seated next to him, his mother's coffin perched at the end of the aisle. The hiss of whispered blame settled around them like burning incense.

He blinked the image away and moved to a pew. In the quiet stillness, he again felt the weight of his past pressing in. Zak's appeal, urgent according to Webb, seemed vague and mysterious in a way uncharacteristic of the straightforward priest. He had said Blanca needed his help but for what purpose? Did he not know or just decline to say?

He let his gaze wander across the dark wood of the altar, the painted statues of saints, the stained glass speckled with shadow. The world of border crossings and cartels seemed remote and unreal. He leaned against the cool wood, hoping to somehow capture the peace of the place.

A door opened and closed behind him. Seconds later a hand landed on his shoulder, followed by Zak's round face. He studied Maves with his walnut eyes, at once hard yet approachable, seeming to reflect contrary souls, one ruthless, the other forgiving.

"Thank you for coming, Maves," he said, moving beside him. "I know I must have alarmed your son by my talk, but I fear we are entering a dangerous time. The cartels grow bolder. They threaten people, ordinary people, into committing illegal acts.

"One of my parishioners tapped the church's phone lines for them. They threatened to harm his family if he did not agree. He has two daughters. I do not blame him for this. I would likely do the same."

"What of Blanca, Zak? Is she in some sort of trouble?"

"This I do not know, Maves. She called asking that I contact you. She again needs your help. But she sounded different in a way I cannot explain, hesitant and evasive when I asked why. I am concerned for her welfare, and for her state of mind."

"Then I'll leave right away. Where is she?"

"That also I cannot explain. The address she gave me is in Del Rio." He stood. "Maves, I would like to accompany you, if you will allow it. I feel I must see her in person. As it happens, I am due to meet another priest in Del Rio this afternoon."

"There's nothing more you can tell me about her?" he asked, frustrated by the mysterious request.

"Unfortunately, no, I am at a loss." He started down the aisle. "But we must be on our way. I will gather my things and meet you at the street."

An hour later Maves turned off the main road onto a pitted side street lined with dilapidated frame houses, their yards scattered with castoff furniture and old tires. Trash from overfull cans littered the curb. A stray dog loped along the roadside, dodging cars.

Zak pointed him to a red-roofed house, the cracked and peeling walls a homely amalgam of stucco and cinder block. Iron bars crossed the high windows. Behind a chain link fence, the gravestones of a family cemetery glittered in the midday sun. Maves pulled to the curb and cut the engine.

He sat for a moment and studied the house and graveyard, wondering what might bring Blanca to such a place. Zak's words of concern filled his thoughts. Was she acting strangely and, if so, why? The house was certainly out of character.

Zak stared at the building in silence, his expression a puzzling mixture of sadness and consternation. Maves wondered what had come over him. He started out of the van and then paused as the door to the house opened and a young man stepped into the indigo shade of the small porch. His arms held a dense filigree of tattoos that melded with the black of his t-shirt. A crimson goatee sprouted from his chin.

Maves had an instant distrust of the man. He watched him glide along the walkway, his moves furtive and catlike. Vaulting the fence, he disappeared around the corner. Zak turned to him with a questioning look, the same suspicion in his eyes. Maves again started out the door but Zak grabbed his wrist.

"Perhaps we should delay leaving for a moment in case there are other guests."

Reading his thoughts, Maves nodded, his uncertainty over Blanca's motives pulling at him. How did she know the tattooed man? What business did he have with her? Why had she chosen to live in such a place? He could not begin to guess.

Deciding enough time had passed, they approached the house. Zak rapped his scar-lined knuckles on the doorframe. Footsteps sounded inside and the door opened to a stout, tea-colored woman in a nurse's uniform. She eyed Maves warily. Then, spotting Zak's collar, she gasped and took a step back.

"Forgive me, Father, I am… I am… I must go."

She grabbed her purse and brushed past him, hurrying down the steps to a shining black sedan tucked in an alleyway opposite them. The car had no license plates. Jumping in, she sped off in a spray of gravel.

Maves glanced at Zak and turned back to the house. The door stood half open. He stepped through and pivoted a slow circle. Filled with chairs, end tables and magazines, the room had the look of a medical clinic. A window of frosted glass above a short counter completed the effect.

Confused, he surveyed the room again. The difference between the outside and where he now stood was striking.

He wondered what connection Blanca might have to a clinic. Was she sick? Could that be the reason she had asked for his help?

He watched Zak roam the room, puzzling again over the change in him. Though saying little, he had seemed on edge from the moment of their arrival. A troubled stare had replaced his usual calm gaze.

A door closed somewhere beyond the frosted glass followed by footsteps again creaking across the floorboards. Seconds later a heavy-set man in horn-rimmed glasses and white lab coat emerged from an adjacent hallway. Spotting them he drew up short, blinking through the thick lenses. His skin shone the color of red clay.

"I am terribly sorry there is no one here to greet you," he said with a lilting accent, glancing around the room. "Yes, terribly sorry I am. But I suppose the staff has left for the day. Why they forgot to lock the door I cannot say. In any event, the clinic is closed for now. I am Dr. Rajiv."

"We're looking for a friend," Maves announced, suddenly aware he did not know Blanca's last name. He shot Zak a questioning glance. "I know her as Blanca Munoz but she may go by her married name."

"Ah," the doctor said, his eyes growing large, "you must be Mr. Van Horn. Yes, yes, she certainly told me to be expecting you, no doubt about it."

"She's not here?"

"No, no, not at all, I am sorry to say." He pulled a scrap of paper from his coat pocket, handing it to him. "But she gave me this note. She said a man will be waiting for you with a package. He will know where the package is to be taken."

Disappointed, Maves studied the crumpled paper. It held only the name and address of a local café.

"Blanca won't be there?"

"I think not," he mumbled as he gave Zak a nervous glance. "No, no, I am certain she will not, definitely not… she, uh… she said nothing about a priest."

114

Maves ignored the comment as a mounting frustration crept into his throat.

"Where is she?"

"She was called away suddenly."

"Where to?"

"I do not know this," he said, jerking a handkerchief from his pocket and wiping his face.

"Then *why* was she called away?" he growled, making no effort to hide his anger.

"I am terribly sorry but that is all I know," he answered, his voice rising, "the note and what I've told you. She said nothing more, I'm certain of it. That is all I can…"

"What sort of work do you do here?" Zak interrupted.

The doctor flinched, glancing about the room as if looking for escape.

"A clinic… a clinic… as I have said, this is a clinic," he jabbered, "and we now are closed for business."

"You didn't answer the question," he said, stepping closer.

"What? Yes, yes, of course." Sweat beaded on his cheeks. "We are a clinic and we provide treatment for rare and difficult to cure cancers, if you must know the details."

"Those sorts of treatments are expensive?"

"Yes, yes, quite expensive they are, quite expensive," he answered, running the handkerchief across his brow, "and not the type covered by health insurance. We have an elite clientele, I must say."

"You have no sign or other means of identifying yourself. Why is that?"

"Why? Well, we… we… we wish to protect our patient's privacy. As I have said, they are not the usual patients." He forced a smile. "I am flattered our work is of interest but…"

Zak leaned in, his large hands poised before his chest, one below the other. The image of a boxer flashed through Maves' thoughts.

115

"You are trying to hide?" he continued.

"No, no, I would not put it that way, no. Our patients are wealthy and, as I have said, value their privacy." He waved the handkerchief at the door. "Now, I must be leaving here, big meeting to go to, yes, yes, so you will kindly remove yourselves."

He hurried to the door, holding it open for them. Maves hesitated, unsatisfied with the little they had learned. Zak squinted at the man and then started for the door, motioning Maves to follow.

The deserted street sat quiet beneath the noonday sun. Waves of heat drifted off the pavement. Maves paced before the van, trying to sort through his jumbled thoughts, the questions far outnumbering the answers. Zak stood nearby, lost to his own musings.

"What happened in there?" Maves said, stopping to face him. "What did you see?"

He stared into the distance without answering. Maves waited but he made no move to speak, so he pulled the scrap of paper from his shirt pocket and held it before his face. Coming out of his trance, Zak locked eyes with him for an instant and then he climbed into the van.

Chapter Fourteen

A surreal image of downtown reflected from the windows of the small café, streets and storefronts floating across the glass as if freed from gravity. Maves slowed the van to check the scrap of paper, confirming the address. Nearby buildings stood empty. Bales of castoff clothing stood outside shops selling used appliances and furniture. He parked a block from the café, the strangeness of the last half hour having left him alert and cautious.

Moments later they stepped from the fuming sidewalk into the air-conditioned coolness of the diner. Booths, most of them occupied, lined a row of windows facing the street. Maves found an empty table and sat puzzling over how he would find the man with the package. Zak sat across from him and stared out the window, still brooding in silence.

Maves pondered the change in him. Gone was the relaxed assurance of a man who knows and understands the world and his place in it. Instead, his walnut-hued eyes held a grim resignation, hard and unforgiving, not unlike the rock-strewn land stretching away from them in all directions. He again thought to ask him about it but decided not to, leaving him to his private thoughts. He would talk when he was ready.

The muted click of hard-soled shoes sounded behind him. He turned to find a man waiting at the table's edge, leather briefcase in hand. Without asking, he pulled a chair from a nearby table and sat. His face held the sharp nose and beady eyes of a rodent, the whiskers of his mustache so few as to render it inconsequential.

He looked both directions before lifting the briefcase and setting it on the table, his fingers draped bone-like across the dark leather. Nodding at them each in turn, he flipped open the clasps and pulled out a thin package wrapped in brown paper. An envelope was taped to the top.

Again turning from one to the other he set the package beside the case and tapped the brown paper. Maves began to wonder if the man was capable of speech. He leaned in, seemingly about to speak, when a shadow moved past the window. His smile disappeared at once.

Jumping up, he knocked his chair to the floor before stumbling past the tables and out a rear exit. The blinding light of a sun-drenched alley briefly filled the café, leaving an image of the room floating in space, pale and dreamlike. Maves blinked and turned his gaze to the envelope, ripping it free of the package. The enclosed note held a local address, Blanca's name under it. He realized with regret he had no idea if the handwriting belonged to her.

A hand landed on his shoulder and he turned to find Zak standing over him. Maves studied his round face. A calm determination had replaced the earlier darkness. He pushed the package toward him and nodded to the door.

Moments later they were on the sidewalk, the van a half-block away. Storefronts and offices lining the street stood quiet. Maves surveyed the scene. The vibrant downtown he had known a decade earlier had vanished, a casualty of the border violence.

Twenty yards ahead, a man stepped from a recessed doorway and began walking toward them. Pale and furtive, he kept his eyes to the pavement. Maves glanced at him and then looked again. His neck held the same scorpion tattoo as the man in Abel's boat.

He shifted the package to his left hand, away from the stranger, and nudged Zak's elbow. He followed Maves' gaze. The man edged toward the street, keeping them between himself and the buildings. An instant later they were even with him.

In a glint of flashing metal a switchblade appeared in his hand. He stepped in front of them, blocking their path. Sunlight sparked off the blade. Holding the knife between his thumb and forefinger, he twisted it back and forth as if admiring the sheen. Then he pointed it at Maves.

"You have something, a package," he said, extending his free hand, "and it belongs to me."

"Who sent you?" He kept the box at his side.

"I didn't come here to talk, old man." He waved the blade in Maves' face. "I want that package... now."

"We're only asking to trade," Zak said, stepping closer, "the box for a little information."

Maves glanced at him, trying to read his movements. The man turned to Zak.

"Since you are a priest I will not cut you... not unless I have to." He turned back to Maves. "But this one looks like he needs a new..."

In a blur of motion Zak's fist caught the man across the chin. He jerked upright, his eyes staring at nothing, and then crumpled to the pavement. Zak grabbed his arms and motioned Maves to take his feet. Moments later they were back in the café.

He was coming to as they set him in a chair and called to a waitress for water. Zak patted him on the cheek. His eyes fluttered open.

"What... what happened?" he mumbled, his jaw already beginning to swell. He stared at Zak's clerical collar. "A priest... I must be... am I dying, Father?"

Zak leaned in inches from his face. A glass appeared in his hand.

"You're going to be alright, son. You passed out and hit your head on the pavement. You must be dehydrated."

He held the water to his lips.

"I passed out?" he mumbled.

"You were about to tell me... how did you know to wait for us?"

The man drank, wincing as the glass touched his split lip. His eyes never left Zak's face. Grasping the man's shoulder, he repeated the question. He said nothing.

All at once he stood, braced himself on the chair and turned, scrambling past the tables and out the door before disappearing. Zak turned to Maves and sighed. Then he started for the exit.

119

Stepping back into the fuming heat of midday, Maves tried to clear his mind. Nothing made sense. At least he had Blanca's address. The possibility of seeing her again filled his thoughts, her dark eyes, her glowing skin.

They walked to the van in silence and Zak climbed in, his face solemn. Sensing he might want a moment to himself, Maves hesitated by the door. No doubt the irony of a priest disarming a robber by force had not escaped him. After a moment, he noticed Maves through the window and motioned him inside with a quick nod.

"I will ask your pardon and God's forgiveness for that unfortunate display," he said, rubbing his knuckles. "I don't know what came over me."

"Whatever it was, I'm glad of it."

"I should have been more patient with that poor soul, more talk and less action."

"Your action kept me from getting a new whatever it was he wanted to give me."

"A haircut, do you think?" Zak gave him a wink.

Maves snorted. "A scalp, maybe."

"Maves," he said, his expression turning grave, "you must take care. I fear Blanca is caught up in a dangerous game. I only wish I could have seen her, talked to her myself, but I have run out of time. I must collect my priest and return to Quintero."

A quarter-hour later Maves watched Zak disappear through the ornate doors of a brick church flanked by a sprawling school and rectory. He checked the address on the scrap of paper and turned the van a half-circle, heading south. The border stood less than a mile away. Brightly painted taco stands, pawn shops and Mexican bakeries lined the street, their signs in both English and Spanish.

He entered a tattered neighborhood and a yellow duplex appeared midway down the block, wedged into a row of white frame houses like a bad tooth. A hot breeze swirled through the window. He slowed the van and angled onto the grass, parking in front of a vacant house with a plastic Santa and sleigh topping the roof, a disconcerting sight in mid-summer.

He pulled the note from his shirt pocket and peered at it, searching for a clue as to why Blanca had again asked for his help. Despite the strange turn of events, he still worried she might have some rare form of cancer, a cancer that might take her before he had a chance to... He let the thought die, unable to finish.

He crossed the street, the package in hand, and passed through a fenced garden separating one side of the duplex from the other. A tiny porch fronted the doorway. He pushed the doorbell once, then again. Curtains rustled in a nearby window and seconds later the door flew open. Blanca stood at the threshold, wide-eyed. He had never seen her as beautiful.

"You came," she said, reaching for him. "I was afraid I had asked too much of you, that you would finally say no to me."

She pulled him inside and disappeared without a word. He set the package on an end table and glanced around the room, surprised at the expensive furnishings. A hand carved walnut chest sat before a leather couch and settee. Oil paintings in gilded frames scattered the walls. Through an open door he spotted the edge of a four-poster bed.

She reappeared with an open bottle of wine and two glasses, nodding him to the sofa. Moving next to him, she filled the glasses and handed him one, raising hers to his. He nearly drained the glass in one swallow. Her black eyes seemed to draw him in, their dark beauty mesmerizing.

"At last, we have a private moment," she said, taking his hand, "just a man and woman together."

"Are you alright, Blanca?" He studied her face. "I mean your health, is your health good?"

She put a hand to her face. "But of course, Maves, why do you ask this?"

121

"The address you gave… the clinic…"

"Oh, yes," she said, waving off his concern, "the doctor, he is only helping me."

"You're not sick then?"

"My heart is till beating."

"I'm relieved to hear it."

"Would you like to feel so you can be sure?"

She took his hand, pressing it to her chest, leaned in and kissed him. The heat of her breath, the satin-like feel of her skin surged through him. Wrapping her arms around his neck, she pulled him closer, molding her form to his. He eased her back onto the couch and the world faded to nothing, leaving only her touch, her smell.

For a moment, he felt as if time had come unmoored, as if they had returned to the tiny stucco house near Crystal City, the house he had found for her, the house with the turquoise walls, the creaking bed. Memories swirled about him in a blur of fleeting images. Nothing had changed yet everything had.

He felt her hands move to his chest. Pushing him back, she slipped from beneath him and stood. He fumbled with the buttons of her blouse. Moving his hands away, she pulled him upright. Then, without a word, she turned and led him into the bedroom.

Maves jerked upright. A low morning sun streamed through lace curtains, falling across the hardwood floor in gold filigree. The vaguely threatening hum of a ceiling fan turned overhead, as if voices conspired just beyond his hearing. Then all at once the events of the previous day came rushing back.

He jumped from the bed and slipped on his shirt, awkward in the knowledge of how he must look to Blanca after fifteen years. Her perfume still clung to his clothes. The whistle of a tea kettle drifted through the doorway, mixing with the soft slapping of footsteps on the tile floor.

An unbidden memory came to him of the last time he had seen Webb's mother. Barefoot, her shoes in hand, she stood beside her car, disappointment and anger captured in her green eyes. He knew then and still felt the terrible power of his selfishness. Though he had known women in the years since, he had always kept a distance, somehow unable to move past that singular moment. He would not allow himself to hope this time would prove different.

His thoughts shifted to the afternoon and the unanswered questions surrounding the package. Before he could sort through them Blanca appeared in the doorway in a silk robe that clung to her like a second skin. She moved to where he stood and pressed herself against him.

"You are troubled by our love-making?" she said, peering up at him.

"No", he lied.

"You are still a passionate lover, Maves."

"Blanca, I, uh… I need to ask…" he stammered, the heat of her body surging through him. "What I mean is…"

"Not now, Maves," she said, putting a finger to his lips. "We have little time and I still need your help. The package, it must be traded for another."

"But a man tried to steal that box, Blanca. Something is not right here."

"There is much crime along the border."

"No, it's more than that," he persisted. "He knew I would have the package. I'm sure of it. You need to tell me what this is all about."

"In the package is money," she said, sighing. "I hope to buy papers for the women like Frida, passports, birth certificates, to help them gain asylum. They flee for their lives and leave with nothing. They will have much trouble without such papers."

"How did the man know I would have the money?"

"The cartels, they have ears everywhere, eyes everywhere," she said, holding his gaze. "It is the way of life here."

"And the doctor, how is he involved?"

"He has contacts in Mexico."

"He seemed nervous, like he was hiding something."

"That is his nature, Maves." She took his hand in hers. "Sometimes people just want to help."

"I suppose you could be right," he admitted, wanting to believe her.

"Then you will take the package for me and retrieve the other?"

"Yes, Blanca, I'll take it."

"The trip, it is long." She kissed him before turning for the door. "I will make coffee."

He watched her disappear around the corner, scarcely able to believe she wanted him again. A vague thought pulled at the back of his mind, lost but still nagging from its dim corner. Was she caught up in some perilous game as Zak had said? If so, why would she not say so? Did it even matter? That he would do what she asked, regardless, he was certain. He could be sure of little else.

Chapter Fifteen

The truck topped a ridgeline and a rusted-out trailer house came into view beside a clutch of towering cottonwood trees. Their hand-sized leaves fluttered in the midday heat. Webb surveyed the scene. Broken down cars lay slumped about the yard like wounded animals. In the open door of a faded sedan a young girl sat with her head down, a book in her lap.

Webb motioned Frida to back the truck away from the ridge and then he returned to the hilltop, crouching in the tall grass and studying their route, thinking it best to stay clear of people. The road they were following passed close to the trailer before disappearing over a distant rise. He searched the area for another way past.

In a swale to his left, out of the trailer's sight, a barn sat beside a metal windmill, its arrow-shaped tail reading 'Aermotor' in sun-bleached red. Piped water flowed from the pump into a nearby cement tank. Almost hidden in the tall grass, twin ruts of a seldom-used path wound from the barn up the hill before joining the road not far from where he stood. He hustled back to the truck, hoping the road continued past the barn.

Moments later Frida eased the truck next to the building. He climbed out and peered around the corner. Though barely visible, the path continued down the slope and around a thicket, ending at an open gate, the highway just beyond.

He was about to motion her forward when he spotted the outline of a car bumper glinting through the brush. Keeping low, he crept behind the tank and peeked over the top. The green and white of a Border Patrol truck winked through the tree line. Cursing under his breath, he scrambled back to the barn. Frida stood waiting in the shade of the door.

"Better find a comfortable place to sit," he said. "We're stuck here for awhile."

"You saw something?"

"The Border Patrol is camped out next to our only way out of here." He nodded toward the windmill. "At least we have water."

She slipped into the relative cool beyond the doorway, Webb following, and they stood together surveying the dim interior. A double row of empty stalls, their gateposts hung with dust-covered bridles, faced a wide aisle that ended in an open space crowded with a stair-step wall of hay. The bales stretched almost to the ceiling. She climbed onto the lowest tier, leaned back and looked around the room, a dejected frown on her face.

"I can't believe I'm back in another barn," she sighed.

Webb watched her, surprised at the change. In a sudden moment, she had become impossibly young and vulnerable. The defiant woman who earlier had confronted a dangerous man now sat with her chin on her knees, straw scattered confetti-like through her auburn hair. He had a sudden urge to go to her, to put his arms around her, to feel her breath on his face. He wiped the beads of sweat from his lip.

A light breeze passed through the room, stirring the bridles, offering a brief respite from the fuming heat. She leaned back against the straw and closed her eyes. Seeing his chance, he climbed onto the platform and moved beside her.

"I'm so tired," she mumbled. "It seems all I've done my whole life is run from one place to the next."

"We'll be out of here before you know it," he said, trying to sound reassuring. "With any luck the agents will move on and by nightfall we'll be back at home sitting on the porch, sipping something cold and watching the stars rise above the hills."

"You make it sound so nice."

He peered at her profile, again struck by her beauty.

"You'll be safe there."

126

"Will I?" she said, opening her eyes. "I've forgotten what it's like to feel safe, to have a home."

She turned as if expecting a reply. Instead, he bent and kissed her. She hesitated for an instant and then leaned into him, pulling him closer, threading her fingers through his hair. He ran his hand down her neck and to the first button of her blouse. Her breath quickened. Then suddenly she pulled back.

"No, Webb, I must not," she whispered, pressing her hands to his chest.

"What's wrong?"

"Did you forget I'm still married?"

"I remember," he said in disbelief, "that you sent your husband to prison."

"Yes, but I cannot be with another man. My church forbids it."

"You don't really believe all that."

"Yes, Webb, I do."

"But why?"

"Why? What do I have to count on, Webb? I have nothing. The church gives me something solid in my life, something certain."

"But, Frida…"

"What about you?"

"What about me?" he grumbled, frustrated.

"What do *you* believe?"

"Nothing," he snapped.

"But you must have something."

"Not that I've noticed."

"You don't go to church?"

"Not since my mother died."

"Oh Webb," she said softly, "do you know how sad that sounds?"

"Sad or not, it's just the way it is," he answered, turning away. "Sometimes things work out, most of the time they don't. A kid has a mother and then he doesn't. God, if there is one, doesn't factor in."

"You don't believe in God?" she gasped.

"I don't know... maybe." He tried to soften his tone, again facing her. "But I don't see what God has to do with you and me."

"You could be married too for all I know."

He stared at her, feeling the blood drain from his face. A swirl of conflicting emotions gripped him. The wreckage of his past flashed before him, the doomed romances, the one night stands, all culminating in a failed engagement to a woman who left him for his boss. Citing his quick temper, his inapproachability, she blamed him for their falling out, as if his faults justified her betrayal. Barely able to listen, he had realized with disgust her words held a perfect description of Maves.

"Well, Webb, are you?"

"Once I... I..." he stammered, at a loss for words.

He looked away. She bent, trying to see his face.

"What is it, Webb? What happened?"

He slumped against the hay, feeling defeated, Frida's rejection just another in a long list of failures. The only surprise was that her rebuff surprised him at all, he mused bitterly. She still faced him, waiting for an answer.

"Won't you talk to me, Webb?" she said softly. "I'll listen without judging, I promise."

A part of him wanted to stand up and walk out the door, the other part felt compelled to tell her. He searched for a place to start, finally looking up and meeting her gaze.

"I'm not married, Frida." The words seemed to come without thought. "The truth is I haven't had much luck with women."

"Have you never been married, Webb?"

"I came close once."

"And?"

"She left me for another guy. How's that for trite?"

"Just because something is common doesn't mean it hurts any less."

128

He grunted a noncommittal response. Looking at him askance, she continued.

"Was she very cruel?"

"About like you'd expect."

"So the breakup was her fault?"

"Like I said, she left me."

"That's not what I mean."

"What do you mean?"

"A relationship is a two-way street."

"Now you're the one with the clichés."

"But talking about it helps, don't you think?"

"I suppose so," he answered, disarmed by her hopeful tone.

"How are you doing now?"

"I'll survive."

"You're starting to sound like your father."

"Don't compare me with Maves," he grumbled. "I'm not him."

"You're right. I won't do it again." She peered at him for a moment. "He's not so bad, you know."

"You don't have him for a father."

"What I mean is being a little like him might not be so bad."

"The last thing I want is to be like him."

"Webb, you could do worse that take after him. He is a good man. Just go easy on the strong and silent part."

"My fiancé... my *ex*-fiancé said I never talked to her, never let her in. That's why she left me, or one reason anyway."

"That doesn't really fit what I've seen."

"Maybe it was just an excuse."

"Or maybe it was more complicated than that."

"What do you mean?"

"Maybe you picked her because she was someone you couldn't talk to, who you couldn't be yourself with."

"Why on earth would I do that?"

"Maybe it was your way of keeping your distance, keeping yourself protected. You and Maves have that in common."

"How many times do I have to say it? I'm not him."

"No, Webb, you're not. I see all sorts of differences between the two of you. You're sensitive to the needs of others, and you have an artistic side. To be honest, I can't imagine having a conversation like this with him. But we're influenced by our parents whether we like it or not. Wishing doesn't make it disappear."

"Thank you, doctor, for your opinion. But I think I've had enough head-shrinking for one…"

A twig snapped beyond the doorway. He looked up to find the girl from the trailer standing at the threshold, the book still in her hands. A tangled mane of blonde curls framed her face. She stared at him as if unsure whether to enter or bolt.

"You can come in if you want to." He raised a hand and gently waved her forward. "We're just resting in the cool air for a minute."

She hesitated, her face somber, and then stepped through. Frida slid off the hay.

"My name is Frida," she said, moving closer, "what's yours?"

The girl looked past her, eyeing Webb with suspicion.

"That's my friend, Webb." Frida motioned him over. "Webb, come meet, ah… I'm sorry but I don't know your name."

"You found my secret place," she announced.

"Your secret place?"

"This is where I come," she replied, waving the book in a half-circle, "when I want to hide from…"

She pointed out the door. Webb eased next to Frida and smiled reassuringly. The last thing he wanted was the girl telling someone their whereabouts.

"We won't tell anyone this is your hiding place," he said, bending toward her, "if you won't tell your parents we're resting here."

"They're not my parents!" she shouted.

"Okay." He took a step back. "Where are they, your parents?"

"I don't have a daddy anymore," she said, scowling at him, "and my momma left with her new boyfriend two weeks ago."

Frida knelt and pointed to the book. The girl shifted her gaze.

"You like to read?"

She nodded.

"I like books too, especially *Anne of Green Gables*. Have you read it?"

She stared at her without answering. Frida reached out and took her hand.

"Will you tell me your name?"

She cut her eyes at Webb and then studied Frida's face as if deciding whether to answer. Finally, she nodded an agreement.

"I'm Mariah Brownlee."

"So, you're staying at that trailer up the hill until your mother returns?"

"She's not coming back, not ever," she said, her voice just above a whisper.

"Not ever?"

"That's what Anvil said."

"Who's Anvil?"

"He's momma's old boyfriend." A look of resignation crossed her face. "She gave me to him only she didn't ask permission. She just left a note."

"Your mother gave you to her old boyfriend?"

"He was her boyfriend once but he's married to another lady and she came back. Now she lives in the trailer too."

"Do you like living with them?"

"She's a witch," she sneered, "but he's worse. He treats Ewan like a dog."

"Who is Ewan?"

"If it wasn't for him I would have run away a long time ago. He's fifteen. He hurt his hand protecting me from Anvil. Anvil is his dad."

"Is there anyone else living there?"

"Ewan's sister, April, is adopted. She's younger than him and real quiet. I think it's because she's going to have a baby."

"She's pregnant," Frida gasped, "and not even fifteen?"

"I think she might only be thirteen."

"I'm not surprised you want to run away."

"The worst part is Anvil is always bumping up against me and touching me. He says it's not on purpose but I can tell he's lying."

Footsteps sounded outside the barn and seconds later a boy appeared in the doorway, his arm in a sling. A maze of scratches and scrapes crisscrossed his scalp. Blonde hair sprouted between the scabs like fresh-cut wheat. He studied them, his gaze without emotion, until his eyes fell on Mariah. A flicker of feeling crossed his face.

She ran to him and took his hand, dragging him inside. He tensed as he moved closer, eyeing Webb the way an animal might a baited trap. He moved in front of Mariah.

"What do you want?"

"How did you know we were here?" Webb glanced at the doorway. "Is anyone with you?"

"Relax, I was looking for Mariah. I'm on my own." He pointed a finger at Webb. "But you didn't answer my question. Why are you here?"

"We just need a place to rest out of the heat. We'll be leaving soon."

"You need a place to rest, huh?" He turned from one to the other, a look of understanding crossing his face. "You're hiding from the Border Patrol, aren't you?"

"It's not like it seems. We just…"

"Don't worry," he interrupted, "everything's copacetic. You have your needs, I have mine."

Webb squinted at him. "And yours would be what, exactly?"

"I saw the neighbor's truck out there." He gestured outside, ignoring the question. "I guess old Mr. Janacek let you have it."

"I had car trouble. We're only borrowing it."

"Yeah, well, he couldn't give it to you even if he wanted to. He's been in the old-folks home for the last six months. Poor guy doesn't even know his own name."

"You've made your point," he groused, losing his patience. "Are you after money? Well, you can save your breath. I'm broke."

"What I want," he said, pulling Mariah to his side, "is for you to take her with you when you leave."

She looked up at him, her eyes wide with disbelief.

"No!" she yelled, struggling free. "I want to stay here with you."

Running to the bales, she pressed herself against them. Frida knelt next to her.

"You don't know what you're asking," Webb said, trying to reason with him. "We don't have the right to take a little girl just because someone wants us to."

"Trust me. She needs to leave this place."

"There are agencies that deal with this sort of thing. That's where she needs to go."

"Alright then, take her there. Anywhere would be better than here."

"You can forget about it. Turn us in if you want to but we're not taking her."

Frida wiped the tears from Mariah's face and took her hand, leading her to where Ewan stood. She studied him a moment.

"Tell me what happened to you," she said softly, pointing her chin at his head. "I think it may help us."

"You mean this work of art?" He ran a hand across his scalp, his voice bitter. "I had let my hair grow out. It was awesome, my best feature. I come from a poor family so I get no respect at school but the hair made a difference, a true difference. People finally treated me like a real person.

"Then one day my stepmother slapped Mariah so I stepped in, grabbed her by the throat and told her if she ever did it again she'd get worse than a slap from me. That night she and my father snuck into my room while I was asleep. Before I knew what was happening they grabbed me, held me down and shaved my head. They said the long hair made me disrespectful and had to go.

"Girls won't even look at me now. Those are the ones that aren't laughing. I don't need to tell you what the jocks say."

"That's what you want to protect Mariah from, the reason you want us to take her?"

He stared at her, saying nothing. She stepped closer.

"There's something else, isn't there, something worse."

He nodded, his eyes dark.

"You have to take her," he whispered.

"Tell me about your sister. How old is she?"

"She'll be fourteen next month."

"Is it true she's going to have a baby?"

He turned to Mariah, his voice calm, matter of fact. "Do you remember where I keep the bucket?"

"I remember," she answered, her eyes sparkling. "It's up the windmill ladder."

"Will you bring us some water?"

She sprinted out the door without answering. He waited for her disappear and then turned back to Frida, locking eyes with her.

"She turns eleven next month. She can't be here much longer. Do you understand what I'm telling you? I will do whatever I have to but I'm not here every moment of every day. You have to take her."

Webb moved next to Frida and peered into the boy's face.

"You're telling us that your father is the baby's father?"

He nodded. Webb leaned in, his face inches away.

"Don't lie to us so we'll take the girl. This is serious business. We're talking prison time."

"He's a bastard. I hope he rots in jail. I should've done something for April but I didn't realize what was happening until it was too late. Now that she's showing he won't touch her.

"Mariah is a different story. It's only a matter of time. I'll kill him if he touches her. I'm totally serious. I have the means and I will keep him away."

"How will it affect her," Frida said, "if you're the one that ends up going to jail?"

"If it means he's not around to hurt her," he answered, his voice flat, "then it's a fair trade."

"You don't know what you're saying." Webb waved off his comment. "All you have to do is call the authorities and report what he's done to your sister."

"Don't you think I've tried that? They don't believe anything I say."

"Why wouldn't they?"

"I've run away, punched holes walls, broken stuff. My parents have turned me in more than once even when they caused the problem. The law believes the adult, not the fifteen-year-old kid."

"Webb," she said, turning to face him, "I believe him."

"Whether we believe him or not isn't the point. This is not our problem."

She grabbed his arm and pulled him down the aisle.

"We can't let this boy ruin his life," she whispered. "We have to take her with us."

"Damn it, Frida, the world is full of heartache," he hissed. "We can't fix every problem out there."

"But that's the point, Webb. We've come across these children and now we have the chance to help them."

"We can't get involved."

"We're already involved."

They turned as Mariah reappeared, bucket in hand, her face flushed. She hurried to where Ewan stood.

"Look at them, Webb," she whispered. "Are you telling me you can just walk away?"

He watched Mariah dip a ladle into the bucket and hand it to Ewan. An image of himself as a child, motherless and plagued with self-doubt, drifted like smoke through his thoughts. His troubles, though real, could not compare to theirs. He turned his gaze to the doorway, watching dust swirl among the shadows, waiting for darkness to come.

Chapter Sixteen

Webb crept around the barn, kneeling behind the water tank and peering over the top. Nothing stirred in the shallow valley below him. To his back, a streak of red split the western sky like a wound, staining the scrub-strewn scene in crimson. Ropes of cloud drifted overhead, surreal in the eerie light.

He studied the tree line flanking the gate. The green and white of truck fenders no longer glinted through the thicket. The Border Patrol finally had left.

He slipped back into the barn and minutes later they were on their way, bumping down the narrow path in the creaking truck, Mariah on the seat between them. He cast a furtive glance her direction, hoping he was right in agreeing to take her. Ewan had refused to go with them despite Frida's pleas. He would not leave his sister.

The trees fell away and the trailer appeared a hundred yards to their right, still visible beneath the glowing dusk. Light spilled from a front window. Silhouetted figures moved behind the curtains like specters, appearing and disappearing, growing large and then small. Webb stopped the truck, disturbed by the look of it.

An instant later the front door burst open and Ewan stumbled down the stairs, landing face first in a pool of light. The sling hung from his neck like a giant bandana. He rolled onto his back, cradling his arm.

"Ewan!" Mariah screamed.

Anvil appeared in the doorway, his bearded face twisted with anger, followed by a stout woman. A length of electric cord dangled from her hand. Clambering down the stairs, Anvil fell onto him, lifting his shirt. Then the woman raised the thick cord above her head, bringing it down on his bare back with a sickening thwack.

"Webb," Frida gasped, shielding Mariah's eyes, "you have to do something."

He leapt from the truck and sprinted through the darkness, ignoring the tall grass grabbing at his feet. The woman raised the cord again and brought it down. Ewan cried out. Seconds later Webb burst into the light, throwing himself onto Anvil. They tumbled into the dirt. The woman turned, whipping the thick cord across his back.

Ewan scrambled to his feet and ran toward her, ducking as she swung again. Grabbing the cord with his good arm, he yanked it free and raised it over his head. She stared at him, eyes wide, and then scurried back through the door.

He rushed to where Webb had Anvil pinned to the ground. Grabbing the cord from him, Webb deftly looped it around Anvil's neck, jerking it up and back. He stopped struggling at once. Then Webb bound his wrists with the free end and stood, putting a foot to his neck. Ewan grabbed his arm.

"Don't hurt him."

"Move enough," he said, ignoring him, "and you just might strangle yourself. Not that it would be any big loss."

Anvil groaned as he pressed his shoe to the cord. He turned to Ewan and motioned toward the trailer.

"Are there any weapons inside?"

"They have a shotgun but I took the shells." He nodded at the sling. "That's how I got this."

"And you don't want me to hurt him?"

"He didn't mean to do it," he replied. "He has a problem with anger because of the war and…"

"Why should you care what I do to him?" he interrupted, his voice rising with every word. "Look what he's done to you."

"He's my father," he muttered.

"And a damn poor one."

Frida appeared at his shoulder, scowling. She nudged Mariah toward Ewan.

"Please take her back to the truck."

He nodded and took her hand, disappearing beyond the edge of light. Frida pointed a finger into Webb's face.

"You should be ashamed, showing off your cruelty," she hissed. "Don't you think that boy has seen enough violence? Already he has the habit of solving problems with force."

"You wanted me to stop this bastard, didn't you?"

"Yes, but not to become like him. What is it with men and physical violence?"

He pressed his heel into Anvil's back, eliciting a low moan. "You saw what he did to the boy."

"Is that what you want, for Ewan to take after a man like that?"

"You know I don't."

"The boy is still watching, you know, watching and learning."

He moved his foot and knelt beside Anvil, bending close to his ear.

"Now, you listen up," he growled under his breath. "Ewan and Mariah are coming with us. Don't even think about trying to stop us or we might have to get the law involved. That would be your bad luck. From what I hear they have no mercy on child abusers."

Within minutes they were past the gate, the headlights cutting a dim wedge through the tree-choked highway. Webb glanced at his passengers. Ewan sat wedged next to him, Mariah in his lap. Frida leaned on the dashboard peering into the darkness.

He tried to work out how he had started the day with a job interview, a job that surely was no longer an option, and ended up with a young girl and a teenager. He had no idea what he would do with them or, worse, what Maves would say when he found out. To complicate matters, Frida was still angry with him.

He glanced at her reflection in the glass, wishing despite himself he could find a way to win her over. A part of him saw no future in such a hope. The wall of her belief would always stand between them. But his feeling for her remained despite the obstacles. He stared into the darkness as the miles drifted past in a blur of asphalt and brush, offering nothing but a momentary distraction from his restless thoughts.

The next morning, he stood in the dining room doorway blinking the sleep from his eyes. Streaks of honey-colored sunlight angled across the floor like bars on a golden cage. In the far corner a tangled pile of rumpled blankets marked the makeshift sleeping pallet he had set up the night before. He watched the rise and fall of Ewan's chest, his sleeping face a gruesome map of bruises, some purple, some already fading to a dirty yellow. He turned away, angered by the sight.

Taking a breath, he forced his gaze to the living room couch where Mariah lay curled beneath the bedclothes deep in sleep. He could not help but see a terrible vulnerability in her young face.

"At least for now they're safe," he muttered to himself. He would not allow his thoughts further.

The aroma of coffee drifted from the kitchen. Frida appeared in the doorway, the collie at her feet and motioned him inside with a quick nod. A plate of toast and another of bacon sat on the table. Handing him a mug, she pointed him to a chair and closed the door.

"They must be exhausted," she whispered, sitting opposite him. "I haven't heard a peep since we got home."

"Should we wake them?"

"Let them sleep." She picked up a slice of toast and then dropped it. "I can always make more breakfast."

"They've been through a lot."

"We all have. And I was wrong," she said, reaching across the table to touch the bluish knot below his eye. "I shouldn't have been so hard on you last night. I know you were only trying to help the boy."

140

The warmth of her fingers stirred him. He leaned toward her and she locked eyes with him briefly. Then she pulled back and let her hand drop to Pilar's head.

"No, you were right," he said, realizing his mistake. "Ewan needs to see that a man can act without losing control. I had to get Anvil off him but I should've stopped there. Instead, I went too far. I'll handle things differently next time."

"I hope there is no next time." She turned to the window, for a moment lost to her thoughts. "Oh, Webb, I want to have just one day where nothing bad happens. I won't complain, I promise."

"You'll be bored in no time," he chuckled, relieved to sidestep the awkward moment.

She frowned, feigning offense. "That's not true."

"Well, see. Before you know it you'll be begging Maves to take you on his next call."

"Speaking of your father, I thought he would be back by now. Should we be worried that we haven't heard from him?"

"He said he might need to turn off his phone, and he asked me to take his calls."

"Will you know what to do?"

"I helped out around here when I was a younger. But I'm praying I don't have to find out how much I've forgotten."

As if in answer, the clinic doorbell rang. He sighed and gulped his coffee.

"You see what praying gets me?"

"Maybe God has something in mind for you."

He snorted. "You mean something like torture?"

"Webb, you're incorrigible," she muttered.

"Come on," he said, standing, "I may need your help."

They slipped out the back door and crossed the yard, rounding the corner of the garage, the clinic just beyond. A horse trailer stood in the driveway. Webb checked the office but found it empty. He motioned Frida to follow.

141

Moments later they stepped through the back door and into the covered arena. A chestnut-colored pony stood just inside the corral, a blood-stained bandage taped to its withers. The horse eyed him listlessly, its head drooping.

A potbellied man in a felt Stetson and khaki suit appeared in the stable doorway. Sunlight glinted off his newly shined boots. Spotting Webb, he hustled to the corral and ripped off his hat, giving Frida a slight nod before turning his attention to him.

"My daughter's pony was gored by a Longhorn bull," he said, breathless. "She's only eleven. She'll be devastated if we lose her."

Webb glanced at the crimson bandage sagging from the mare's shoulder, blood trailing below it in narrow streaks. A wave of panic swept over him. If forced to, he might remember how to tend a minor cut or scrape, but he knew nothing about serious wounds. Doubt, familiar and intimidating, filled his mind.

"The horse needs a vet right away," the man continued, "and I understand you're one of the best, Mr. Van Horn. I'm Lars Landrith and I'll pay whatever…"

Webb raised a hand to stop him and then jerked it back, startled by the sight of his trembling fingers.

"My father is who you're looking for," he said, sticking his hands in his pockets, "not me."

"But… but…" he sputtered. "You're not a Van Horn?"

"I'm Webb Van Horn." He tried to sound confident. "My father is out and I don't know when he'll be back. You'll need to try another vet."

"She won't make it." He jerked a wallet from his pocket. "I have money."

"I'm sorry, Mr. Landrith. Another clinic is your best bet."

"But look at her." He pointed to the horse. "How am I going to take her anywhere? She can barely stand."

Webb glanced at the horse, knowing the man was right.

"We'll help get her into the trailer," he muttered, unable to face him.

He stared into the corral feeling powerless. The mare stood before him, shivering in spite of the heat. Frida moved next to him.

"Webb, she looks bad," she said, her voice a near-whisper. "You must not delay."

"And do what?" he hissed. "I've never stitched up a gored horse. I doubt even Maves has."

"You can help her, I know you can. All you have to do is remember."

"It all happened so long ago, Frida. I doubt I can remember a thing."

"Whether you can or not, you are her only hope."

He stared at her, unable to deny the truth of her words. If he did nothing the mare would die. He had no choice but to try. He turned at once and pushed through the gate, hoping his shaking fingers would remember what to do.

"Get the leather case from the office," he called over his shoulder, "and meet me inside."

Within minutes he had a half-dozen needles threaded and set atop of the case alongside two filled syringes. The horse gave no resistance as he hobbled her back leg. Frida stood at her neck, gripping the halter and speaking to her in low tones.

Webb peeled back the bandage and examined the area. The mare flinched but otherwise remained still. Mr. Landrith took one look and retreated to a bench at the far side of the corral, his face pale. To Webb's relief the blood oozed rather than flowed from the exposed wound. He probed the ragged edge with his fingertips. The injury appeared more gash than puncture.

Taking a syringe, he traced a circle of numbing injections around the tear. Then he traded the syringe for a needle. Frida deftly sponged the wound with gauze as he

143

slipped the needle through the torn flesh, sewing the gash together from the inside out.

Frida handed him one needle after the other, all the while speaking to the mare in a hushed and rambling monologue of Spanish. He understood little. But something in the lilting rhythm of her words eased the ache in his fingers. To his surprise, her hands seemed to anticipate his every move, as if she had done it all before. More than once, she pointed out a part of the wound needing attention.

After what seemed hours, he tied and clipped the final stitch, leaving a small gap at the bottom for drainage. Dropping the instruments into the case, he pulled out a second syringe, this one filled with antibiotic. He slipped the needle under the mare's hide. She turned and snorted as if ready to be rid of him but he thought he spotted a brightness to her eye that had been missing earlier.

He examined the wound once more and then leaned his back against the fence, massaging his hands. Mr. Landrith sprang from the bench, taking a quick glance at the stitches before facing him. A hint of color had returned to his face.

"You had me going there for a minute, Mr. Van Horn," he said, his voice excited, "with all that talk of your father being the vet. I figured you were capable of fine work and I was right, sure enough. She'll be good as new in no time."

"I was just lucky. The injury wasn't as bad as it could've been."

"Nonsense!" he barked. "In my business we see shoddy work all the time. I know quality when I see it."

"Like I said, my father is the vet of the family."

"Sure, sure, you can drop the act now."

"But…"

"I know the work of a professional when I see it."

"Alright," he said, giving up, "bring her back in a week."

144

He pulled a bottle from the case and handed it to him.

"In the meantime, keep the wound clean and put this in her feed."

Relieved to be finished, Webb watched him disappear around the corner, the limping mare in tow. Frida snapped the case shut, stood and faced him.

"It's true what he said. I watched you put in every stitch. You're an artist."

"Don't get carried away."

"Admit it, Webb, you did well... and because of you a little girl has her horse again."

"I didn't think I could do it," he said, surprised to have avoided disaster. "But once I started it all came back, all the memories of stitching wounds or closing incisions while Maves stood by watching. I guess I had forgotten all he let me do."

"It must have taken a lot of patience to let a boy learn when he could have done it quicker himself."

He gave no answer, taken aback by the thought. Maves had always been demanding, his expectations seemingly unattainable to a young boy. But could the pushing, the critiquing, even the criticizing have been Maves' way of insuring he became skilled rather than merely adequate in whatever work he chose? Looking back now it seemed possible, even probable.

He was about to tell her so when the muted neigh of a horse drifted past. For a moment, he thought Mr. Landrith had returned with the pony. Then the sound came again, louder than before, and he turned to find a smoke-gray horse leaning out of the stable window.

"There's a... who left..." he stammered, glancing around the corral, "where did that horse come from?"

"Marley's here!" she yelled, rushing through the gate.

He followed her into the cluttered confines of the unused stable. The tall gelding, pale and ghost-like beneath the dim light, eyed him from behind the stall door.

145

"Welcome to your new home, Marley," she murmured, stroking his jaw.

"What's he doing here?" He peered at the horse. "He doesn't look sick."

"Marley belongs to Maves."

"Maves owning a horse," he snorted, "is about as likely as me owning a Cadillac."

"Then you have an expensive car in your future," she quipped. "Gil Shannon couldn't keep Marley anymore so he gave him to Maves. Gil must have brought him while we were gone."

"I can't believe Maves agreed to it."

"People can change, Webb, even your father."

Her gaze shifted past him to the doorway and he turned to find Mariah standing at the threshold, her cheeks streaked with tears. Frida ran to her.

"What is it, sweetheart?" She brushed away the tears. "Did you think we had left you?"

"No," she said, shaking her head.

"You had a bad dream?"

She shook her head again.

"Then what's happened?"

"Ewan sent me. He said to tell you there's a man at the door." She pointed to the house. "He has a badge."

Frida gasped and pulled her close. Webb sprinted out the door, rounding the arena and stopping at the corner. A sheriff's cruiser sat blocking the drive. He hurried back into the stable, pointing Frida to the back wall.

"There's a storage room in the corner. Hide in there."

"But what if it's not me they're after. What if Anvil called them?" She held Mariah to her chest. "Webb, you must not let them find her."

"Take her and stay out of sight. I'll figure out something."

Moments later he stepped into the living room. Ewan loitered by the door as if ready to bolt. A red-faced deputy stood nearby, a notepad in one hand, a paper cup in the

146

other. His nametag read 'Officer Herman Stoll'. A wad of chewing tobacco bulged in his cheek. Webb glanced at Ewan before approaching the man.

"What brings you here, officer?" he said, trying to sound unconcerned as they shook hands. "If you're looking for my father, he's away on business."

His coal-chip eyes studied Webb a moment. Then he spit into the cup and set it on a side table.

"I'm looking for the driver of a Ford sedan found parked on a ranch two counties over. The name on the registration is a Webb Van Horn, and this house is listed as his permanent address. You wouldn't happen to be him now would you?"

"Yes but I can explain..."

"Just one moment, please sir." He raised a hand to stop him. "A truck from that same ranch went missing, a truck that fits the description of the one parked in your driveway. You know anything about that?"

"Well, the car... the Ford..." he stammered, "a rock must've..."

"Old Mr. Janacek," Ewan interrupted, "he promised me that truck when I was old enough to get my license. But then his mind went bad and he ended up in the nursing home before he could sell it to me. He and I talked about it so many times I thought it would be okay to borrow it."

"You admit you took the truck," the deputy said, looking at him askance, "and you don't think that's stealing?"

"Like I told you," he said, his tone defensive, "Mr. Janacek promised me."

"We had planned," Webb jumped in, "to contact the Janacek family and ask about buying the truck. We were on our way to look it over, make sure it was drivable, when the Ford broke down."

The deputy rolled the tobacco in his cheek, flipped through his notepad, and eyed them again.

"You're telling me you borrowed the truck with the intent to purchase it?"

"Is that so hard to believe? The old man is incapacitated. If he had been there we would have taken it for a long drive to make sure it was worth buying. That old truck had seen heavy use."

"A test drive is not the same as taking the truck to your home," he said, spitting into the cup.

"We were stuck out there. My car was not drivable. The old man, the truck's owner, had promised a chance to buy it. It isn't like we went there intending to steal a vehicle."

He peered at his notes again. Webb gave Ewan a knowing look before the deputy lifted his gaze.

"The Ford sedan was called in by Border Patrol agents busting up an illegal alien operation. You know anything about that?"

"Are you telling me we almost stumbled on human traffickers? From what I hear, those are dangerous people."

"Yes sir, you could say that. There's been a lot of activity up this way." He held up the cup, ready to spit, then hesitated. "So you saw nothing suspicious?"

Webb turned his eyes to Ewan. "Did you see anything, son?"

"Everything was real quiet with Mr. Janacek gone."

"Well," Webb shrugged, "I guess we're no help."

A look of consternation crossed the deputy's face. He spit into the cup and slammed it on the table, wiping a dribble of juice from his chin with a quick jerk of his hand.

"You could say that too," he grumbled. "Well then, I'll be off. You'd best contact the Janacek family right away or I'll be back out here and it won't be so pleasant."

He started for the door and Webb called after him, pointing to the tobacco-stained cup.

"You may want to take that with you, Deputy Stoll."

148

He grabbed the cup and hurried out the door. Webb watched him through the window, making sure the cruiser disappeared from view before he turned to Ewan.

"That was some quick thinking. But don't make a habit of lying to the authorities."

"I'm not sure I said anything that wasn't true. He did promise to sell me the truck, for a good price too."

"In any event, we need to get that truck back over there soon."

"You mean I can't keep it?"

"No, you can't keep it. You heard what the deputy said."

"But I just thought..."

Frida rushed into the room pulling Mariah behind her.

"Oh, thank God you're still here," she said, breathless. "I heard the car leave and feared they had taken you with them."

"They found my car and then discovered the truck was missing. Thanks to Ewan's quick thinking we were able to talk our way out of it."

"We are safe then?"

"I'm not so sure."

"What will we do, Webb?"

"Please take Mariah to the kitchen," he said to Ewan, "and close the door. There's bacon and toast on the table."

"I'll make you something hot for breakfast in a moment," she called after them.

"I need time to think." He pulled a phone from his pants pocket. "But first I have to call children's services."

"Webb, you mustn't."

"We don't have a choice."

"We can't just hand them over as if we'd found a lost coat."

"Frida..."

"They'll stick them in some sort of terrible home where no one cares a thing about them."

"Frida, you know we can't keep them."

"Why can't we?"

"It doesn't work that way. We could be arrested for kidnapping."

"They'll have to find us first."

He sighed, seeing the determination in her eyes.

"I suppose we can postpone a short while," he muttered. "But there's one call I won't put off. We have to tell them what's happened to Ewan's sister."

He made the anonymous report and set down the phone, thinking again of Maves, both dreading and hoping for his quick return. Taking on an unwanted collie or horse was one thing, but Maves had little toleration for children. He could almost imagine the heated exchange.

The worrisome sense he had felt earlier returned and he puzzled over the irony of Maves venturing back near the scene of his injury, Blanca again the cause. Her hold over him was unsettling. What was she after, and why did she need him this time? He could not guess. He only hoped Maves would keep his wits about him while traversing that lawless place.

Chapter Seventeen

A wedge-shaped thunderhead loomed above the horizon, hatchet-like and blood red in the morning haze. Maves stood on a low rise squinting into the sunlight. Without checking he knew the canyon where he was injured stood less than a mile to the east. He peered at the torn landscape, trying to banish the thought.

Below him an abandoned town sat at the edge of a deep gash in the earth. Nothing stirred on the weed-littered streets. The sheer cliffs beyond looked eerily like the canyon where Riley Banks lost his life.

He tried to resurrect a vague thought buried in his consciousness, the same thought that had followed Zak's warning to take care. There had been something more in his words, something unsaid yet palpable, something to do with Blanca. She too had seemed to hold back, but to what purpose he could not say.

He backtracked to where Abel waited in the shade of his green and white panel truck. Eyeing Maves, he tugged on his mustache as if considering his words. He pointed his chin at the bleak scene below them.

"Your woman friend sure knows how to jerk your chain, sending you way out to no hombres land on the hottest day of the year. I think it's about time you told me how you know this chica."

"I'm not much bothered by the heat," he said, ignoring the question. "Besides, September is a month away and it's always the hottest month in this part of the world. I once saw it..."

"It's a short leash too," he said, grinning.

"I'm not on anyone's leash," he snapped. "I'm just a messenger."

"A messenger blinded by love."

"Nonsense. This is business, pure and simple."

"What kind of business goes on out here other than the illegal kind? Come on, Maves, I come all this way to help out, I deserve to know something about this woman."

"Like I told you," he grumbled, "she's getting important papers for the women refugees she helps so they can get asylum."

"If any of those refugees need a place to stay, I got room… as long as they're fine-looking."

"Abel, you have a one track mind."

"I have my priorities. I appreciate beautiful women and don't mind admitting it, unlike some people I know."

"My priority is delivering a package."

"Speaking of good-looking women," he continued, "I ran into Rosie last week when I was in San Antonio. She looked good, Maves, I mean finger-licking good. We had a beer and talked over all the old times. Too bad she's still married. This guy makes the third Mr. Rosie."

"I wouldn't think being married matters to you."

"Not to me, but it does to her. Anyway, she said something I meant to tell you only I can't remember just now." He pointed a finger at Maves. "Wait, it'll come to me. A beer might help. You bring any in that ice chest?"

"No, I did not bring any," he barked. "I need you alert. I don't much like the look of our meeting place."

"No, it looks like trouble." He peered at the dilapidated buildings, most of the roofs sagging or missing altogether. "The border has to be somewhere below that big cliff. That damn drop must be four hundred feet or more. I hope it keeps the drug runners away."

Maves stared down the slope, tempted to tell him all that had happened since Blanca had reentered his life. But words kept slipping away, writhing in his thoughts like landed fish, impossible to hold for more than an instant. Giving up, he jerked open the door and motioned Abel insise.

They bumped down a rugged path that smoothed and leveled as they neared the town. Abel stopped before a two-story building of weathered shiplap, the roof a mere shell of beams and rafters. A sign over the door read 'Mecum Hotel'. Shards of glass clung to the upper windows, reflecting indigo hues of the sunless canyon below.

Maves surveyed the buildings along the street, all in some state of disrepair, all seeming to be empty. The remains of a windmill moaned in the shifting wind, high-pitched and drawn like the cry of a wounded animal. Opposite him a side street held a scattering of hollowed-out shacks, some with stables. Past the houses the road disappeared from view, the far side of the canyon taking its place.

A squat man appeared in the shadow of the nearest shack. Maves nudged Abel. This was not the sort of meeting he had imagined. A feeling of unease swept over him and he wondered again if Blanca was, as Zak feared, playing some dangerous game.

Then the man stepped from the shadows. The white smear of a smile crossed his ruddy face. His manner casual and friendly, he waved them closer. Maves glanced at Abel and started toward the man, chiding himself for his rush to judgment. All was going according to Blanca's instructions. He would no doubt complete the trade and return by nightfall.

The man's round head and flattened nose held the disarming look of a cartoon character. A spout of blonde hair rose from the top of his head like a fountain. He raised both hands at their approach as if to apologize for their bleak surroundings. His smile dimmed only slightly.

"For a minute you had me fooled," he chuckled, squinting up at him. He stood a head shorter than Maves. "When I saw that green and white truck of yours I thought maybe the law had decided to pay me a visit."

"You're not the first to think that," Maves said, shaking his hand. "The truck belongs to my friend here, Abel. I'm Maves Va..."

"Surnames are not advisable in this business," he interrupted. "I'm Harlan."

"I understand, Harlan. We'd like to finish up and be on our way as soon as possible."

"Yes, and the sooner we do so the better." He glanced around, his smile vanishing. "Business dealings have become very unpredictable on the border, unpredictable and unsafe. You have the package?"

"It's in the truck." He nodded up the street. "If you'll meet me there, we can make the trade and get out of your hair."

"You mean what little I have left?" he laughed, running a hand across his scalp.

"Losing hair is a fact of life for most men... except Abel, that is. I'll see you at the truck."

He pivoted, took a step and then stopped as two men, one tall, the other dark and stocky, stepped from the porch of the abandoned hotel. Shotguns at their sides, they started down the street, an old man wedged between them. A thick beard framed his umber face in white. Sunlight glinted off his bleeding forehead.

Stopping before them, the men released their hold and pushed him into the street. He fell at Maves' feet.

"Forgive my weakness, Mr. Van Horn," he pleaded in a thick accent, fear twisting his features. "I had no choice but to tell them of you. They threatened to cut off my ears and bury me to my neck in the way of the Comanche."

"What's your name?"

"I am Narciso Garza," he said, wiping the sweat from his eyes.

"You brought the delivery?"

"Si, and now they have it. I got here early and they were waiting for me with their guns."

"And now it's time for you to leave," Harlan sneered, still smiling. "The road is behind you."

154

"But the land has nothing for many miles, twenty or more" he said, squinting up at the dome of sky. "The heat, it is too much."

"He's right." Maves glared at Harlan. "There's no shade and no water."

"I don't remember," he replied, his smile vanishing, "asking for your opinion."

"I'm telling you anyway," he growled.

"My, aren't we the feisty one?"

"I know this place, this land. I know how unforgiving it is. He won't make it without water."

"Well, we wouldn't want that now would we?"

He stepped inside the shack and then reappeared with a plastic bottle of water. His other hand held a pocket knife. Ambling to where the old man stood, he raised the bottle and thrust the knifepoint into the plastic before tossing it to the ground. Narciso stared at the bottle in disbelief then pounced on it, pressing his mouth to the hole.

"Now, unless you want to end up like that bottle, you should make tracks out of here fast as you can."

"But I…"

"Having trouble hearing," he said, holding the knife to the light, "are we, old man?"

He scrambled to his feet. Maves watched him scurry up the slope until, glancing over his shoulder one last time, he disappeared over the rise. Maves dropped his gaze and spit, disgust bitter on his tongue. Then he turned, biting back a growing anger. Abel locked eyes with him and gave his head a slight shake as if to urge restraint.

Harlan folded the knife and stuffed it in his pocket, moving to where they stood. Maves wondered if he and Abel would suffer the same humiliation as the old man. The men holding the shotguns stood by without expression.

Harlan nodded and one of them entered Abel's truck, emerging seconds later with the box. Ripping off the lid, he pulled out a stack of greenbacks and held them up.

155

Harlan's over-white smile returned and he leaned in close, his face within inches of Maves.

"It looks like we're in business, Mr. Van Horn. Your partners were foolish enough to send cash, so we know they have money to spend. I imagine they'll be willing to spend a little more on getting their friends back with their ears still attached. What do you think?"

"I think if anyone should lose their ears and be buried to the neck," he grumbled, "it's you."

"Too bad you're worth something to me. I enjoy doing things to people like you, painful things, unimaginable things." He turned his gaze on Abel. "I don't suppose your hairy friend shares your love of trouble, does he?"

"Don't pay any attention to Maves," Abel said, winking. "He has a thing about old people. I think it's because he's a vet, so he likes picking up strays, helping old ladies across the street, that kind of thing. You know the type."

"They call them Boy Scouts."

"Yeah, something like that. Anyway, he just gets overexcited when he sees some old person all upset. That old guy, he'll be alright. Take my word for it. My old man was just like him, complaining about one thing and another, sounding like he was about to take his last breath, then the next thing you know he's drinking you under the table. I mean the old dude was tough. I remember one New Year…

"You more than make up for your partner's silence," he interrupted, his smile vanishing, "don't you?"

"You mean Maves? Talking to him is like talking to yourself. I mean, he almost never…"

"Enough!" he shouted, motioning to the two men. "Tie them up and hide them behind the stable in case the old man does make it out alive and we have unexpected guests. In that eventuality…" he turned back to Abel, his

156

smile returning, "we'll just shove the *evidence* off the cliff."

"Evidence?" he said, his eyes wide. "You mean Maves and me?"

"That's very astute of you," he sniped.

"That's one deep canyon. You'd throw us over the edge just to be rid of us?"

"Keep talking," he snipped, "and you'll find out."

The tall man kept his shotgun trained on them while the other bound their wrists behind them with a thick hemp rope. Leading them to the stable, he kicked Abel in the ribs, sending him to the ground. Maves landed next to him. He pushed himself against the building, edging his back up the splintered wall.

Harlan reappeared and smiled down at him. "I must go negotiate a price for you. Unfortunately, phones are useless in this godforsaken place."

"How can you know who to contact?" Maves studied his reaction.

"Are you so parochial," he sneered, "as to imagine I'm some sort of amateur?"

"Then why not tell us?"

"I know the same way I knew you would come here. I have my sources. Besides, rather than deal with your employer, I'm selling you to the cartel. They've finally discovered the lucrative value of kidnapping gringos."

"How long will this negotiation take?"

"My, you do like your questions. But you've wasted enough of my time." He gestured at the dark man. "Benito will be back to keep you company until our return."

Maves watched the men leave. He turned his attention to the narrow space between the stable and canyon. The earth sloped away from him at a steep pitch, ending at a sheer cliff twenty yards beyond. The yawning drop was dizzying even from where he sat.

To his left, a short post jutted from the dirt. A heavy chain drooped from a metal ring, disappearing beneath the rocky soil before reemerging inches from his feet. To his immediate right, just past Abel, a pile of wooden slats sat adjacent to a flatbed trailer of rusted iron. A stone wedged beneath the nearest wheel was all that kept it from rolling down the slope and off the edge.

He studied the trailer frame, eventually spotting a thick hook beneath it partially hidden by the hitch. An idea came to him at once. He kicked Abel's shoe and nodded at the slats.

"Think you could use one of those boards to snag that chain," he whispered, "if I talked you through it?"

"What are you up to, Maves?" he hissed, glancing at the pile. "Whatever it is, I don't like it. That Harlan may be a creep but he was right about you. You go looking for trouble."

"You want to take a swan dive off that cliff?"

"Don't start in on the cliff," he cringed. "I've heard enough from the little man already."

"Then slide over there and grab a board."

"What if Benny comes back?"

"That's a good reason to hurry."

"Why not just untie me?"

"He has a shotgun, remember? Besides which I'm tied too tight and he's not likely to get close enough to surprise."

"What if he catches us? I don't need another kick in the ribs."

"The ground is rocky enough. We'll hear him coming."

"Okay, Maves," he sighed, "I give. What's the plan?"

"You back up to those slats and get a hold of one, then lift that chain and hook it under the frame."

"That's some magic trick but I'll try anything to keep on solid ground." He turned his back to the stack of wood. "Say abracadabra and tell me where to go, Houdini."

He slid to the pile at Maves direction and grabbed an inch-wide slat, slipping it under the chain and lifting it.

158

With a muted clink of metal the links emerged from the rocky soil. He lowered it and stabbed at the end link, trying to force the slat through. After several failures, he slumped forward.

"This damn behind the back business is killing my arms. I think the slat is too big for that little hole. How about I find a way break off the end?"

At Maves' direction, he slipped the slat between the frame and an angular support then gave the stick a quick jerk. The wood snapped with ease, leaving a sharp point. He stabbed at the chain again, snagging a link on the fourth attempt and then maneuvering the length under the frame. With a clank the trailer was attached. Maves kicked dirt back over the chain. Moments later a van topped the rise and disappeared in a swirl of dust.

"Okay," Abel groaned, "I did your trick. Now what happens?"

"We wait."

"We wait? What do we wait for?"

Maves stared at him, offering no answer. He leaned back and cast his gaze over the post and trailer.

"Maves, you sly devil," he whispered, grinning, "I've never known you to be so underhanded. It's not like you to sneak around."

"I don't plan to be bought and sold like someone's prize bull," he said, spitting into the dirt.

Seconds later Benito rounded the nearest shack and squatted in the shade of a stunted tree, pulling the stub of a cigar from his shirt pocket and lighting it. Blue smoke swirled about his face. He squinted at the cloudless sky and then disappeared inside the shack, reemerging with a small chair and setting it in a narrow band of shade cast by the roofline. He sat, leaned against the wall and pulled a knife from his boot, idly trimming his fingernails.

Maves watched his movements with interest, wondering if their plan had any real chance of success. Blanca's face flashed through his thoughts. Would she be willing to pay for their release? To his dismay, he found he had no answer. He could not help doubting her now.

All at once he realized he must tell Abel everything. He might not have another chance. As if reading his thoughts, Abel leaned toward him.

"I sit here with nothing to do," he said, "and I finally remember what Rosie told me. She…"

"I have something I need to say first," he interrupted. "Earlier, you asked about the woman I've been helping, the reason we're here now. The truth is she's the one from the bar in Piedras Negras, the small one, the friend of Rosie's. Her name is Blanca."

"You don't think I figured that out already, Maves? I just didn't say anything because I could see Webb didn't know and I wasn't going to be the one to tell him. Plus, I wanted to see if you'd ever come clean."

"You know about the affair?"

"Maves, don't you think Rosie would've told me? Back then we spent a lot of time together. We were, you know, close."

"Did you know that Webb's mother left me because of it," he replied, the words bitter on his tongue, "that he's never forgiven me for hurting her the way I did, that I've never forgiven myself?"

"No, my friend," he answered, his voice somber, "I didn't know that part of the story."

A mix of relief and shame filled his throat. Recalling his regret over keeping the truth from Webb, he vowed not to repeat his mistake.

"I'm sorry I never told you," he managed.

"No big deal. Forget about it."

"You've been a good friend and deserve better."

"We all make mistakes, Maves."

"I just couldn't get past my pride… and my shame."

"The past is sometimes hard to shake, amigo."

"How can those days seem like yesterday when they happened so long ago?"

160

"Time is like that. But you can't beat yourself up over what's done, Maves. You have to leave it behind."

"I wish it was that easy." He took a breath, compelled to face the rest of the story. "Tell me what you learned from Rosie."

"Well, I said she told me the whole story back then but she left out one part, the part I was about to tell you. It has to do with Blanca."

"Do I want to hear it?"

"Probably not when you have your hands tied behind your back…" he said and then paused, "but then again, maybe it's the best time. This way you can't kill the messenger."

"Sounds like more bad news."

"You might say that."

"Then get it over with."

"Okay, so I was working the Ordaz charm on Rosie, hoping she was about to ditch hubby number three and I might have a chance to comfort her a little before number four…"

"Can't you just give me the news," he groused, "without turning it into a novel?"

"Do you want to hear it or not?"

"Go on, then," he muttered.

"So I was chatting her up when all of a sudden she up and tells me that while you two were together, Blanca was also messing around with Riley Banks."

Maves stared at him in disbelief, his mind racing. Abel peered into his face.

"Maybe we should talk about this later. You're not looking so good."

"No, I want to hear it all."

"Rosie said they had a place across the border where they met," he continued. "Blanca made her promise not to tell anyone."

"She got it wrong," he said, grabbing at whatever memory he could find. "That happened after I stopped seeing her. She was lonely and..."

"No, Maves," he interrupted, "I'm sure I heard her right. I asked all kinds of questions about it. She told me Blanca was real careful, that she started seeing Riley a month before you and her got together."

"Did Riley know about me?"

"That I can't say," he said, studying his face. "But better to hear the truth from me than not hear it at all, isn't it?"

Maves turned away, unable to accept the news. He tried to convince himself Rosie was mistaken or Abel misheard her. Yet the nagging doubts would not leave him.

The sound of an approaching car pulled him back into the moment and he looked up, spotting a cloud of dust rising over the ridgeline. Seconds later Harlan's van crested the rise. Benito jabbed the knife in the dirt and jumped from the chair, vanishing around the corner. Maves nudged Abel with his foot.

"When they show up," he said, nodding toward the shack, "ask for water. Act like you're sick from the heat."

Harlan rounded the shack, followed by Benito and his tall companion. Maves studied their approach, trying to will their movements. The tall man hung back while Harlan stepped closer, his over-white smile returning. Benito moved next to him.

"Our negotiations went nicely... and lucratively. We have only a short while to wait in this interminable heat and then it's off to a beautiful island cooled by tropical breezes and an endless supply of frozen drinks."

"Speaking of the heat," Maves said, nodding at Abel, "your money ticket over here isn't doing so well."

"I drank too much beer last night," he croaked, his head drooping, "and now I'm paying for it. I need some water."

"Well, unlike the old man, you're too valuable to let die. Just to show how generous I am, I'll let you have two bottles... if, that is, they don't go empty first."

He nodded and the tall man vanished, returning moments later with the bottles. Smiling, Harlan pulled out his pocket knife and started toward them, Benito at his side. Abel gave Maves a quick wink and then staggered to his feet, lunging at Harlan, his eyes wild.

"Give me that water you bastard!"

"Do something, Benito!" he screamed, recoiling.

Benito brought the shotgun across Abel's face, sending him to the ground. Seeing his chance, Maves kicked the stone from beneath the trailer. The iron wheel lurched forward, unnoticed by the men, quickly picking up speed on the steep grade.

Abel rolled onto his back, groaning. Benito moved over him and raised the gun. Hoping he had acted in time, Maves scrambled to his feet as memories of Riley Banks swirled about him like windblown dust. He could not allow another friend to die.

The chain sprang from the dirt and raced forward, pulled taut by the post. Still off to one side, the tall man looked on, preoccupied with Abel's fate. Maves leapt at him, his shoulder lowered, throwing his full weight into the man's chest. The shotgun skittered beneath the shack. The man stumbled backwards, grabbing at the small tree, peeling off a branch and holding it before his face as if somehow it could tell him what was happening. Then he disappeared over the cliff.

Maves rolled over, watching Benito turn toward the oncoming grind of iron on stone. He made no sound as the chain caught him in the gut, taking his breath and throwing him backwards. An instant later the links slammed into Harlan, riding up his chest to his neck, dragging him along before they both vanished over the edge. The crash of metal against stone rose from the canyon.

Maves rose to his knees and then stood, staggering to where Benito's knife jutted from the ground. Turning his back, he knelt and pulled it free, deftly flipping the blade and sawing through the rope. Then he moved over Abel, still splayed across the dirt, and cut him free. He pushed himself onto an elbow, wincing as he fingered the knot below his eye.

"Your harebrained scheme worked," he grumbled, glancing at the empty ledge, "except for my rifle-whipping."

Maves helped him to his feet. "Flat on your back is where you needed to be."

"Yeah, but I had that all worked out," he continued. "I was going to pass out on my own. I didn't need Benny's help. Now I feel like I got kicked by one of your horses."

They turned as a moan drifted up from the canyon rim. Seconds later, Harlan crawled over the edge, his face scraped and bloody. Spotting them, he scurried between the outer shacks, heading away from the town. Abel staggered a few steps and then stopped, bent over with pain.

"I'll go after him," he said, his face in his hands, "as soon as my head stops exploding."

"No, we'll let him find out what it's like walking out of here."

He helped Abel into the panel truck and then collected the boxes from Harlan's van, tossing the keys into the scrub in case he tried to circle back. He set the packages in the truck, almost dropping the box brought by the old man. The contents rattled with a faint clink of glass. He put his ear to the top and shook it. There was no doubt. The package Blanca told him held refugee's papers instead contained something else.

He stared at the cardboard and tape, tempted to rip it open and see for himself. Questions about her filled his mind. If she had lied to him about Riley, how else might she have deceived him? Or did she lie to Riley as well? If he questioned her would he lose her just when she had

164

taken him back? It seemed likely. Climbing into the truck, he realized he had little choice but to act as if he knew none of it.

Chapter Eighteen

Maves wrestled the panel truck along the rutted road, doing his best to dodge the potholes. The rock-strewn land vibrated with heat. His head in his hands, Abel groaned with every bump. Behind him the glass contents of the package rattled like alarm bells.

A plume of dust appeared over the next rise. Maves stopped and climbed out. Taking a pair of binoculars from behind the seat, he trotted up the hill, dropped to his knees just short of the top and raised the glasses. A dust-covered chartreuse sedan raced toward them, oblivious of the potholes. He counted five men, two in front and three in back. Rifles stuck from the windows like thorns on a cactus. He scanned the horizon for another way out, finding nothing.

Retreating to the truck, he scrambled inside and jammed the gears into reverse. Abel sat up with a start. Maves made no effort to explain, instead wheeling a half-circle and backtracking toward the town. The approaching rumble of a powerful engine drifted through his window. There was no outrunning the car.

With a sudden jerk of the wheel he left the road, speeding between stands of creosote and yucca toward the canyon edge. Abel pressed himself against the seatback. Yards from the cliff, he stomped the brake pedal, sending the truck into a sliding stop.

He scanned the canyon wall, first in one direction and then the other. The desert stretched uninterrupted and razor-straight to their left. To their right, a rain-eroded gouge sloped toward the canyon. Shifting into four-wheel drive, he eased the truck down the steep grade, hoping the small ravine was deep enough to hide them.

Moments later they had reached the bottom. The sheer drop of the cliff stood just beyond. He dared venture no closer. Still pressed to the seatback, Abel squinted at him.

"You want to tell me why you're driving like some madman?" he grumbled. "This is my truck, you know, and I like it plenty."

"Harlan's friends got here earlier that I thought they would."

"You mean the damn cartel," he craned his neck toward the ridgeline, "they're here already?"

"Let's hope they're in too much of a hurry to notice us."

The deep rumble grew steadily louder and then moved past, echoing off the canyon walls. A heavy silence settled over them. Occasional voices drifted in and out of hearing, feral and animal-like. Abel leaned out the passenger window, peering up and down the canyon.

"I don't like it, Maves. If they spot us we got no way out of here."

"I'm hoping we're out of their sight."

"Me, I like to do better than hope," he said, scrambling out of the truck, "when I'm playing hide and seek with drug-runners and murderers."

Maves watched him weave through the boulders to canyon wall and then quickly return. He stuck his head through the window.

"There's a ledge going down into the canyon," he said, panting.

Maves squinted at him. "I thought you were afraid of heights."

"That was just me messing with the little man." He craned his neck toward the drop-off. "How far it goes I can't tell but I'm game to try it."

"You want to crawl down a sheer cliff?"

"I doubt those hombres have the cojones to follow me," he said, grinning. "The big question is, does Maves Van Horn?"

Before he could answer the engine rumble rose above the canyon like thunder. He hurried out of the truck, glancing toward the road as he matched Abel's footsteps

167

down the rugged slope. A sudden wind rose from the canyon, coursing past them.

In a matter of feet the ground fell away. Before them a narrow band of stone scarcely wide enough for a man angled down the sheer wall, disappearing around a rocky point. Scattered with sharp hoodoos of stone, the canyon floor stretched below them like a grinning mouth.

Maves hesitated at the drop-off, watching as Abel teetered along the slim pathway. The engine rumble eased, slowing as it drew nearer. Seconds later the sound stopped, followed by the slamming of car doors.

Guessing he had little time, Maves slid one foot onto the ledge, dragging the other behind it. A ribbon of dust poured off the path, floating up and past him on the rising air. He pressed himself to the wall and shuffled downward, keeping his gaze from the yawning space behind him.

Excited voices called out in Spanish, the words slurred by the shifting wind. They had spotted the truck. Try as he might, he understood little else. Within moments he had rounded the pointed outcropping of sandstone. The path continued but Abel was nowhere in sight. A wave of panic ripped through him. Forcing himself to turn, he peered down into the canyon, searching among the hoodoos and boulders, fearing what he might find. The scrub-strewn floor stood empty.

A whisper of voices drifted up from the ledge below him, hushed but just within hearing. He shuffled along the trail. Beyond another bend the path widened, opening onto a shallow cave etched onto the canyon face by eons of wind and rain. In its center, a thin stream meandered from a tiny spring-fed pool, disappearing over the cliff. Narciso Garza squatted beside the water. Abel crouched next to him.

"Look who I found," Abel said, waving him over, "a fellow mountain goat."

"Yes, Mr. Van Horn," the old man chuckled, "I found this place by following a herd of wild goats."

"Narciso," Abel said, winking, "since we're sharing your hideout you better call him Maves."

"Welcome to my cave, Maves."

Relieved to see them, Maves stepped into the cramped space.

"I'm glad to see you proved Harlan wrong."

"After I left you, I heard his van coming so I ran from the road. I thought he had changed his mind and came to kill me." He ran a finger across his throat. "Then I saw the goats and followed them here. You see, they brought me to water. I think I owe them my life."

Maves knelt next to him. Abel dipped his hand in the pool, raising it to his mouth.

"Not bad for goat water, Maves. I think it got rid of my headache."

"That's because you're part goat," he quipped.

"We could've waited out those damn hombres in here, but I guess we don't need to now."

Maves turned his ear toward the trail, straining to listen. Except for the shifting wind, the canyon stood silent.

"You think they left?"

"Sure they left, Maves."

"You're certain?"

"Didn't you hear them?"

"I must've been preoccupied with staying alive."

"We listened to them go. You can hear that big engine for miles. They got to be halfway to Del Rio by now."

"I say good riddance to them all."

"I bet they thought my truck was the real Border Patrol, not Abel's border taxi service, huh Narciso?" he said, clasping his shoulder. "Our friend here lost his wheels, Maves."

"Yes, I am now without my favorite truck," he sighed. "Harlan's men, they pushed it off the cliff."

"If it's any consolation," Maves said, nodding toward the canyon, "those men joined your truck."

"I thought as much. Here the sound, it travels like the wind." He crossed himself. "God forgive me, but I am not sorry for the evil bastards."

Maves studied the old man a moment, wondering at his role in Blanca's plan. He leaned toward him.

"Narciso, I hope you don't mind my asking, but who had you deliver the package?"

He ran a hand through his beard, considering the question.

"My daughter, she had the cancer," he sighed. "All the doctors said she would die, but a doctor, Dr. Rajiv, said he could save her. I sold my house to pay for the medicine. My daughter lives but I owe him much money so I must do what he asks of me while I am in his debt."

"What's inside the box?"

"This I do not know," he replied, pulling at his beard, "but I wonder also. The box a young man gave to me in Mexico, in the alley behind a hospital. I told him I did not like the look of it. Why not meet me at the front door, I said. Was he trying to hide something?"

"Who was this man?"

"I did not know him but he wore a white coat. I think he must be a student, some day to be a doctor."

Maves turned his gaze to the dark shadow of the canyon, his troubled thoughts made more so by the news. Little made sense. Why had Blanca side-stepped his queries time and again? Was she in truth helping refugees? Or were her motives altogether selfish? He stood and started back up the trail with reluctance, realizing he could not continue without knowing.

A cloudless sky rose above Blanca's yellow duplex, the low sun casting thin shadows along one side. Maves stood on the doorstep. Questions crowded his thoughts, questions only she could answer. Yet the risk of losing her had kept him silent.

He leaned past the small entryway and peered between the curtains, hoping to catch a glimpse of her. Instead he found the room vacant. He stepped into the flowerbed and bent for a better view. The antiques, the paintings, even the four-poster bed were gone. From what he could see, the entire place appeared empty.

He moved back onto the porch and rang the bell. The apartment stood silent. He pounded the door with his fist. Still nothing. He brought the palm of his hand against the heavy wood, fighting a growing frustration. Then a door opened behind him, followed by the hoarse twang of a woman's voice.

"She hightailed it out of there, honey, sometime after six."

He turned to find a middle-aged woman standing in the opposite doorway. She wore a flowered robe and slippers in spite of the heat. A lime-green scarf covered her copper-colored hair.

"I saw them in the alleyway early this morning," she continued, "just after you left out of here." A half-smoked cigarette jutted from the corner of her mouth, jumping with every word. "There were four of them whispering and tippy-toeing around, trying to be real quiet while they loaded up a flat-bed truck with all her fu-fu stuff."

"Where did she go?" he asked, not knowing what else to say.

"I'm sorry to disappoint, sweetheart, but there's not a chance in hell I would I know *that*. She had no use for the likes of me. I got no money, no fancy stuff, no big car. I barely scrape by, if you know what I mean, hand to mouth, the whole bit."

"Any idea why she left?"

"I'm just a river of disappointment for you, honey." She dropped the cigarette on the pavement, crushing under her toe. "Nothing I hate worse than to disappoint a good-looking man."

"Do you remember anything else?"

"She was in a hurry by the look of it, and those with her were some rough-looking men. I wouldn't want to meet them in a dark alley, if you know what I mean. Just peeking through the blinds at them gave me the willies." She glanced inside. "I got supper on so I need to go tend it, sweetheart."

She disappeared through the door. He ambled back across the weed-lined street and climbed into the van. Though he felt a need to return home and tend his practice, he decided instead to seek out Zak. Perhaps he knew, or at least suspected, more than he was telling.

A half-hour later he parked outside Our Lady of Guadalupe Church, alone in the stifling heat of early evening. He hoped Zak was inside. Above the two-columned bell tower, shafts of sunlight split the yellow-gold haze, sending indigo shadows across the empty street.

Within moments he had slipped into the cool confines of the sanctuary. He cradled the box with one arm. On impulse he had decided to have Zak pass it on to her. Moving midway down the aisle, he set the package on a seat and sat beside it, leaning back. A part of him wished he could simply stretch out on the pew and sleep for hours.

He longed for escape. Blanca's reappearance had changed everything. The quiet life he had known now seemed a distant and surreal memory, leaving him no choice but to press on. His eyes drifted shut.

He dreamed of her again. Standing before him, she drew close, her eyes luminous yet forbidding in their dark mystery, as if they knew him better than he knew himself. She pressed his fingers to her cheek.

Her lips moved as if to speak. Instead Frida's voice whispered his name. He blinked and suddenly she stood in Blanca's place, her auburn hair swirling about her like wildfire. Taking his hand from her face, she pressed it to her chest.

He jerked awake. Seconds later a hand landed on his shoulder and then Zak's round face appeared above him.

172

"I didn't think you had much use for church," he said, smirking, "but you're looking right at home, Maves."

"Excuse my manners, Zak," he said, trying to shake off the disturbing image. "I must've nodded off."

"I'm glad to see you in any event." He moved next to him. "Ever since I left you I've had a bad feeling about this errand of Blanca's."

"Your intuition was right on target. I don't know how but I'm pretty sure she's mixed up in something risky, not to mention outside the law. I'm hoping you can tell me what."

He stared into the distance as if unsure how to answer. Maves studied him, trying to guess at his thoughts. After a moment, he looked up.

"When you saw Blanca," he finally said, "did you happen to ask her about the clinic?"

"I did. She said the doctor is helping with her refugee work, that he has contacts in Mexico."

"Yes, that would fit." He pointed to the package. "And the box, did she tell you what it contains?"

"What are you getting at, Zak?" he asked, anxious to know the truth.

"When we were at the clinic I was bothered by the secrecy, by the so-called elite patients it serves. But I am often plagued by such distances between rich and poor." He pointed a finger into the air. "Then all at once it came to me. I had heard the doctor's name before, something to do with the illicit transport of medicines."

"He was arrested?"

"No, he has been suspected only. The authorities are unable to find proof."

"You think Blanca is mixed up in some medicine scam?"

"I do not want to believe such things of Blanca. But a little voice keeps telling me otherwise."

"I don't know what to believe."

173

"So *that* is why you come to this place of belief, eh?" he chuckled.

Standing, Maves lifted the box from the pew. After what he'd heard he figured it best to keep it.

"She wasn't at home when I tried to deliver this," he said, nodding at the package. "If she shows up, please tell her I have it."

Zak's gaze lingered on the package. Everything pointed to Blanca's involvement in something illegal, probably involving the clinic. For an instant Maves considered telling him of the faint clinking of glass inside the box but decided against it. He needed time to think.

Part Three

Let the whiteness of bones atone to forgetfulness.
There is no life in them. As I am forgotten
And would be forgotten, so I would forget

-T. S. Eliot

Chapter Nineteen

Hours later Maves angled the van through his gate and up the gravel drive. The house stood dark except for a single porch light. Shadows cast by the glow stretched down the stairs and across the drive like grasping fingers. He cut the engine and sat for a moment, the earlier exhaustion returning, his head swimming with all that had happened the previous week.

He climbed out and started for the house but stopped at the sight of a figure lurking in the corner. For a moment he wondered if his mind was playing tricks. He blinked and peered into the shadows.

"You look like you could use a beer," Webb's voice called from the porch.

He stepped into the light. Maves squinted up at him.

"Are you waiting up for me?" he asked, surprised but grateful.

"When you called you sounded tired," he said, shrugging, "so I thought…"

"I'm not too tired for a beer." He mounted the stairs.

"Have a seat." Webb pointed him to a chair. "I'll be right back."

"You don't want me to come in with you?" he said half-heartedly, glad to stay put.

"It's nice out here." He pointed to the chair again. "Besides, I have something important to tell you."

"You're taking over the practice so I can retire?"

"You're tired alright," he quipped, "and beginning to hallucinate."

He disappeared through the door. Maves eased onto the chair and peered into the darkness. Wind turbines winked along the horizon like crimson stars. Swirling around him, a brisk wind rattled the porch shutters. The warm air felt strangely comforting. A surprising contentedness settled over him, as if he'd passed through a violent storm intact.

Webb reappeared and handed him a bottle. Taking the chair opposite, he studied his father, preparing himself for the argument he knew was to come. Maves sipped his beer in silence. His expression revealed little. If he was curious about Webb's comment he hid it well.

"I get the feeling you want to tell me this news," he finally said, "before we go inside."

Webb guzzled half his bottle, stalling while he searched his mind for an answer. Deciding to start with the facts, he took a breath and locked eyes with him.

"There's a teenager sleeping in the dining room, and a ten year old girl on the couch."

Maves stared at him, trying to make sense of it.

"They're staying the night?"

"It looks that way."

"Who do they belong to?"

"You might say they're homeless."

"I might say or you might?" he said, his tone skeptical.

"We were faced with a situation and we did our best to handle it," he continued. "You'll remember I had a job interview in Hondo. Frida talked me into taking her along."

"She did the same to me, said she's afraid of being left alone."

"Unfortunately, we ran into the Border Patrol."

Webb told him the whole story, ending with Frida's plea to keep Mariah and Ewan with them rather than hand them over to the authorities. Maves sat speechless. A wave of conflicting emotions washed over him and suddenly he felt unmoored from all he knew, all he counted on. The sense that his old life had vanished forever came rushing back, palpable and real. Webb set aside his bottle and leaned toward him.

"Now don't get yourself all worked up, Maves." He tried to sound confident. "I admit I was reluctant to keep them at first but…"

"I don't like the idea of sticking your nose in someone else's business," he interrupted, "but I won't oppose it."

"Frida refused to leave," he continued, "without taking…"

"I might have done the same in your shoes," he added, surprising himself.

"Are you feeling alright, Maves?" Webb stared at him in disbelief.

"Funny how a woman can change things," he admitted, "don't you think?"

"You believe we were right to take them?"

"It's a risky move. But difficult circumstances require difficult decisions. I'm proud of you for taking that risk, Webb."

"Well, I…" he muttered, at a loss for words.

"An old friend of mine is a judge." He stood and drained his beer. "I'll give him a call in the morning. We'll know more then. Now I need to sleep."

Webb looked up at him, startled by the change. Beneath the dim porch light he had trouble believing his father stood before him rather than some stranger. Maves squinted down at him and then started for the door. In that instant he thought he glimpsed a familiar look, intense and determined, in his good eye.

The following morning a stern-faced secretary with red hair and lipstick ushered Maves into a wood-paneled office laid out in a perfect square, its frosted glass door reading 'Henson Stiles, District Judge, 33rd Judicial District'. Having insisted on coming along, Webb moved behind him like a second shadow.

Floor to ceiling bookshelves crammed with leather-bound legal texts filled three sides of the room. The fourth wall held a broad row of windows overlooking the courthouse lawn and the two-lane highway beyond. Behind a massive oak desk, a man in a black robe stood mumbling to himself and scribbling into a thick file. A matt of white hair topped his head.

Without looking up, he waved them to a chair. Maves studied his meaty features, trying to make out the red-faced boy he had known as a child. Slapping the file closed, he pushed it aside and pulled out an even thicker folder. He tapped his forefinger on the cover and raised his eyes.

"How'd we get so old, Maves?"

"You haven't changed since high school, Henny," he said, shaking his hand, "except for that hair. I think you must be part sheep."

"Well, you would know." He leaned on the desk and eyed him. "That is, unless you've retired."

"I wouldn't know what to do with myself."

"Vera says I'd be hell to live with." He tapped the file again, a look of concern crossing his face. "You say this boy is staying at your house?"

"He is, at least for now."

"Maves, are you sure you know what you're doing?"

"He's a runaway, Henny."

"We've got shelters for runaway teenagers."

"He says he won't go, that he'll live on the streets first."

"And you're prepared to have him in your house?"

"He has nowhere else to go."

"With all due respect, Your Honor," Webb jumped in, "he's better off with us."

He turned a disapproving gaze on Webb.

"Who is this with you, Maves?" he asked, never taking his eyes off him.

"He's my son, Webb. He knows the boy so I thought he could help."

"Now I do feel old," he sighed. "You were just a kid the last time I saw you. How well do you know this teenager?"

"Well enough to know he can't remain in his home."

179

"I can't argue with that. His father is a menace in more ways than one." He passed his palm over the file as if blessing it. "But the boy has troubles of his own."

"Who wouldn't in a house like that?" Webb replied, feeling protective.

Henny lifted a pipe from a rack and gazed at it wistfully before returning it.

"You don't know, do you?"

"What do you mean?"

"This boy has a significant history."

"What does that mean, 'significant history'?"

"I believe I'll decline to elaborate. I don't want to poison the well. Let's just say some bad things have happened in that home."

"At least tell us what sort of bad things."

"A child, an eight-year-old girl, died under suspicious circumstances. They ruled it an accidental death. And this boy we're talking about has a long history of trouble with the law, fighting, destroying property, getting kicked out of school. He's been in and out of detention. That's the sort of history that leads to unpredictable behavior, sometimes to violence."

"The poor kid..." Webb muttered.

"He needs our support not our pity," Maves grumbled.

"You sure you want to take that on?" Henny turned to face him. "He could become a threat at any moment."

An image of his own teenage years came to him, his father distant and bitter, never failing to find fault, backhanding him with little provocation. For an instant he could hear him. Then Frida's voice replaced the angry rant, pleading with him to let Ewan and Mariah stay even though he had already agreed to it.

"I don't see that we have a choice in the matter, Henny. Will you help convince the authorities? We intend to keep him until we can find an acceptable alternative. It's the right thing to do."

180

"You always were a self-righteous so and so, Maves Van Horn. That's coming from a judge, mind you. But I suppose even an ornery sort like you can do some good when the opportunity comes along."

"Then you'll help us?"

"I'll be in touch. In the meantime, Maves, watch your back."

A crinkling light filled the cloudless sky, paling the dust-filled shadows between the house and stable, casting the torn horizon in relief. Mariah held tight to Marley's braided lead, her jaw set, her gaze intent. Frida walked behind, coaching her as she led the big horse from the stable into the corral. Webb watched from the kitchen doorway.

Frida made a circle with her hand, motioning Mariah around the perimeter in their morning ritual. The gray horse limped alongside, occasionally nibbling at her halo of blonde hair. On their third pass, Frida stopped her and palpated the horseshoe-shaped wound below Marley's shoulder. Then she sent her off again.

Webb crossed the yard to where she stood with her elbows on the fence. The collie lay curled at her feet. He studied her the way she had the horse, admiring yet analytical. After a moment, she turned and squinted at him.

"What?"

"You know more than you've let on," he said, half-smiling.

"How do you mean?"

"Don't play dumb."

"I don't know what you're talking about," she said, avoiding his gaze.

"I saw how you handled Landrith's pony. You knew exactly what to do, how to assist without getting in the way, how to point out the right spot for a stitch without seeming to, how to catch what I was missing. I'll bet you

181

could've done the whole thing by yourself. Come on, Frida, out with it."

She locked eyes with him for an instant and then turned back to the corral.

"Before I met my husband I was in medical school."

He stared at her in disbelief. "You're a doctor?"

"No, Webb," she answered, disappointment filling her voice, "I never finished. I had completed the coursework and was in the final month of my residency when my mother became gravely ill. She still lived on the plantation, an hour from the nearest town and two day's travel from the university. I had no choice but to leave school and care for her.

"After she died I felt I could not continue my former life. She never told me but the plantation was deeply in debt. The bank and creditors took everything. Suddenly I had no money, no income, no place to live. And once I left school my student loan came due. I became so depressed I wished for a terrible illness to end all my troubles. You see, the church would not allow me to take my own life.

"That's when I met my husband. He paid off all the bills and gave me a house to live in. I never asked where the money came from. I had wished for an end to all my problems and God sent him, so I let him take care of me. I hope you can understand that, Webb.

"Later I realized what a mistake I had made. But you see, at the time I was not myself and my thinking was far from clear."

"You'd had one disappointment after another," he said, wishing he could take her in his arms. "You'd just lost your mother. You had to be at a low point. That's when we're most vulnerable, most prone to making bad decisions."

"And so I made one that changed my life."

"And now you're trying to correct that mistake."

"I suppose that counts for something."

"Would you finish medical school if you could?"

"I can't help but wonder what my life would be like if I had finished, especially now when I watch Maves at work. But it was so long ago, Webb, and in a place I can never return. Things are not so easy to arrange here."

"You once told me I was wrong for not following my dream. Now it's my turn. You have to finish medical school, Frida. Medicine was what you wanted once and it can be again."

"You make it sound so simple."

"Not simple but possible."

Mariah stopped in front of them and pulled on the horse's lead, bringing his muzzle to eye-level.

"I think she's forgotten us, Marley."

Frida stepped onto the bottom rail and leaned over the fence, cupping a hand around the horse's ear.

"Don't listen to her, Marley," she said beneath her breath. "She's doing a fine job of rehabilitating your shoulder. You may even be able to take her for a ride soon."

Mariah jumped up the fence, facing her through the rails.

"Please let him now, Frida," she pleaded. "He's ready, he told me so."

"He did, did he?" she chuckled.

Maves called from the back stoop and waved them over. Moments later they filed into the kitchen. Webb stopped before the table, Mariah at his hip. Since arriving, she had kept herself beside him at every opportunity, as if the sight of Anvil writhing in the dirt hogtied and screaming had made him her protector.

Ewan slouched behind the table, a dejected look on his face. Puzzled, Webb started to ask why but Maves caught his eye, warning him off.

"We just learned," he announced from the head of the table, "there's to be a placement hearing before a judge tomorrow morning."

"Oh, Maves," Frida gasped, moving next to him, "this worries me."

"Let's not get ahead of ourselves. It's a hearing, not a trial."

"Maves," she whispered, "do they mean to take Ewan and Mariah from us?"

"Children's Services mentioned the boy only." He tried to sound reassuring. "I don't believe there's cause for worry just…"

"Excuse me, Maves." She stepped back, glaring at him, "He has a name, you know."

He squinted at her, confused by her quick change in mood.

"What?"

"He has," she repeated slowly, "a name."

"I know he has a name," he replied.

"Well, it's not 'the boy'," she continued, hands on her hips. "Ewan has been here a week and I haven't once heard you call him by name."

"The reason," he said, waving off the remark, "is that I've hardly talked to him."

"And you probably think that's just dandy," she sneered.

He nodded toward the table.

"I don't think it's proper to argue in front of the children."

"I'm fifteen," Ewan groused, "not a child."

"Let her talk." Webb put a hand on his arm. "She can handle him without your help."

Frustrated, Maves sighed and set his palms on the table, looking at them each in turn.

"Ewan, you have to be at the courthouse tomorrow morning at eight o'clock. I'll be the one to take you so I expect you to be up in plenty of time. Frida will stay here and look after Mariah."

"No, Maves," she said, leaning in, "I want to go too."

"You can't risk it with all the law enforcement hanging around the courthouse."

"But Maves," she pleaded, "I can help. I know I can."

"Mariah needs you here."

"There's not a hearing for her as well?" Webb asked.

"No one has reported her missing. To them she doesn't exist."

"Oh, Maves," Frida sighed, "it sounds so sad when you say it like that."

"Alright then, let's try this. We get to keep her with us because the authorities haven't found out about her yet."

Webb glanced at Ewan, "Why such a short notice for something as important as a hearing?"

"There's a backlog and they had an unexpected opening. I decided not to argue and told them we'd be there."

"But I thought Henny… I mean Judge Stiles was going to talk to them."

"He's done what he could."

"It's been nice knowing you all," Ewan grumbled. "I'll write from whatever hellhole they send me to."

"Ewan, you must not talk that way." Frida moved beside him. She peered across the table. "You will convince them he should stay, won't you?"

Chapter Twenty

The courthouse roof stood blood-red against a morning sky salted with clouds. Sunlight glinted off car windows. Despite the early hour, the air was thick with heat.

Maves stood on the sidewalk and waited in awkward silence, venturing an occasional glance at Ewan. His attempt to start a conversation with the boy had stalled almost from the start. Eyes downcast, Ewan sulked in the dappled shade of a nearby tree.

Webb would know what to say, he admitted to himself. He scanned the street, hoping to find him on his way from the parking lot. The sundrenched lawn stretched past the limestone building, the meager trees scattered across it promising little relief. Webb was nowhere in sight.

He thought again of his easy way with the boy, and even more so with Mariah. He had taken responsibility for them without complaint, and when he spoke they responded, clearly wanting to please him. Maves had looked on with admiration and a touch of envy at how quickly he had gained their trust. Watching at Ewan now, he regretted that he had not told Webb so.

Ewan flinched, suddenly coming to life, his eyes fixed on the far side of the square. Without a word he slipped next to him. Maves followed his gaze across the lawn, spotting a stout woman charging toward them, her fleshy arms swinging, a scowl twisting her face. Within seconds she was on them.

"Your father is in jail thanks to you, you little monster," she hissed, thrusting a finger at him, "you and your friends."

"Now hold on there." Maves raised a hand to stop her. "That's no way to talk to the boy."

"I know the real truth," she continued, ignoring him, "and I mean to tell the law. It was you that got the girl pregnant, not poor Anvil."

"That's a lie!" he shouted. "I know it and you know it."

"Don't you dare call me a liar, boy!"

"You saw what he was up to," he sneered, "and you let it happen."

"You got no right to go accusing me!" she screamed.

"He deserves jail for what he did," he yelled, "and you ought to be in there with him!"

She swung a meaty fist, catching him on the jaw, and he staggered backwards, tumbling to the ground. Maves grabbed her wrist and swung her around, pressing her arm to her back.

"Ewan is not to be hit," he bent close to her ear, "not now, not ever. Do you understand me?"

"You'll get yours, mister," she growled, "you and the boy both. Anvil won't forget who turned him in."

"He's where he belongs and if the law works right that's where he'll stay. Now, we're due in court. Otherwise, I'd find a deputy to escort you out of here. Instead I'll just have to tell them I witnessed a woman assaulting a child. No doubt they'll want to look into that."

He released his grip and she hurried off toward the street, glancing over her shoulder as she melded with the crowd. He watched after her.

"That was the stepmother Webb told me about?"

"She's the witch, alright," he answered, still on the ground. "But she's not my stepmother, not really. They're not married."

Maves pulled him to his feet.

"She was wrong to treat you that way."

"I'm used to it."

"It's not a good thing to get used to that sort of treatment."

"Do you think my father," he said, keeping his eyes on the crowd, "really is in jail?"

Maves watched him pace the sidewalk, his gaze never leaving the courthouse steps. More than the anger stirring in him at the boy's treatment, Maves felt a deep sadness over his plight. At his age he should be thinking of girls and cars. Instead, he spent his time worrying about keeping Mariah safe and finding a place to live.

The crowd began to move into the courthouse and Maves motioned him toward the door. Moments later they stepped into a cavernous room lined with wooden benches. A center aisle ended in a low stage topped with a high, broad desk.

Maves followed him down the aisle. His sullen demeanor seemed to return with every step. As they reached the second row a door opened behind the stage and a man in uniform rounded one end, announcing the judge.

Seconds later a woman wearing a black satin robe appeared behind the desk. A steak of gray bisected her dark hair. The nameplate before her read 'J. Carlene Justice'. She peered over her reading glasses, scanning the crowd, her gaze finally settling on Ewan. A look of consternation spread across her face. Fumbling with her glasses, she rifled through a thick stack of papers and then raised her eyes.

"Mister Fisk," she said in a formal tone, "I must tell you that I'm less than pleased to see you in my courtroom again. As I recall, the last time we spoke you assured me I would not see you again... ever."

"But I didn't ask to come here," he complained. "Children's Services..."

She raised a hand to stop him. "You talk, Mister Fisk, only when asked to. Otherwise, you maintain silence in my courtroom. Am I understood?"

"But what if..."

"Mister Fisk," she interrupted, "do you understand me?"

188

He nodded dejectedly and slumped against the seatback. She motioned the room to sit. A clerk appeared at her side and began thumbing through the stack of papers, speaking to her in low tones. The low murmur of voices drifted across the courtroom. An instant later Webb slipped in next to them.

"The parking lot was full," he whispered between breaths. "I didn't think I'd make it in time."

Maves said nothing of the earlier incident, deciding to spare Ewan the aggravation.

"You haven't missed much."

Webb leaned forward, looking past him.

"He doesn't look too happy."

"The judge seems to have taken a special interest in him."

"That doesn't sound good. She looks like she won't tolerate much nonsense." He squinted down the aisle. "That can't be her real name."

"You might laugh but I'm hoping she lives up to it."

The clerk vanished and she turned back to the courtroom, her gaze again drifting to Ewan.

"Mister Fisk, I have been made aware of the recent events. Your father appears to be unable to care for you now that he is, shall we say, indisposed, and your so-called stepmother is deemed unfit."

"Then Judge, please," he said, jumping to his feet, "you have to get my sister out of there. She…"

"You are a slow learner, Mister Fisk," she barked, pointing a finger at him before softening her tone, "but your concern is well-placed. I will tell you that your sister is now in a safe place where she will receive the proper care until she... well, enough said. Our concern today is a suitable placement for you."

He started to speak and Maves grabbed him by the shoulder, pulling him back onto the bench. Shaking off his hand, he slouched low in the seat, his face sullen.

"Unfortunately, your age and history present us with limited options," she continued. "You have shown you need a high level of supervision, especially during these summer months when you have so much idle time on your hands, too much time in my judgment. If I had the resources I would see that you spend your time in a constructive enterprise."

"Maves," Webb whispered, "we have to do something."

He glanced at the boy, his mind searching for a solution. An image of Frida holding the reigns of a sick horse came to him and he knew at once what he would do. He took a breath and stood.

"Therefore," she continued, "it is my opinion that a group home is your best..."

She peered down at him.

"Yes, what is it?"

"Your Honor, I believe I can offer an option that will satisfy your conditions."

"And you are...?"

"I'm Maves Van Horn and I have a veterinary..."

She raised a hand to stop him. "Did you say your name is Van Horn?"

"Yes and I wanted to..."

"You're the vet that saved my sorrel mare after she got into some bad feed." She leaned across the desk, the hint of a smile crossing her lips. "I own the J Bar J ranch over near Camp Verde."

He recalled the case at once. "The mare foundered on green alfalfa."

"That's right. I wasn't at home but my foreman told me how quickly you diagnosed her after the other vet had failed to help. She was in a bad way by then."

"I just got lucky and happened to spot the field on my way in."

"You're too modest, Mr. Van Horn" Her gaze briefly wandered to Ewan. "Now what were you saying about an option?"

"I'm offering to make the boy my assistant until school starts back."

Ewan sat up, his expression less than pleased. Maves glanced at him before continuing.

"He'll have to get up early, keep track of the instruments and medicines, help with the animals. The work requires taking responsibility for yourself, staying organized, finishing what you start, skills all young people need in life."

"That's very generous of you but I doubt a teenager is capable of…"

Ewan jumped to his feet.

"Who says I want to be an assistant?"

"Mister Fisk, what did I tell you about speaking out of turn?"

"But it's my life he's talking about."

"You have another idea?"

"No," he muttered, "but I don't know anything about taking care of sick animals."

He lowered himself back onto the bench, looking dejected. Webb slipped next to him.

"Listen to me, Ewan," he whispered, "I know how smart you are. Focus on what you can do, not on what you can't."

The judge leaned on the desk, peering at him over her glasses.

"Mister Fisk, do you suppose you could learn how to care for these animals?"

"I don't know." He cast Webb a rueful glance. "I guess so."

"Well then, we still have the problem of your living arrangement. You cannot go back to your home. You know that, don't you?"

"I don't have a home," he grumbled.

"Now, there is something we can agree on."

He said nothing in response. The judge turned her gaze on Maves.

"Mr. Van Horn, I understand he has been staying at your house temporarily."

He nodded. She turned back to the papers, again thumbing through them.

"And he has had no trouble?" she said without looking up.

Maves glanced down at Ewan, his elbows on his knees, his head down. He tried to imagine the world through his eyes, the eyes of a homeless teenager, unsure who to trust or what violence the future held.

"Your Honor, the boy..." he started then corrected himself, "Ewan has settled in just fine and..."

He hesitated, realizing the importance of what he was about to say. She leaned over the desk, waiting.

"Yes, Mr. Van Horn?"

"He should continue with us. What I mean to say is... I believe living there at the house is best for him right now. Unless you or someone else convinces me otherwise, I want him to stay put."

Webb jumped to his feet, shocked by what he'd heard. For the second time in two days Maves had surprised him.

Chapter Twenty-one

Ewan unloaded the last of the boxes, carrying them through the garage and into the examining room. The collie danced beside him. Maves watched for a moment to be sure he found the correct cabinet or drawer for the medications, syringes and dressings. Beneath the boy's perpetual scowl he thought he spotted a hint of pride.

His thoughts kept drifting to Blanca and the mysterious package. He had tried repeatedly to reach her without success. Zak had heard nothing as well. Though his suspicions remained, he sensed something more disturbing in her disappearance, a change of course that signaled a new danger.

Mariah appeared in the doorway and motioned him to join her. Leaving Ewan to his work, he followed her through, squinting into the midday sunlight past the arena. Marley stood at the corral fence half-asleep, his head drooping. Mariah put a finger to her lips, barely able to contain herself.

Tiptoeing across the sun-drenched dirt, she crept toward the horse from behind, careful to avoid his notice. Within seconds she was crouching beside him. His head dripped lower in the noonday heat.

Giving Maves a mischievous grin, she stretched her forefinger toward his muzzle and glanced back once again. Then she flicked his lower lip. The big horse snorted and jerked upright, tossing his head back while she squealed with laughter.

Maves did his best to give her a stern look but felt the hint of a smile cross his face. He pointed her to the driveway where Webb and Frida stood waiting to take her clothes shopping.

"When you get back," he called, motioning to the stable, "take him inside and give him his feed."

He watched after them as the truck turned onto the roadway and disappeared from view. Moments later a car appeared at the gate, bouncing up the drive and sliding to a stop, its horn blaring. Within seconds Ewan burst through the office doorway.

"There's an injured dog," he said, breathless, "a retriever."

"Tell the owners to take it to another veterinarian." He waved him back through the door. "I'm a large animal vet."

"They aren't the owners. They just spotted him by the side of the road."

"Large animal vets treat farm animals," he continued matter-of-factly, "like horses, cows and sheep."

"But he needs help now."

"Notice that you didn't hear dogs mentioned on that list."

"But he's hurt."

"I don't treat pets," he grumbled.

"They said he's hurt bad. Please just take a look at him," he pleaded. "He could die before they find another vet."

Maves squinted at him, in no mood to venture outside his expertise. But the anguish on the boy's face moved him in spite of his reticence. He sighed and pointed him back through the doorway.

Within minutes they had reached the dog, a male Labrador retriever, his yellow fur stained crimson. He lay stretched on his side, panting. Maves knelt to examine the injury. The dog's left rear leg bent at an unnatural angle, a jagged gash running above it. The retriever made no movement as he palpated the site.

Ewan appeared with the leather case. He knelt and stared at the open wound, his face pale. Maves took the case and flipped open the snaps, pulling out a roll of gauze and thrusting it in his face. He flinched and then locked eyes with him.

"If you're going to get sick, go on and get it over with," he said. "Then I need you here if this dog is going to have any chance."

Maves watched him scramble away, falling on his knees and retching into the grass. The sight of him rekindled a memory of Webb as a boy, and he realized with regret he had treated him no better. Ewan crawled back up the slope and crouched next to him.

"How bad is he hurt?"

"It's hard to tell without doing a more thorough exam. First we need to stop this bleeding."

"Will it hurt him?"

"I'll give him a shot so he won't feel... damn it to hell," he barked, peering into the case. "I forgot to restock the vials. We'll have to do without."

He pulled out a small towel and handed it to him.

"Put this across his head to calm him. You'll have to hold him down and help me at the same time. Can you do that?"

He nodded and draped the towel over the dog's head. Maves threaded a needle and leaned over the retriever.

"Use the gauze to sponge away the blood so I can see what I'm doing." He pointed his chin at the gash. "Watch that he doesn't snap at you."

Maves slipped the needle into one side of the wound, expecting a struggle or at the least a flinch. The dog lay still except for his panting. Setting aside the needle, he grabbed a tongue depressor from the case and ran it along the retriever's feet. No response. Lifting a front leg, he pressed his palm against the paw. The leg offered no resistance whatsoever.

He sighed and turned back to the wound, stitching it together distractedly. Ewan followed his movements, sponging blood from the gash with care. Maves cast him a glance, suddenly overcome with sympathy for the boy. He would take the news hard.

Completing the final stitch, he cleaned the needle and then began pricking the retriever's shoulder with it, moving up and along his neck. The dog gave no response even as the needle drew blood. Ewan sat back on his haunches and watched, a slow realization crossing his face.

"He can't move, can he?" he whispered. "He's paralyzed."

"I don't think he's in too much pain," he answered, doing his best to soften the news. "The accident severed the spinal cord high up on his neck. I'm surprised he's still alive."

"But you can still save him, can't you?"

"The injury is too severe, Ewan."

"But I've seen those shows," he said, leaning closer, "where the dog wheels around with his back legs in a cart."

"His front legs are not..."

"No!" he yelled. His eyes welled with tears. "He can do it. He can have a good life anyway, like those dogs."

"I'm sorry, son. He's too badly hurt. He'll never..."

"Why won't you listen to me?" he cried. "You have to make him better!"

He jumped to his feet, backing away. Maves stood and followed him, struggling to find the words.

"Ewan, I know it's hard to see him like this. But our job is to help and, if beyond our help, to keep him from suffering as much as we're able."

"No, you're wrong!" He turned away, refusing to face him.

"Labradors are bred to retrieve." Maves bent, trying to catch his eye. "That's what they love. That's what they do best. But he'll never walk again, much less retrieve. What sort of life is that?"

"I just want him to get better," he muttered.

"So do I, but wanting won't make it happen." He nodded toward the dog. "I know you don't want him to suffer."

"That's the last thing I want."

196

"Then help me take his suffering away."

"You'll give him a shot?"

"He won't even feel it."

Taking him by the shoulder, Maves guided him back to the retriever and knelt. The boy stretched a tentative hand toward the dog's head, hesitated and then lowered his palm to the damp fur, gently stroking his neck. Maves pulled a syringe from the case and slipped the needle into a small vial of yellow-hued liquid. The bottle hissed between his fingers. He set aside the vial and pinched a wedge of skin above the dog's shoulder.

The syringe poised, he let his gaze drift to where Ewan knelt over the dog. Maves studied his bruised profile, wishing he knew how to ease the boy's anguish. Unable to stall any longer, he raised the syringe but hesitated again, sensing a change in the dog.

The retriever's panting began to slow, his breaths halting and irregular. Ewan sat up, turning to him, confusion in his eyes. He lowered the syringe and started to speak then caught himself, realizing no words could do justice to the moment. Instead he slipped his hand alongside Ewan's, listening as the dog's last breaths mingled with the boy's quiet sobs.

An hour later he angled the van beside the house. The moment he stepped through the front door he sensed something amiss. He pushed Ewan back onto the porch and put a finger to his lips. Turning into the foyer, he crept across the living room to the hallway.

The floorboards creaked along the narrow passage. Pausing at each doorway, he peeked around the corners one by one. Overturned dresser drawers littered the floors, their contents scattered over the beds.

Backtracking, he crossed the living room and eased open the kitchen door. The cabinets and drawers were unmolested but his instinct had been right. Someone had broken into the house. He took a breath, grateful the others were away. Then something moved just out of his vision.

In a sudden clatter of mops and brooms, a dark-haired man burst out the back door, crossing the lawn and disappearing around the corner. Maves hesitated and then started after him, racing down the stairs and past the office. Within seconds he was in the covered arena. Nothing stirred.

To his left the stable door stood half-open. He started toward it. Then Ewan's voice called from the front of the house, yelling his name once and then again.

Pivoting, he sprinted alongside the garage, fear gripping his chest. An engine roared to life beyond the house. Seconds later he rounded the corner.

A black sedan flashed between the trees, speeding toward the gate. Out of breath, he watched it skid over the cattle guard and swerve onto the roadway in a cloud of blue smoke. An instant later it slipped from sight.

He turned to the house, expecting to find Ewan. The porch stood empty. He stumbled up the stairs and through the door, running from room to room but finding no sign of the boy. Fighting a growing panic, he burst back onto the porch. Ewan stood at the bottom step, squinting up at him.

"Aren't you going after him?" He pointed toward the gate.

"What?" he answered, confused by the question. He took a breath, trying to collect himself. "Where have you been?"

"I was waiting at the van, you know, to go chase him."

"I needed to find you first. I was starting to worry he'd taken you with him."

"He didn't want me. He wanted that cardboard box you brought back from wherever you went."

"How do you know?"

"I saw him carry it off." He cast a wistful glance toward the road. "We could've caught him. That was a beater car he was driving."

Suddenly exhausted, Maves lowered himself onto the top step. Ewan peered up at him.

"You don't look so good."

"I couldn't find you and I thought…"

"I'm not some little girl, you know," he snapped, his tone defensive. "I can take care of myself."

"With what you've been through I don't doubt you can."

Ewan studied him a moment, his frown slowly disappearing.

"You were really worried I'd been kidnapped?"

"I won't lie to you." He ran a hand over his face. "For a moment I was more than worried."

"But why would you care?"

"Well, I… I just…" he stammered, overcome with emotion.

"Don't say you feel sorry for me," he barked, his scowl returning. "I'm not pitiful and I don't want anyone treating me like I am."

Maves turned his eyes, searching his mind for the truth while his shortcomings as father to his own son dogged his thoughts. After a moment he motioned down the road.

"I saw how you were with that injured retriever," he replied, speaking without thought. "I watched the care you took to bury him. And I was with you when your step-mother showed up at the courthouse. You had the courage to stand up for yourself even though you were about to go before a judge. A lot of people would just have rolled over and given up at that point.

"More important, I see how you are with Mariah every day, how you want to protect her, make sure she's safe. You showed the same concern for your sister when you were before the judge. I'll admit there's plenty I don't know. But I know I want what's best for you."

Ewan lowered his gaze and sat on the step below him, staring into the distance.

"If you knew everything you wouldn't say that."

"I know enough. The rest doesn't matter."

"No one has ever cared what happened to me," he mumbled, picking at a red-rimmed scab.

"A youngster should never have to say that."

"I always thought it was because…" he added, his voice trailing to nothing.

Maves tried to imagine what he would want to hear.

"I'll listen," he finally said, "if you want to say."

"No, I can't… you won't…"

"Then I'll not bother you about it." He stood as if to end the conversation. "You just let me know if ever you feel ready. I'm always willing…"

"I killed my little sister," he whispered.

Having no idea what to say Maves sat again and laid a hand on his shoulder.

"I didn't mean to," he continued. "I was angry, not at her, at my father. He'd hit me, splitting my lip for using a tool without permission. The anger was intense, like a screaming whistle inside my head that never let up. I couldn't stand it. I knew I had to do something, hit something or break something to make it stop.

"I'd punched holes in the wall before, broken stuff. I wish I'd done something like that again. But the rifle was right there beside the door where my father always left it. Before I realized what was happening it was in my hands.

"The shot sounded like a cannon inside that room. I remember for a moment I had this wonderful feeling of peace even though I knew my father would beat me for what I'd done. Then the screams started outside and that feeling left me forever. I did something terrible and I won't ever get it back."

"You were just a boy, Ewan," he said softly.

"I did what I did. Being young is no excuse."

His voice trailed to a near-whisper. Maves leaned closer.

"But as you yourself said, you didn't mean for it to happen."

"Whether I meant to or not, the fact is I killed her. Nothing will ever change it."

"That's hard knowledge for a man to live with, much less a boy. It will tear you up inside. It's time for you to find a way past it."

"You mean forgive myself for what I did?"

"That's one way to put it."

"You don't understand. It's not that easy."

"It's true," he agreed. "There's nothing easy about forgiveness. But it *is* possible to move on."

He cringed at the irony of his answer, knowing the extent of his own failure. Ewan eyed him skeptically.

"You're sure about that?"

"I am," he lied.

"Well, I'm not," he said dejectedly. "So, you can see why I don't expect anyone to care what happens to me."

"You're wrong there, Ewan, people do care."

"According to my parents I'm getting what I deserve. I have no doubt they're glad to be rid of me."

"I'd say you're better off without them."

"Except that I'm only fifteen and don't have a place to live."

Feeling the sting of his words, Maves nodded behind them.

"This old house isn't much but it'll do for now, won't it?"

"I didn't mean it like that," he mumbled. He motioned toward the van. "Are you sure you don't want to chase that guy?"

Maves could see he was anxious to change the subject. He hesitated, wanting to say something, anything to ease the boy's pain. But then he saw at once it was in truth his own discomfort he wanted to be rid of. He would be selfish to say any more about it.

"Speaking of the bastard," he offered instead, "did he have anything with him besides the box?"

"I don't see how. He was carrying it with both hands, like he thought it might break if he wasn't careful."

Maves mulled over the meaning of his comment.

"That's a helpful observation. I doubt we'll ever have the chance to ask him." He stood and pointed him up the steps. "With all that's happened, we missed lunch. Go on in and find us something to eat. I'll be right along."

Maves lingered on the landing, again puzzling over the package and what connection, if any, the intruder had to Blanca. A part of him wanted to climb into the van and set off searching until he found her. But he would not shirk his promise. Ewan was his responsibility now.

Chapter Twenty-two

Webb pulled to the curb and followed Frida out of the truck. Mariah remained in the cab, her head in a book. As much as he disliked Maves' rattling pickup, he was grateful to have use of it. The result stood before him now in the form of a hundred and fifty year old, tree-shaded house. The former residence and office of a prominent doctor, the two-story home stood above the street on a slight rise. Peeling paint and sagging eaves hinted at a less storied recent past.

Heeding Frida's advice, he had found work with a company restoring historic homes and buildings. Though he had been given only the simplest of jobs so far, he had never known work so gratifying. He lingered on the sidewalk and admired the clean lines of the old Victorian, enjoying the quiet afforded by a Saturday morning visit.

He led her up the stairs and into a high-ceilinged foyer lined with walnut wainscoting. Before them a broad staircase wound to the second floor, narrowing as it stretched upward. To their left, sliding pocket doors opened to a window-lined dining room. Palm trees in the garden beyond vibrated in the morning breeze.

A tile-covered sunroom on their right ended in a set of French doors that opened onto a covered entryway and second garden. Beneath the cover, an unused cobblestone driveway served as a narrow patio. He gestured into the light-filled room.

"A doctor once owned this house." He pointed to the French doors. "Carriages would stop under that covered drive to drop off sick people then he'd see to them in here."

"The house must have been beautiful back then." She turned a slow circle.

Webb let his gaze drift across the warped floor and water-stained wallpaper. A crack zigzagged up the far corner, ending at a shattered stained-glass window.

"I know the place seems a disaster at first glance," he said, facing her again. "But now instead of the damage I see the potential, what it will look like eventually. This old house inspires me, Frida. And I have you to thank."

"I can't imagine why."

"You told me to have a dream and follow it."

"They were only words, Webb. You did the real work."

"No, Frida, if not for your encouragement I wouldn't be here."

"Well, I don't know. But I'm glad you've found work that suits you."

"It does suit me, Frida. I knew from the moment I stepped into this place. I could see the possibilities, the way the house could look with the right planning, and the way the work fits my love of drawing and design. I've already given the owners some new ideas for the project."

"I'm not surprised, Webb."

A muffled ring sounded from his pocket and he pulled out his phone. Maves' voice crackled in his ear.

"You'd best get back straight away," he said, his tone somber. "A deputy just showed up asking for Ewan."

Maves lowered the phone and hurried back to the living room. Ewan sat slumped on the couch, his eyes to the floor. Maves studied him, worried by the look, and then he turned to where Deputy Stoll stood, his lower lip bulging with snuff. He raised a paper cup to his mouth.

"I consider it impolite to dip inside the house," Maves barked, making no effort to hide his irritation. He pointed to the door. "I'd appreciate it if you'd leave that outside."

"The last time I was here," he grumbled, "your son didn't seem to mind."

"Well, that's one in a long list of differences between us."

The officer frowned and then vanished through the door, reappearing moments later, the bulge beneath his lip gone. He jerked a notepad from his shirt pocket and scribbled in silence, pausing to cast Ewan an occasional disapproving glance. Maves stood by, his patience finally giving way to annoyance.

"You plan on telling us why you're here sometime before the next Ice Age?" he quipped.

The deputy scowled at him from behind the notepad. Then he absently pulled a can of snuff from his back pocket, tapping it on the heel of his hand before catching himself. Cramming the can back in place, he jutted his chin at Ewan.

"I'm here to collect your boy," he snarled, "and deliver him to juvenile detention."

He returned to scribbling on the pad. Maves took a breath, trying to corral his frustration.

"You still haven't said why."

"I'm surprised you don't know. He's been reported for the statutory rape of a female minor."

"What?" Ewan jerked upright. "That's a lie!"

Maves laid a hand on his shoulder, keeping him on the couch.

"Who reported him?" he continued.

"His parents made the report just this morning."

"Based on what evidence?"

"The girl, as they say, is with child," he said as if pleased with himself. "I'd say that's pretty good evidence."

Maves stared at him in disbelief.

"You're arresting him based on the word of a *prisoner*?"

"The man bonded out this morning just before he and his wife made the report."

"But what does the girl say? Surely she can clear this up."

"She's not talking, so we've got the word of two adults against a kid who has a long record of run-ins with the law. Who would you believe?"

He stuffed the notepad back into his shirt pocket and pulled out the tin of snuff.

"We consider child abuse cases priority," he continued, "so I came out straightaway. Now I'm due back at the station."

"The man is lying to protect himself. Anyone can see that."

"Maybe he is and maybe he isn't," he said with an unfriendly grin. "But you'll have to take that up with the judge."

He tapped the can on his palm and pointed Ewan toward the door, following him out. At the top of the stairs he paused to stuff a wad of snuff beneath his lip. Then he handcuffed him. Maves watched in mounting frustration, searching his mind for a plan as the deputy led the boy down the steps and into the back of the waiting car.

Seconds later the truck roared up the drive, sliding to a stop beside the house. Webb bolted from the door and circled the car, stopping before Maves.

"What's happened? Why is the deputy here?" He gestured at the cruiser, his voice rising. "What's Ewan doing in his car?"

"His parents claim he's responsible for his sister's pregnancy."

"Of course the old man is denying responsibility." He turned to the officer. "You can't possibly believe him."

"Like I told your father, I just have a job to do here."

"I want to talk to him before you go."

"Make it short," he groused.

Webb stuck his head through the car window. Ewan's eyes stayed to the floor.

"Don't think for a minute we're going to let this happen," he whispered. "The deputy is a bimbo. And what's happening here is wrong. We'll get you out, I promise. Just hang tight until you hear from us."

The boy made no response. Webb pushed away from the car.

"Maves," he said under his breath, "we have to do something."

Maves locked eyes with him, the idea coming to him at once. He bent next to the window and leaned close to Ewan's ear.

"We're going to find your sister and see if she'll tell us the truth. If she'll talk to us then she might be willing to tell the authorities."

He looked up, his eyes dark with emotion.

"I should've known what he was doing to her," he muttered, "but I was just too stupid to see it."

"You're not responsible for everything bad that happens, you know."

"You believe it wasn't me that got her pregnant?"

"Of course I believe you, son."

"I told him if he ever touched her again I'd kill him," he hissed. "I wasn't just talking. I bought a gun from a kid I know and I learned how to use it. I didn't care what he did to me, but she's so small and…"

He dropped his head, unable to finish. Maves leaned close again.

"I can see you love your sister, Ewan. But you won't be much help to her if you end up in prison. Now, I expect you to do what you're told and stay clear of trouble. We'll figure something out. You have my word."

The engine cranked and he stepped away from the window. Moments later Frida appeared beside him, watching as the deputy's car slipped below the hilltop. She pulled back her swirling hair with one hand, holding the auburn strands to her shoulder.

"Where have you been?" he said, glancing toward the house.

"Webb had me hide Mariah inside the truck in case they were looking for one of us." She gazed down the empty highway. "Oh Maves, I wish they had come for me. I so hate to see that poor boy taken away like a criminal."

He nodded in agreement, hoping he could keep his promise.

An hour later, he pulled up to the gate of a rambling house surrounded by a fleur de leis-topped iron fence. A sign spanning the entrance read 'Wellborn Home for Girls'. A second sign along the drive warned against trespassing in crimson letters. Webb peered through the windshield at the forbidding home.

"Are you sure this is the right place?"

"How many homes for pregnant girls can there be way out here?"

"But she could be in San Antonio or Austin, or even Maine for that matter."

"You worry too much," he grumbled. "Remember why we're here."

"The sign says they don't allow visitors." He pointed out the window.

"I don't see any sign."

"But it's over..." he started and then dropped his hand. "Oh, right, I don't see any sign either."

Jumping from the van, he jerked the sign from the ground and tossed it into the weeds.

"I guess we can go right in," he quipped, climbing back into the cab.

Maves parked the van beside the porch and they mounted the wide staircase, stopping before an ornately carved oak door crossed by a head-high row of rectangular windows. Webb rapped his knuckles against the beveled glass. Within seconds a woman's face appeared behind the glass, her eyes wide with surprise. In an instant, her expression changed to annoyance.

"No visitors," she called out, her voice muffled by the heavy door. A nametag hanging from her collar read 'Mrs. Bittern'.

"We can't hear you," Maves called back, his hand cupped behind his ear in feigned ignorance.

She tried again. Webb joined in the ruse, shaking his head. An instant later the door flew open in a clatter of metal latches and locks. The woman stood before them stout and red-faced, her hands on her hips. A beehive of silver hair rose from her head.

"Visitors are expressly forbidden in this house," she announced, "just as the no trespassing sign says. Are you unable to read?"

"What sign do you mean?" Webb asked innocently.

She pointed to where the sign had been, gasped and craned her neck in both directions. Exasperated, she faced them each in turn.

"We are a home for expectant mothers," she said, her voice trembling, "and they must be left in peace at this delicate time."

"We apologize for intruding." Webb did his best to sound sincere. "I'm sure the work you do here is of the utmost importance. But a boy's welfare rests in the hands of one of your residents, his sister."

"We operate in strictest confidentiality." She looked at him askance. "How could you possibly know she's here?"

"How could we know?" He struggled for an answer. "Uh… we have contacts."

"What sort of contacts?" she asked, doubt clear in her voice.

"Our friend, Hen… uh, Judge Henson Stiles is helping us navigate this difficult legal terrain," he lied. "Judge Stiles recommended that we, as representatives of the boy, talk with the girl."

"And your name is?"

"I'm Webb Horner and this is my father, Van."

"Well, I don't know. We are an adoption agency and not beholden to the court…"

Tired of the delay, Maves pointed a finger in her face.

"A boy's future is at stake here," he growled, "a future of success or failure, of following the law or breaking it."

She reared back. "Well, I…"

"Letting us have a brief talk with his sister," he continued, his tone softening, "can make all the difference. Are you sure you want to stand in the way of that?"

"Well, I… I'll need to get the director's permission," she said, moving aside to let them pass, "if you'll wait here."

She disappeared down an adjacent corridor. The high-ceilinged foyer opened onto a circular atrium edged by a winding staircase. The unmistakable cry of a baby drifted from the second-floor landing.

"Our best bet is up there," Maves whispered, pointing up the stairs. "When she returns, tell her I stepped out to take an urgent call."

"You're going alone?"

"She'll come looking for us otherwise."

"How will you know the girl?"

"Ewan has a snapshot," he answered, hoping his memory would serve. "Stall our gray-haired friend as best you can."

He started up the steps without another word. In seconds he had reached the second floor. A tiled corridor lined with doors stretched away from him. The baby's cries drifted past again, along with the soft murmur of a girl's voice. He followed the sound, keeping one eye on the landing.

Slipping along the wall, he paused at each doorway and peeked inside. Most of the rooms stood empty. Thinking of Zak, he said a quick prayer that he would recognize the girl.

He came to the room with the baby, suddenly wondering if Ewan's sister might have already had her child. Peering around the corner, he spotted a young woman sitting before a window, her back to him. He hesitated, unsure whether to approach. Then the baby appeared over her shoulder, its round face the color of coffee.

210

He eased back into the corridor. The murmur of a girl's voice again drifted past him. Moving toward the sound, he stepped into another doorway and peered past the corner. A young girl, frail and birdlike, sat reading aloud, a book across her lap.

He scanned the room looking for her guest but found it otherwise empty. He stepped back and pondered for a moment why she might want to read to herself. Perhaps she was lonely. He leaned past the corner again to see if she matched Ewan's photo. He was as sure as he would ever be. Taking a breath, he stepped inside.

Webb paced the painted tiles of the atrium wishing he had talked Maves into letting him speak with the girl. He hated the waiting. Pausing to listen, he strained to find any sign Maves had found her. Only the baby's cries echoed from the landing, nothing more.

Footsteps sounded along the ground floor corridor, growing steadily louder. Seconds later Mrs. Bittern emerged from the hallway, flanked by two nuns, one in a gray habit, the other in black. The older nun stopped before him and smoothed out her black cloak before extending her hand.

"I am Sister Mary Therese, the head of the home." She looked past him. "I understood there were two of you."

"My father was called away."

"Then please tell me why you have come here, Mr. Horner."

"We're here to speak with a girl, the sister of a boy we're trying to help."

"You have no connection with our church?"

"I'm not sure what you mean," he said, stalling.

"We are a church-affiliated home here, Mr. Horner."

She stepped away, looking as if she might ask him to leave. With a growing sense of panic, he searched his mind for a way to prolong the conversation.

"Father Palamedes Zakros" he blurted out, "…has sent us."

"You know Father Zakros?" she asked, grinning.

"My father has known Father Zak for years," he answered, both surprised and ashamed by the ease of his lying. "In fact, we're helping him with his refugee program."

"We here are quite fond of the father." She gestured around the room. "He has been a great supporter of our girls."

"Then you'll allow me to speak with this boy's sister?" he asked, anxious to avoid getting caught up in his own lies. "As I told Mrs. Bittern, it is of critical importance to her brother's welfare."

"Why, yes, by all means you must…"

She stopped at a loud knocking on the front door. They stood looking at one another and then the pounding repeated, this time with more force. Mrs. Bittern hurried into the foyer and peered through high window then swung the door open. Maves stood before them.

"We have an emergency." He motioned Webb toward the doorway with an urgent wave. "We need to leave right away."

Mrs. Bittern pointed to the second floor. "What about talking to the girl?"

"It'll have to wait," he answered, pulling Webb through and turning to follow.

"But you said it was urgent that you speak with her."

"No time now," he called as they hurried down the stairs.

"But the boy's welfare…" she yelled.

They jumped into the van and sped through the gate, sending a cloud of dust into the air. Webb steadied himself on the dashboard.

"What's the emergency?" he called over the engine noise, his thoughts in chaos. "Has something happened to Ewan?"

212

"Son, you can sure tell a lie," he chuckled as he eased back on the accelerator. "That was impressive, I have to admit."

Webb squinted at him, at once recognizing his scheme.

"There's no emergency, is there?"

"I needed a way to get you out."

"But you found the girl?"

"By now she'll be asking Mrs. Bittern to see Judge Justice so she can tell the truth of what happened to her. Ewan should be out in no time."

Relieved, Webb sat back. An unbidden image of Frida standing beside the corral came to him, her green eyes shining, her hair swirling flame-like before the wind. Try as he might, he could not stop thinking about her.

The vision faded before the shade-dappled roadway. He glanced at his father with a tinge of embarrassment, guessing he would view the infatuation as the foolishness of youth. Yet even Maves seemed different now. If he could change, Frida might also. He stared through the windshield, watching shreds of cloud scud along the horizon, hoping against reason he was right.

Chapter Twenty-three

An August sun sent pools of heat rippling across the highway, the mercurial surface overturning images of trees and farmhouses. Webb surveyed the broken horizon. Clouds of white dust drifted through the still air. Beyond the fence line cattle stood statue-like and panting beneath the dappled shade of live oaks.

His hand draped idly across the steering wheel, he let his gaze drift from the highway to the passenger seat. Ewan leaned against the doorframe, his eyes half-closed. Mariah sat squeezed between them. A book on horse care sat propped on her lap. Hot air whistled through the truck windows, whipping empty beer cans and candy wrappers into a rowdy chorus.

The road dropped into a broad valley thick with sycamore and cottonwood, opening onto a treeless plain. Stretching alongside the road, knee-high grass burnt brown by the summer sun vibrated before a sudden breeze. Mariah slammed the book closed and sat up, craning her neck to see above the dashboard.

"This is the road where I saw the colt," she said, squinting through the windshield. "Please, Webb, can we go see him, please?"

Ewan sat up, dazed and blinking. She pointed to the roadside.

"We have to be real close," she continued, excitement in her voice. "Look, Ewan, I remember that tree."

"You can't remember a tree," he grumbled.

"I can too and I know it's on the way to the colt. We'll be there soon, you'll see. Please stop, Webb," she pleaded. "Please stop so I can talk to him."

"You talk to horses now?" Ewan sniggered. "Do they talk back?"

"You're just jealous because Marley likes me best."

"He only likes you because you feed him."

"That's not true," she said, looking hurt. She pulled on Webb's sleeve. "Please, can we stop?"

"Don't listen to her, Webb. Sunday is my only day off and I don't want to waste it gawking at some nag."

"Don't you know anything?" she snipped. "A nag is an old horse not a baby."

"I don't care what you call it. I don't want to waste my time staring …"

"Enough!" Webb barked, tired of their bickering. "Ewan, I understand you want to make good use of your free time. You're not the only one that has to go back to work tomorrow. But we need to give Frida more time to study."

Ewan slumped onto the seatback. Webb nudged Mariah.

"We'll make this a short visit."

They crossed a one-lane bridge, the rock-strewn creek below it running clear and fast. An instant later a herd of paint horses appeared in a lush meadow bordered by a plank fence. Huddled next to a tan and white mare, a tri-colored colt stood dozing. Webb pulled onto the shoulder and climbed out of the cab, leaning his elbows on the tailgate and motioning Mariah to the fence. Ewan moved beside him.

"I don't understand why someone as old as Frida has to study," he said. "She's not in school."

"Sometimes even people as old as me go back to school," he chuckled.

"What's she studying?"

"She has an important test."

"You mean like a final exam?"

"Frida had mostly finished medical school a long time ago when something happened that kept her from getting her license. Afterwards she pretty much gave up on ever practicing medicine. But it turns out she can get her license after all by completing a few requirements and taking tests called board exams."

"If she passes she'll be a doctor?"

"It looks that way."

Mariah appeared next to him, disappointment in her eyes. He searched her face.

"What's wrong?"

"The colt and his mother decided to leave with the other horses."

"You mean they didn't understand when you talked horse to them?" Ewan teased. "Maybe Marley speaks a different dialect, you know, like the way people talk in Mexico compared to Spain. That's got to be it."

"You don't know everything," she grumbled.

Webb opened the door and motioned her inside.

"We need to be leaving anyway."

"Someday," she announced, "I'm going to get my own ranch and raise horses and have a colt of my very own."

He slid next to her, pulling the door to.

"I have no doubt," he said in all seriousness, "you will do just that."

Minutes later the truck rounded a sloping curve and the house briefly rose above the treetops. Sunlight glinted off the metal roof. Farther on a small sedan appeared alongside the road, the hood up. Webb slowed the truck.

A man stood bent over the car, his head beneath the hood. He ignored them as they crept past. Webb decided he wanted no assistance. Checking the rearview mirror, he watched as the man stood upright and turned to watch them, his face thin and angular, his blonde hair nearly white beneath the midday light. Webb recognized him at once.

"Muntz," he muttered.

He jammed the accelerator to the floor, bouncing across the cattle guard and sliding to a stop before the house. Scrambling from the cab, he leaned through the window, locking eyes with Ewan.

"Keep her in the truck," he whispered. "Get on the floor and stay out of sight."

He pivoted, bolting up the stairs and into the living room. Frida's papers littered the dining table as if she had just stepped out. He called out for her, first down the hall and then off the back stoop. The house stood silent.

He rushed across the yard and into the clinic, bursting through the office doorway. The door to the storage room stood slightly ajar. He slipped across the room, watching over his shoulder for any sign of Muntz.

Taking a hammer from the counter, he wrapped the fingers of his free hand around the knob and eased the door open. A shaft of light split the dark space. Beneath its dim glow, Frida sat crouched against the wall, a scalpel in her fist.

"I'll cut you," she yelled, slicing the air with the blade, "if you come anywhere near me!"

"Frida, it's me," he called to her. "It's Webb."

He dropped the hammer, raising both hands in the air. She squinted into the glare.

"Webb, is it really you?" She cast aside the knife. "My God, Webb, he is here."

"I know." He helped her up. "I saw him."

"Where are the children?"

"They're hiding in the truck."

"You must keep him from taking them."

He peered at her, trying to make sense of her words.

"Why would he want to do that?"

"He said they belong to him. He's crazy, Webb. I saw him though the window. He was banging on the door, yelling that he would take them and kill anyone who tried to stop him."

"That doesn't make any sense."

"But it's true. He said they belong at home not here." She grabbed his arm, her voice pleading. "Please, Webb, you must stop him. It makes no difference he is the boy's father."

Bewildered, he stood staring at her.

"You're saying Muntz in Ewan's father?" he finally said.

"What on earth are you talking about?" She frowned. "Ewan's father is called Anvil and he is here."

Realizing his mistake, he rushed out the door without a word. She hurried after. They rounded the house, threading between the bushes to the truck. He hesitated, fearing what he might find, and then jerked open the door. The cab stood empty.

"Webb," she whispered, her eyes filled with fear, "he has taken them."

"Maybe, but I'm going to check on something. Wait here."

Before she could protest he jogged up the steps to the far end of the porch, hoisting himself on the rail and peering down the road. Anvil's van sat at the bottom of the draw, a hundred yards past the gate. Otherwise, the road was empty. He hurried back to where she stood waiting.

"He's still here. His van is just down the road." He surveyed the house and yard trying to imagine what had happened. "They must have seen him and gone to hide somewhere else."

He started for the house but she grabbed him, holding him back.

"He has an axe."

"Then you wait here."

"No," she answered, her face determined, "I'm coming with you."

They retraced his steps through the house, going room to room but finding no sign of either Ewan or Mariah. Minutes later they stepped onto the back stoop. Nothing stirred. A muted whinny drifted across the yard. Webb peered through the stable window, spotting Marley's gray outline in the shadows, ghostlike and surreal.

Taking Frida's hand, he slipped across the yard, past the corral and into the narrow confines of the stable. He knelt just within the doorway letting his eyes adjust to the dim light. Then he peered down the aisle. A figure lay in the open area beyond the stalls.

He turned and put a finger to his lips, motioning her to wait. With a shake of her head she moved past him to the center of the room. Anvil lay sprawled across the floor, a circle of blood-soaked hay beneath him. A pitchfork jutted from his chest. Frida stared in disbelief at his lifeless face.

"My God, Webb," she gasped. She knelt and checked for a pulse. "Ewan has killed him. They are sure to take him from us now."

"You don't really believe he did this?" he whispered.

"But who else... you think Muntz killed him? But why would he?"

"I don't know."

"Then Ewan could have done it."

"I refuse to believe that," he hissed. "Muntz must've followed us and run into him."

"If he is still here, the children are in danger. We must find them."

Webb peered into the brilliant sunlight beyond the doorway trying to imagine where they might have gone. An image of Marley flashed across his thoughts, his pale form hovering near the window. He leaned close to her ear.

"If you were a ten year old girl," he said beneath his breath, "you'd hide where you felt the safest, wouldn't you?"

She glanced down the corridor. "You think they're with Marley?"

She started toward the stalls but he held her back.

"Muntz may have found them, or he may have them captive in there, or he may be in there by himself." He set a foot on Anvil's chest and pulled the pitchfork free. The tines rang as metal grated against bone.

"Oh, Webb," she grimaced, "must you?"

"I'm not taking any chances."

219

They crept back down the aisle, stopping at the half-door marking Marley's stall. Webb lifted the latch and raised the pitchfork, pushing the door open with his foot. Marley eyed them from the far corner. Behind the big horse, Ewan crouched with his back to the wall, a broken scythe one hand, his free arm around Mariah. At the sight of them she burst into tears. Frida ran to her, pulling her near.

Ewan lowered the blade and slumped against the wall. Webb eased next to him, studying his troubled face.

"You know what happened out there?"

He nodded, staring at nothing.

"The man with the blonde hair is gone?"

He nodded again. Webb rose and pulled a blanket from the half-wall, taking it down the aisle and draping it over Anvil's body. When he returned Ewan faced him. For a moment his lips moved but he made no sound. He took a breath.

"After you left us I spotted him," he managed, "my father I mean. He had a crazy look, the way he looked when he was out of control, when he could hurt you. I knew sooner or later he would check the truck, so I snuck Mariah past the porch when he was in the house. It was her idea we'd be safe in here with Marley.

"But he found us anyway." He pointed to the stall door. "He stood right there with the axe over his head. I saw right away Marley couldn't protect us so I put her behind me and told him to go ahead and kill me but I wouldn't let him get to her. I had that scythe in my hand and probably said a lot of other things too. I don't remember. I wanted so bad to kill him I sort of blacked out.

"Then all of a sudden the blonde-haired man was behind him. I thought I must be hallucinating. Once my father saw him he went completely nuts and grabbed for the man, swinging at him with the axe, pushing him back into the closet. I thought for sure he was killed.

220

"A second later my father stumbled backwards and swayed for a second like he was drunk. Then he fell backwards with the pitchfork sticking out of him. The man jumped from the closet and looked at me like he wanted to say something but turned instead and ran out the door."

Webb said nothing, at a loss for words. Ewan leaned against the wall and closed his eyes.

"I know I should feel bad," he muttered, "but the truth is I don't feel anything. He would've killed me. My own father and he would've if he'd had the chance. There was no way I was going to let him get to her, not while I was alive."

Webb sat back, torn between speaking and saying nothing. As much as he wanted to help, he sensed Ewan needed his presence more than his sympathy. Being there with him was what mattered.

Chapter Twenty-four

A week later, Webb paused at the soft murmur of voices drifting through the living room doorway. He peeked around the corner. Frida sat leaning back against the sofa cushions, her eyes closed, while Mariah read from *To Kill a Mockingbird*. She paused in mid-sentence and Frida sat up, peering over her shoulder.

"Did you find a word you haven't seen before?" she asked, running her fingers over the page.

"No, I can read all the words."

"Then you have a question?"

"No," she answered, looking up at her, "I don't have one."

"Then what is it?" She brushed the hair from her forehead.

"Scout doesn't have a mother."

"That's right."

"Her mother died?"

"Yes, Mariah, she did. That's the way the author, Harper Lee, wrote the story."

"Ewan's mother died too."

"I know," she sighed. "He told me."

"Why did she have to die?"

"She was very sick. Sometimes that happens with very sick people."

"Like Scout's mother?"

"I suppose so."

"But sometimes mothers just leave."

"Yes, Mariah, sadly that is also true."

"Scout doesn't have a mother," she said, her voice pensive, "and I don't have a mother."

"I know, sweetheart."

Webb watched Frida stroke her hair, doing what little she could when words were no longer of use. A part of him wanted to go to her, to lean close, to tell her what he truly felt. But he did nothing, held back by his pride.

After a moment he stepped through the doorway. They both turned, their faces brightening at the site of him. He paused to savor the moment, knowing it could disappear at any time. Mariah jumped from the couch and started toward him.

"I just saw the mailman drive off," he said, motioning toward the door. "Your package might be here."

She pivoted and vanished in a clatter of footsteps. Frida faced him, her face full of questions.

"What are you up to, Mr. Van Horn?"

"Mariah and I have an agreement."

"What sort of agreement?"

Before he could answer she burst back through the door with a small package in her hands. Tossing a stack letters in Frida's lap, she tore open the box and pulled out a thin paperback book. Without a word she sat and began thumbing through the pages. Frida collected the envelopes and moved to where Webb stood watching.

"Now what about this agreement of yours?" she whispered.

"I told her I'd let her choose a book each month if she'd promise to read them. We're a long way from a library."

She pulled an envelope from the stack and held it to the light. Then she slid her finger under the seal, lifting out the letter.

"Well, you're very thoughtful," she said, glancing at the paper and then jerking it open.

"Besides," he continued, "as hard as it is to get kids to read nowadays, I had to do something. Ewan spends all his spare time playing computer..."

"Oh my God!" she gasped.

She looked up at him, her face pale.

"What is it, Frida?"

"My husband... my husband has been killed."

"Your husband is..."

"He is dead."

223

She collapsed onto the couch. Webb moved next to her, his mind racing.

"You're sure about this? He's really dead?"

His voice seemed to belong to someone else. She held up the letter, her hand trembling.

"There was a fight between gangs in the prison. Others were killed as well."

"Then it must be true."

"Still, I can't believe he is…"

"Frida, you're free," he blurted.

"I am free?"

"Think what that means," he added, his voice hopeful.

"I don't know what to think," she muttered.

He took her hand in his and she looked up at him, her expression dazed. He bent close to her.

"Now we can…" he whispered.

"No, Webb," she said, drawing back, "you must not say such things."

"But he's no longer in the way."

She stared at him, her eyes filling with tears.

"Why are you crying," he said, confused by her reaction, "when you ought to be celebrating?"

"He was my husband, Webb."

"But he wanted you dead."

"These things are not so easy for a woman," she murmured, brushing away the tears. "Can I truly be a widow?"

Mariah scrambled onto the couch, squeezing next to her. The crunch of car wheels on gravel drifted through the screen door. Dispirited by her rejection, Webb stood and pushed through the door, stepping onto the porch. The van sat parked down the slope in the shade of a scrub oak.

Ewan slid out of the passenger door, his expression both exhausted and elated. A blood-spattered apron drooped from his neck.

"You look like a butcher," Webb called from the top step.

"I stitched up a bull's privates but he didn't much like it." He paused to inspect the apron. "And I only threw up once."

Maves followed him to the porch and clasped a hand on his shoulder.

"I don't believe I've ever seen a worse-behaved animal," he added. "You could see he was ornery just by looking at him. Those black eyes showed pure meanness."

"I'd be mean too," Webb quipped, "if my privates needed sewing."

"He did a fine job in spite of the animal."

He started up the steps. Webb raised a hand to stop him.

"Better wait out here, Maves."

"And the reason would be?"

"Frida just learned her husband is dead."

"I thought he was in jail."

"The prison gangs went at each other and he lost."

"From what I heard she should be celebrating."

"Don't tell her."

"You made that mistake already?"

"More or less," he muttered.

"Well, we'll give her some time and then go check on her. It has to be a shock." He nodded up the driveway. "In the meantime, there's beer in the office refrigerator. We can wait back there."

"Can I have one too?" Ewan said optimistically.

"In your case," he said, squinting at him with mock disapproval. "I spell beer S-O-D-A."

They disappeared around the corner. Webb started down the stairs and then stopped as a police cruiser turned into the drive. A sense of dread swept over him. Within seconds an officer wearing a dark blue uniform emerged from the car. Across the cruiser's front fender a city seal read 'San Antonio Police Department'.

Wearing sunglasses and a blue cap pulled low, he resembled any other police officer. He stopped at the foot of the stairs and surveyed the house before turning to Webb and removing his cap. Cropped on the sides, blonde hair sprung from the top of his head in a thick matt.

Maves rounded the corner. Ewan followed close behind but seeing the car hesitated and then ducked behind the porch. The officer glanced in Maves' direction, keeping his attention on the house. He fidgeted with his cap for a moment as if unsure how to begin.

"I'm looking for the Van Horn residence," he finally said, gesturing at the porch, "and I believe this is the correct address."

"That's right." Webb stepped off the stairs. "This is the place."

Maves moved to where the officer stood waiting.

"I'm Maves Van Horn," he said, shaking his hand. "What brings you all the way out here?"

The officer removed his sunglasses and reached into his shirt pocket, pulling out a thick rectangle of paper. Without a word, he unfolded the sheets and handed them to Maves.

"I'd appreciate it," he said, glancing at the papers before passing them to Webb, "if you would just tell us what this is about."

"I wanted you to know I have all the necessary paperwork verifying who I am and why I'm here, all signed by a local judge."

"Alright then, I'll bite." Maves peered at him. "Why are you here?"

"I'm looking for Mariah Brownlee," he said, motioning up the stairs, "and I understand she's staying at this address."

Webb glanced at his brass nametag, finally able to see past the reflection, spotting the name etched across it in capital letters. He looked at the man askance, wondering if Mariah's mother somehow had arranged a scam to get her back.

"You're a relation?" he asked, watching his reaction.

226

"I'm her father."

Webb cut his eyes at Maves but before he had a chance to absorb the meaning the officer pointed to the papers.

"The reason I didn't call, the reason I wanted to have everything in order before I came here, is that I realize this is unexpected news. The message said as much."

"What message is that?" Maves asked, trying to piece together the story.

"I'll need to go back a bit to answer," he said, taking a breath. "Mariah's mother and I got married right out of high school. She was pregnant. You've heard the story before, no doubt. They rarely turn out well. Ours was no exception. Mariah's mother is as wild as they come and had no business having a child.

"I tried to make the best of it and do right by Mariah. I went to night school, got into law enforcement and found the work suited me. Mariah's mother went the other direction. One day she just disappeared, taking Mariah with her.

"I've been looking for my daughter ever since. I had no luck until I got an anonymous email. The writer said he found me using the internet." His gaze wandered back to the house. "Based on that and the writing, I figure he's probably young, maybe a teenager."

Webb studied the papers, all of which seemed official and in order. Judge Justice's signature crossed the final page.

He turned as the door behind him creaked open. Mariah stood at the top of the stairs, Frida beside her. He could see they had been listening. Mariah peered down at the officer, on her face a mixture of hope and fear. His face held the same expression. Frida led her down the steps and knelt beside her, whispering in her ear. She moved next to Webb and leaned into him as she eyed the man. After a moment, he nudged her to where her father stood waiting.

Webb watched him take her hand, bending his face close to hers and speaking to her in soft tones, and for an instant he tried but could not envision having a daughter of his own. His gaze drifted to where Frida crouched in the grass, her eyes filled with a sadness and longing he could scarcely imagine. Her entire world had changed in minutes. In spite of the chaos or perhaps because of it she seemed even more beautiful than ever, and despite his efforts he found himself wanting her.

The living room curtains moved behind him and he glimpsed Ewan peeking through. He backtracked up the stairs and to the door, slipping inside. Ewan moved away from the window and sat on the couch, staring at the floor, elbows on his knees. Webb sat next to him.

"How did you locate him?"

"I did a search. It didn't take long. I decided a cop had to be better than her mother or some lame foster home so I used a bogus email and gave him your address." He looked up. "Was I wrong?"

"Seeing them just now is your answer." He stood. "Come on, let's join them."

"I'm staying here," he said, looking away.

"I won't tell anyone you sent the email."

"I don't care about that."

"Then let's go."

"I can't."

"But Mariah will be leaving soon."

"I know."

"You have to say goodbye to her, Ewan."

He kept his eyes to the floor.

"I never thought it through this far," he muttered, half to himself. "I just wanted to find her father for her. Then all of a sudden he shows up."

"And that's a good thing."

"But she won't be here anymore."

"I'm going to miss her too. We all will."

"You don't understand."

228

"What don't I understand?"

"Mariah is special," he whispered, his voice choked with emotion. "She stuck by me always, any time I got in trouble, when my hair was gone and everyone else was laughing at me, during the time my hand and arm were both hurt and I couldn't do anything for myself.

"I can't imagine her not being around." A pain-filled grin crossed his lips. "And I did it all to myself. That's totally inept, wouldn't you say?"

"No, I would not say. You were right to find him, Ewan. Now you owe it to yourself, and to Mariah, to go say a proper goodbye, knowing there's sadness in it but also knowing the good you've done."

He sat for a moment lost to his thoughts. Then a gradual acceptance filled his face and he stood, his expression pained but determined.

"I need you to let me go out there on my own."

Without waiting for a reply he turned and started for the door, hesitating for a moment and glancing back before stepping through.

Chapter Twenty-five

Ewan stuffed the last of the syringes into the leather satchel, snapping shut the brass latches and sliding the case into the rear of the van. He lingered a moment, going through drawers and cabinets, double-checking supplies he had restocked only days earlier. Unnoticed, Maves looked on.

In the weeks since his father's death he had seemed like any teenager, one moment childlike, the next mature beyond his years. But overall he had adopted a new attitude, an unmistakable pride in his work. That he would soon turn sixteen no doubt had something to do with the difference, but Maves guessed there was more to it.

The restocking complete, he swung the door closed and started for the clinic. Maves stepped into the doorway, keys in hand, and jingled them before his face.

"Are you teasing me for a reason?" He squinted at him.

"Alright," Maves shrugged, "if you don't want to drive then…"

"I didn't say that," he half-yelled.

"So you do want to drive. Do you have a license?"

"You *are* teasing me. You know I don't."

"But you already know how?"

"Webb let me drive Mr. Janacek's truck around the ranch a little when we returned it. I did alright."

He thrust out a hand and Maves peered into his palm.

"So, you're telling me you don't need any practice?"

He jerked his hand away.

"Uh… no," he mumbled, "I could use some practice."

"Ah, now we're getting somewhere. You do need some time behind the wheel."

"Yes," he sighed, "I need the practice."

"Well then, time's a wasting."

He handed over the keys and Ewan hurried into the van, turning the engine and shifting into reverse even before Maves had closed the door. He eased the van down the drive and paused at the gate.

"Is it alright if we go to town?" He cast Maves a quick glance, looking a tad suspicious he thought.

"You're the one driving," he answered, his tone matter of fact.

He edged onto the blacktop as if the van might break into pieces at the slightest bump, creeping along for a quarter mile until, exasperated by the slow pace, Maves leaned over jammed his foot to the floor. The engine roared to life.

Minutes later the town came into view. Maves pointed him down a wooded side street lined with frame houses, their shapes and colors like variations on a theme. They wound from one neighborhood to the next, occasionally pausing to practice parking while Maves barked out directions from the curb.

At a broad intersection the town square appeared through a tunnel of live oaks. Ewan cast him a quick glance, turning onto the street before he could object. Within seconds he had pulled before the courthouse.

"As long as I'm here, I might as well go ahead and get my license," he said as if commenting on the weather.

"What are you talking about?"

"That is, unless you're against me having it."

"Why would I bring you out here if I was against it? This isn't exactly my idea of a good time. The problem is you're not sixteen yet."

"But I can drive well enough?"

"You're passable."

"So you don't have a problem with me having a license?"

"Of course I don't," he said, eyeing him skeptically. "What's with all the questions?"

"Webb told me a person can get a hardship license at age fifteen."

"He did what?"

231

"You just need a good reason."

"Webb knows this for a fact?"

"I don't have any parents," he continued. "That sounds like as good a reason as any."

"What are you in such a hurry for?"

"I want to buy Mr. Janacek's truck before the family sells it to somebody else."

"You have the money?"

"My father was a tightwad, so I inherited enough."

"Well, you have it all planned out," he groused. "What do you need me for?"

"I need you to vouch for me."

"If Webb knows so much," he grumbled, "he can do it."

"But I was hoping it would be you."

"You wouldn't rather have Webb?"

"I want you to be the one."

"Driving is a big responsibility. You think you're ready?"

"You know me better than anyone. What do you think?"

Maves studied him, considering the question. Then he nodded and pointed him out the door. Moments later they stood in the doorway of a wood-paneled office fronted by a heavy desk. A middle-aged woman in reading glasses sat behind it thumbing through a thick folder. He nudged Ewan toward her.

"Well?" she said, squinting at him over her glasses.

"I'm here to see the judge," he mumbled.

A frown spread across her face like a tremor, sending tiny cracks through her make-up. She slammed the folder shut.

"You need an appointment," she snapped. "But this is the judge's consultation time so she isn't available for appointments, much less drop-ins such as yourself. You will kindly leave."

"But the judge told me to come in any time."

"Well now," she said with a strained smile, "I'm sure you think you're a special case. But I can assure you that on her consultation day she doesn't see even the specialist of cases."

"Does it make any difference," he said hopefully, "if I'm here for a consultation?"

"Nice try, sonny," she snipped, "but the answer is still the same."

"If I could only tell the judge why I'm here…"

He laid his palms on the desktop and leaned toward her. Her smile vanished.

"Off my desk!" she barked.

He jerked back his hands. She looked past him to where Maves stood watching from the doorway.

"Just because the judge has a soft spot for juvenile delinquents does not mean they can take liberties in this office." She glared at him over her glasses. "Are you just going to stand there and let him be disrespectful?"

"The only disrespect I see," he answered, stepping into the room, "is on your part, not his."

"I don't know what you mean," she said, eyeing him with disdain.

"You're confusing persistence with disrespect."

"I'll not be lectured to like a child."

"In spite of your obvious prejudice," he continued, "not every teenager is a delinquent."

"Well," she huffed, "never in my life have I heard such rudeness. I want you to leave this office now."

"Frank honesty can seem a little rude, I'll admit that. But the boy has been nothing but polite."

"I asked you to leave."

"I heard you."

"Well then…"

"We'll leave," he said, laying a hand on Ewan's shoulder, "but I have to wonder if this judge, whoever he is, knows how you treat his visitors."

"Why don't you just ask him?" a woman's voice called from behind them.

He turned to find Carlene Justice standing in the doorway. He glanced around the room.

"This is your office?"

"I see you've finally decided to seek emancipation, Mister Fisk," she said, disregarding his question.

"But, no, I'm just…" he stammered.

"Don't worry." She cut her eyes at the woman. "Despite the rumors, I make time for something as important as this."

"But I don't…"

"It's no problem, Mister Fisk, I can assure you." She pointed him into a chair. "Mrs. Hyde will get your file and draw up the papers post haste."

Casting worried glances at the woman, he inched the chair away from the desk and sat. Maves ran a hand across his jaw.

"There seems to be a misunderstanding," he said, confused by the exchange.

"Then you and I must discuss it, Mr. Van Horn." She ushered him into an inner office and closed the door. "Or may I call you Maves?"

"Of course, but I thought he was here for a hardship driver's license."

"Yes," she sighed, "I wasn't thinking. Until he turns sixteen he'll need that license."

She opened the door and called out the additional instructions. Maves watched her move, transfixed by the curve of her hips, the shape of her mouth. He suddenly realized he had never actually looked at her, never before noticed her beauty, seeing her as a judge and nothing more.

She closed the door and ran a hand through her salt and pepper hair, locking eyes with him. In that instant he sensed something from her, something personal, as if she wanted more from him than a simple business meeting.

"What's this about, uh… uh… about emancipation?" he stammered, trying to hide his awkwardness.

"It's perfectly unremarkable," she said in a matter of fact tone before leading him to a pair of chairs separated by a small table, "and to be expected under these circumstances."

"I mean what *is* it exactly, Judge?"

She sat across from him, moving her chair closer. Her normally intense gaze softened as she peered at him.

"Won't you call me Carlene?" she finally said.

He struggled to keep his thoughts on Ewan. Light glinted off her hair, sparking along the thin strands of gray.

"How will emancipation help him, Carlene?"

Saying her name sent a jolt down the back of his neck. He tried to stay calm. She sat back and studied him with interest.

"Emancipation is simply freedom," she replied, somehow making the word sound erotic. "He'll be declared an adult in the eyes of the law. Does that help?"

"Uh… sure." The two words were all he could manage.

"You don't like the idea?"

"It's just that… he's only a teenager, Carlene."

"He's a teenager with no family, Maves, at least not that we've been able to locate. He is, sadly, on his own."

"He has us, Webb and me."

"He knows that. But it's what he wants, Maves. He's trying to take some control over his life."

"You believe he's ready?"

"The law says a minor considered for emancipation must be able to support and manage his own affairs. He has an inheritance, a place to live and, thanks to you, a job. That's a decent start."

"I'll be the first to admit he's made a lot of progress but are you sure about this?"

"Maves," she said, leaning toward him, "I may not always show it but I've taken a special interest in Ewan. I

235

believe you and I share that interest. Between the two of us we can get him through adolescence in one piece, don't you think?"

"I suppose I ought to be proud of him."

"So you'll help me keep an eye on him?"

"I didn't do so well at my first attempt to parent a teenager, Carlene."

"I'm a pretty good judge of character. You'll do fine."

"I wish I was so sure."

She studied him a moment before moving to the edge of her chair, her blue eyes gleaming.

"I have another proposal," she said, "if you're willing to take a chance."

She sat waiting for an answer. Flecks of yellow dotting her blue eyes flashed like fool's gold. He hesitated for an instant, thinking of Blanca, and then gave his head a tentative nod.

"I'm listening."

"I'd like your opinion on something. Meet me at the quarter horse races on Saturday and I'll explain."

Unsure of her intentions he hesitated again, trying to decide if the meeting was social or professional. She gave an impatient sigh.

"I'm not much of a gambler," he said finally.

"This is not about gambling."

"What then?"

She sat back and eyed him like a cat might a mouse, a playful challenge in her voice.

"Come and find out."

Chapter Twenty-six

Maves stepped away from the ticket counter, passing through a wooden stile and handing his ticket to a pink-faced man in a pearl-buttoned western shirt. The words 'Gillespie County Fair' in blue stitching crested his vest pocket. He tore the ticket in half and handed back the stub with a polite nod.

Leaving the entry, he strode along the gravel walk and breathed in the straw-tinged air, trying to recall when he had last visited the fairgrounds. To the east a gibbous moon shone pearl-like above the horizon. All at once a wave of memories flooded his thoughts, he and Webb's mother strolling that same path, his arm around her shoulder, her hand in his back pocket. Strings of colored lights crisscrossed the dance floor, swaying before a gentle breeze.

Pulling him back into the present, a young girl in a white lace blouse and suede lederhosen appeared before him. A single plait of braided hair traced a circle around her head, the honey-blonde hue much like his late wife's. Crossing from shoulder to hip, a purple sash held the word 'Duchess' in red glitter. She handed him a flier for the upcoming rodeo with a shy smile and vanished into the crowd.

He started toward the track, dodging drink vendors and betting lines, the acrid odor of stabled livestock wafting past him in waves. Carlene had suggested they meet beneath the stands. He surveyed the bustling scene. Blue-lipped children chased each other through the crowd, stopping long enough to slurp multicolored snow cones before starting again. Men in straw hats and pressed jeans loitered beneath the stairs in tight groups, studying racing programs and talking amongst themselves. Brightly clad women hurried toward the betting booths.

Giving up on spotting her among the crowd, he stepped into the relative cool of the ticket counter shade, buying a handful of wooden beer tokens stamped with the inked image of a foaming stein. He moved to the adjacent beer stand and slapped two coins on the counter. A man behind the counter turned at the sound. A damp, beer-stained apron stretched across his belly, straining at the ties. He reached up and touched a thick finger to the side of his nose.

"I can tell," he announced, a slight accent bending his words, "it's the German beer you want, yeah?"

"You have the dark?"

"Sure, I got it right here, nice and cold for a hot day like this one, yeah?" He fished two cans from a metal trough, toweling them off with his apron and setting them on the counter. "I sweat so much back here I'm about ready for one myself."

"It's hot alright." Maves tossed another token onto the counter. "Have one on me."

"A good dark one, yeah?" the man called as he moved away.

A beer in each hand, he pushed into the crowd. A voice announcing the first race echoed overhead. Between the stands he glimpsed a line of jockeys perched atop their horses, their brightly-hued jerseys already dark with sweat. The sleek horses paraded along the track railing, some calm, others wide-eyed and jerking at their reins.

The jockeys began to circle back toward the starting gates. Deciding to check the grandstand for Carlene, he elbowed his way up the stairway. A hot wind blowing in off the track coursed past him, whistling through the metal rafters. He could find no sign of her.

He made his way back down the stairs, wondering if she had changed her mind. He again puzzled over the mysterious nature of their meeting. Was her interest personal or professional? Either way he had a growing sense he might never know.

As he reached the bottom step a woman's voice called from beyond the crowd. He craned his neck, scanning the sea of people but finding no sign of her. Then suddenly the crowd parted and she appeared beneath the dappled shade of the beer garden, racing program in hand. She motioned him over with an energetic wave.

He dove back into the crowd, winding his way through the fuming heat of the plaza, the beer garden's tempting oasis of shade pulling him through the mass of people. The cans dripped sweat over his fingers and onto his jeans, spreading in dark patches across his thighs.

All at once the crowd again fell away and she reappeared only yards from him, still waiting beneath the vine-covered entrance, her blue eyes sparking with flashes of gold. He came to an abrupt stop, taken aback by how good he felt seeing her. In his awkwardness, he popped open a can and downed half.

"You must be thirsty," she quipped, a mischievous glint to her eye.

"I, uh…" he stammered. "It's hot out."

He handed her the other beer, wincing at his poor reply. She pressed the can to her forehead and studied him. He took another long gulp.

"It's not that you were beginning to think I'd changed my mind?" she asked.

"No, I… I…" he sputtered, nearly choking.

"Not at the least bit?"

"I wouldn't put it like that, exactly," he hedged.

"After all, I'm the one who was late getting here."

"I admit I had started to wonder."

"I'm sorry, Maves." She ran a tentative hand down his arm. "I got a call just as I was leaving, an important one."

"Something to do with court?"

"I won't bore you with the details." She pulled him into the shade. "You'll get overheated if you're not careful. Where's your hat?"

"I consider it impolite to wear a hat in a woman's presence."

"My, are you always so formal?"

"It's how I was raised."

"Well, I'm flattered by the thought. But it wouldn't do if you got heat stroke because of me."

At a loss for words, he gulped the rest of his beer. She grabbed his arm and moved to an empty table.

"Aren't you wondering," she said, pushing him into a chair, "why I asked you here?"

"Of course I…"

He stopped as the public-address speakers blared overhead, announcing the start of the race. She made no move toward the track so he stayed put. Within seconds a blur of color and hide thundered past the railing, throwing up an orange cloud of dust. Scattered cheers and moans drifted over the stands. She leaned across the table and held out her hand.

"Will you come with me to see something?"

They made their way through the crowd and moments later stopped before a makeshift corral of metal fencing tucked behind the jockeys' quarters. A handful of horses milled about the grass-covered circle, sniffing the air and nickering at the passing racehorses. Their dust-covered backs and uncombed coats stood in stark contrast to the sleek horses in the paddock.

At Carlene's approach a sorrel mare turned from the others, ambling toward her with a noticeable limp. Maves studied her approach, noting the twelve-inch scar running from knee to fetlock. Carlene glanced at him and reached a hand between the rails. The mare nuzzled at her palm.

"That horse is lucky to be walking by the look of her scar," he observed. "The owner must be fond of her. Care like that is costly."

"She has no owner. None of them do."

"Why are they here?"

"All these horses raced once," she continued, "some here, some in Mexico. This one understands Spanish. She has a racing name but I call her Dulce, for her sweet nature."

"She's what you wanted to show me?"

"Not just her. I wanted you to see them all. These horses will never race again, Maves, not a one. At this level, owners aren't inclined to keep an unproductive horse. They can't afford to. And they're not able to sell them due to their condition. They all need medical care of one sort or another. So, typically, they euthanize them."

"I've heard of such practice but it sickens me to see it up close." He let his gaze wander over the small herd. "They're all to be put down?"

"Except that I've offered to take them."

"The whole lot?"

"I inherited a five-hundred-acre ranch from my father. Most of it is good grazing and suitable for horses."

"Even so, taking on a bunch of broken down racehorses is a big commitment in time and expense, not to mention veterinary care."

"That's why I asked you here, Maves. I intend to set up a nonprofit to rescue horses like these and I hoped you might join me in making it happen. I supply the place and you your knowledge. Sounds like we'd make a good team, don't you think? What do you say?"

He looked out over the small herd, surprised by how disappointed he felt. He had begun to imagine her interest in him was personal.

"You asked me here to discuss business," he said half to himself, astonished by his stupidity.

"Oh my…" she gasped. "You thought this was a date, didn't you?"

"No, I..." he started then caught himself, determined to be truthful with her. He'd seen enough of deception and lies. "Well, I thought maybe… but please let's just forget it."

"Don't give up so easily, Maves Van Horn."

"I don't want to make any more fool of myself than I already have."

"Does it matter that I'm flattered?"

241

"You're… you mean you're not offended?"

"No, I'd even…"

A shrill ringing rose above the noise of the crowd, stopping her. She rifled through her purse, lifting out the phone and pressing it to her ear. Maves watched a mix of annoyance and regret cross her face. After a few curt replies, she returned the phone and looked up at him, disappointment in her eyes.

"A child has gone missing. I have to okay a warrant to search the stepfather's home but I need to review the case file first. I'm so sorry, Maves." She took his hand. "I hope I'll see you again."

She turned and vanished behind the milling crowd. He leaned onto the metal fence, admiring the smooth lines of the sorrel mare as a tentative hope passed over him like a zephyr.

Chapter Twenty-seven

Maves set down the phone and stared through the open door into the bright light of late summer. Indigo shadows stretched beneath the covered arena, the sun-drenched corral beyond it vibrating in the midday heat. Half-asleep, Marley hung his dappled head through the stable window.

Maves noticed little of it, his thoughts mired in a maze of unanswered questions, all leading back to Blanca. Zak's words, mysterious in their paucity, still sounded in his ear. He claimed to have answered the riddle of the package but refused to say more over the phone. More troubling, he had implied news of Blanca without ever mentioning her name.

Two hours later he sat peering through the windshield at the low buildings of Quintero. The two-columned bell tower fronting Our Lady of Guadalupe Church stood brilliant white beneath the slanting sunlight. As if sensing his arrival, Zak waited in the doorway.

Maves joined him and they passed through the foyer into the dim confines of the sanctuary. Though warm, the musty air lay cool against the dampness of his sweat-stained shirt. Zak motioned him to a pew. He clasped his scarred boxer's hands, sitting for a moment with his head down.

"The girl, Maves, first you must tell me of her," he muttered, raising his walnut-hued eyes. "She has settled in?"

Maves heard an uncharacteristic vulnerability beneath his words, as if his question went beyond mere interest.

"By girl, do you mean Frida?"

Zak nodded and leaned in close.

"Is she well?"

"She seems to be."

"She is safe there with you and your son?"

"Other than one incident," he replied, studying his reaction, "I believe she is."

243

"An incident, you say?" he asked, breathless. "What sort of incident?"

"She had a close call with the authorities." He puzzled over his sudden interest. "But she came through it alright. Is there a reason you're so concerned?"

He drew back as if dodging a punch, but made no effort to answer. Maves decided to press the issue.

"What are you not telling me, Zak? Is there something I need to know about her?"

He turned his gaze, seeming to sink into the pew, a look of resignation gradually filling his face. He raised a thick finger and pointed to the ceiling.

"Why did God give us the gift of shame, Maves?" he mused. "Have you ever thought to ask yourself such a question?"

"Zak, only you would call shame a gift."

"But a gift it is, a gift of self-knowledge, a reminder of our flaws, our misdeeds, our weaknesses."

"I'm plenty aware of my shortcomings. I don't need reminding." He eyed him, wondering what he was avoiding. "What does this have to do with Frida?"

"It is not of her I must tell you... or not of her only. You see, Frida is my daughter."

"She's your daughter?" He glanced over his shoulder, lowering his voice as if someone might be listening. "But how could... Zak, you're a priest."

"Yes, I am a priest but one with a less then spotless past. I will tell of it if you will allow me."

He took a breath and raised his meaty hands, studying them as if reading a map.

"After I left boxing I was a priest in Guatemala and still quite young. There I had a time of much difficulty. I questioned whether God had called me to this work or whether I had made the decision as an impulsive and flawed young man. Perhaps, as you once said, I sought to escape my guilt over killing a man by entering the

244

priesthood. This I pondered for some time, a time of much sadness.

"Then a beautiful young woman grieving over the death of her husband came to see me. I was distraught over my crisis of faith and she over her loss. We became quite close. In our intimacy we found comfort for a short time.

"Eventually she returned to her coffee plantation, many hours away. I went back to my duties, knowing my sin but determined to move past it. You see, helping her through her grief helped me move beyond my own.

"Only much later did I learn there was a child. Through my contacts I was able to keep track of her, do what little I could for her, until I learned of her need for asylum."

"Frida knows nothing of this?"

"I have given the matter much thought and believe it best to honor her mother's decision in this instance. Frida believes her father died before she was born. I will not complicate her life by taking that from her. Instead I must be content to watch over her and assist where I can. I trust you will keep my confidence in this."

"We both have mistakes we'd like to forget. Have you told anyone else?"

"Other than you, only Blanca knows."

Unable to speak, Maves stared at him, the mere sound of her name catching in his throat. Zak nodded his understanding.

"I see you still have feelings for her."

"What of her, Zak? Do you have news?"

"You can ask her yourself."

"What do you mean?"

"If all goes according to plan, she will arrive very soon."

"She's coming here?"

"She expects to find me. But I am leaving you to talk with her. I know you have questions. But keep your wits about you, Maves. I am less than certain of her intentions."

"What about the package? Do you know what was in it?"

"I am hoping Blanca will answer that question for me." He stood. "Now I must go."

"But if you know, why not tell me yourself?

"I ask only that you have faith, my friend."

He disappeared through the altar door. Maves watched after him, puzzled by his mysterious behavior. What might cause the normally steely priest to act so strangely? He could find no sense to it.

A shaft of sunlight sliced the aisle, interrupting his ruminations. He turned to the foyer. Silhouetted by a wall of stained glass, Blanca stood like an apparition. A chill shot down his spine at the sight of her.

Moments later she slipped next to him, taking his hand. An image of their last meeting flashed through his thoughts, the four-poster bed, the thin fabric of her robe clinging to her like a second skin. He swallowed and tried to clear his head, reminding himself of questions that had long dogged him.

"Maves," she whispered, glancing around the sanctuary, "why are you here?"

"Zak wanted to talk." He peered into her face. "Blanca, what happened…?"

"But where is he?" she interrupted, dropping his hand. "He is supposed to be here. It is of much importance."

"He left."

"But I must see him."

"Blanca, where have you been?" he continued. "I'd given up trying to reach you."

"I… I was… there were complications."

"What sorts of complications make a person just disappear?"

"As I said…"

"I went back to your duplex. The place was empty. What happened?"

"My circumstances, they… well, they became unsettled."

"That's not good enough, Blanca," he pressed, surprised at the anger in his voice. "You asked for my help and then you vanished without a trace."

"But Maves…"

"You could've gotten word to me," he muttered, frustrated by her evasion, "some way or another."

"I must speak with Zak," she said, glancing at the exit, "or I must leave."

"You're not even asking about the package, Blanca. Why is that?"

"The package?"

"You asked me to retrieve a package for you but you don't seem to care about it now."

"I… I have more important concerns."

"You don't care that it was stolen?"

"But of course," she said, clearly flustered, "I am concerned any time we…"

"What was in the package, Blanca?"

"I, uh… well, I…" she stammered, avoiding his gaze. She again glanced at the exit and then faced him, her eyes flashing. "You understand nothing of life for a woman in this place. There are difficulties, many difficulties."

"It's easy to make excuses."

"A woman does what she must," she hissed, "a woman who was left by you to fend for herself."

"This is not about me."

"Because of you," she continued, "I have had to do things, things of which you will never know."

"You didn't answer the question" he pressed.

She leaned toward him, again taking his hand, her eyes dark and luminous, filled with hurt.

"Maves, what has come over you?" she pleaded. "You are cruel to me."

He squinted at her, unwilling to fall for her act.

"Tell me what was in the package, Blanca."

All at once her face transformed into a mask of calm.

"As I told you," she replied, her composure returning, "in the box were papers for the refugees. Losing it is unfortunate, true, but such things happen on the border. The cartels, they…"

"I don't want to hear any more blaming the cartels!" he barked. "You're hiding something and you know it."

"Then I have nothing more to say to you." She glared at him, disdain clear in her eyes.

"The box had glass in it, probably small bottles of some sort."

"Perhaps someone sent perfume to one of the refugees," she sneered, "if there are still a few gentlemen left in the world."

"You don't believe that any more than I do. Tell me what you're hiding."

Her phone buzzed and she glanced at the screen before jumping from the pew. She hesitated as if she might speak but turned instead, hurrying down the aisle without looking back. Maves watched after her. A sense that he would never see her again gripped him, settling like a stone in his chest. Zak appeared from behind the altar.

"You are not looking so well, my friend."

"She wouldn't talk to me, Zak. I can't understand what's happened to her."

"I had hoped I was wrong."

"What's it all about, the package, her disappearance?"

"I have something to show you," he said, motioning toward the door, "if you will allow it."

Minutes later they stood before the heavy wooden doors of a tattered three story building overlooking the Rio Grande. The weathered brick glowed orange beneath the midday glare. A block to the south cars and people moved across the border bridge in a steady stream.

Maves followed him into a sparsely furnished lobby scattered with people. Within seconds the pungent smell of antiseptic enveloped him, acrid and choking. He took a breath and surveyed the high-ceilinged room. Fluorescent light reflected off the polished floors in shimmering waves. A brass sign on the wall read 'St. Clare Children's Hospital' in raised letters.

Zak led him through a set of double doors and down a long corridor that ended in an open room lined with beds. They circled the floor. Small figures, some with woolen caps pulled low over their ears, lay covered in blankets, seeming almost unrecognizable as children. Stands of intravenous fluid crowded the walls. The plastic tubes snaked among the bedside tables like vines.

Zak eased next to a sleeping girl. Her sallow skin shone wax-like beneath the garish light. Taking her hand in his, he stood over her for a full minute whispering a silent prayer. Maves peered into her face, imagining Mariah in her place, her features gaunt, her hair and eyebrows missing. The knot tightened in his chest. Zak turned to him and grasped his arm, pulling him to the rail.

"She is beautiful even in her illness," he whispered.

"Is she why you brought me here?"

"She is," he said, sweeping his arm in a broad arc, "as they all are."

"Why bring me to a children's hospital, Zak?"

"This is a cancer ward, Maves." He tucked the blanket around her shoulders. "She has brain cancer."

"Can they help her?"

"Her type of cancer is curable," he replied, shaking his head in dismay, "but she will not be long with us."

"I'm sorry to hear it. But I still don't understand why we're here."

"We are here because she did not get the proper medication."

Maves stared at him, trying to pull the pieces together, the clinic, the packages, the rattling glass. He turned his eyes to the girl, a part of him unable to believe she would not live.

"You're telling me Blanca has something to do with this?" He pointed to her, his hand shaking. "You're saying she's behind a young girl's death?"

Zak ran his fingers across the girl's forehead.

"Her family lives in Mexico. She was treated at a hospital across the border, as were most of these children, the sickest of them. When so many failed to respond to the treatment the hospital suspected a problem with the medication. Upon investigating, they discovered the cancer medications had been tampered with, diluted to a third the normal strength."

"Someone is stealing cancer medication?"

"Worse than the stealing is the result that now surrounds us."

"But why steal cancer drugs?"

"The medication is very costly, Maves."

"You mean costly like the medication used at the clinic we visited, the clinic Blanca sent me to?"

"Soon after we arrived I began to suspect something amiss. As I told you, I had heard stories about the doctor. When I checked further I learned of the tampering. A great profit can be made by selling stolen drugs on the black market."

"What sort of person cheats children out of life-saving medicine in exchange for money?" Maves muttered half to himself, incredulous.

"Greed truly is a deadly sin, Maves. For a time I could not let myself believe Blanca would involve herself in such a cruel undertaking. Even now I still hold out hope I am wrong. But I fear I am only fooling myself." He sighed. "I asked you here because I hoped she might be truthful with you, of all people. I was mistaken. Now it seems she trusts no one."

Maves turned his eyes, no longer able to look into the girl's frail but beautiful face. He glanced at the rows of beds, the small bundled figures. For a moment he tried to convince himself Blanca's involvement was a mistake, some grand misreading of the facts, but soon he gave up, exhausted by the effort.

"I must attend a rally protesting the mistreatment of immigrants." Zak grasped his shoulder. "I hope you will accompany me to the bridge. I am feeling a little low just now."

Unable to speak Maves nodded his agreement, grateful for an excuse to leave.

Chapter Twenty-eight

Zak moved along the broken sidewalks of downtown in a brooding silence. Maves walked beside him. A sudden flash of pain shot through his leg, white-hot and familiar, and by habit he paused to run his fingers across the dime-sized scar. Squinting into the crystalline sunlight he stood still, determined to keep the memory at bay.

He started again. Images of the children's hospital drifted in and out of his thoughts, disturbing and dreamlike in their unreality. He wondered if the same was true for his companion.

Zak motioned him to stop as a line of flower-laden cars marking a funeral rounded the corner and rolled past. Maves watched after the procession, seeing in it a troubling harbinger. Oven-like heat fumed between the tightly-packed buildings. Above the rooftops, cottonwoods edging the river vibrated before the breeze. As far as he could tell, they seemed to be paralleling the border rather than moving toward it.

Zak paused at an intersection, peering in both directions before pointing to a low-roofed building wedged between an abandoned warehouse and tattoo parlor. The windowless purple and orange façade read 'Cantina Orozco' in turquoise letters. Without a word he started toward it.

Moments later they stepped into the bar's dim foyer. Maves stood waiting, unable to make out anything other than neon beer signs. Within seconds a scattering of mismatched tables and chairs emerged out of the darkness. Otherwise the room stood empty. Zak took his arm, leading him to a corner table.

A man wearing a dirty apron appeared, setting an unmarked bottle of red wine and two glasses on the table. He gestured to Zak in pantomime briefly before returning to the bar. Zak filled each glass, handing one to Maves. He nodded toward the bartender.

"He was shot in the head by a gang for serving rival members. Though he survived, he no longer can speak."

He downed his glass in one swallow and refilled it. Maves glanced around the dilapidated bar.

"What are we doing here, Zak?"

"May goodness prevail," he said, raising his glass, "in this troubled world."

"I thought we were going to an immigration rally."

"Before I call on others to do what is right, I must admit where I have gone wrong."

Maves watched him again drain the glass.

"That sounds an awful lot like confession," he said, refilling his own.

"Yes, a priest confessing to an unbeliever may seem comical. But there is something more I must tell you."

"It's about Blanca, isn't it?"

"Unfortunately, yes." He raised the bottle again, pouring as he spoke. "You see, once she learned that Frida is my daughter she began asking for favors."

"You mean blackmail?"

"She never actually threatened to tell my secret but made it clear I must grant her requests. In return, she agreed to bring Frida to safety."

"What sort of requests?"

"Because of my refugee work, I have contacts in customs. She asked that I arrange for her packages to pass through without scrutiny. She explained that the boxes contained refugees' papers and if found might result in targeting those whose documents were inside. At the time it seemed an unorthodox but not unreasonable request.

"Then when we visited the clinic I began to fear the packages held another purpose. At that point I abandoned our arrangement. When I confronted her she refused to explain and instead began bringing the packages across outside of customs."

"And using me," he said, grimacing at the thought, "to help her steal medication from children, children who would die without it."

"Yes, I did not realize at first what the boxes held. But when I finally saw the purpose I became physically ill." He set his palms on the table, locking eyes with Maves. "You know we must stop her."

"She might tell the church about Frida."

"I will not fear the truth of my past. I care only because of how the news might affect Frida. Otherwise, I will face my punishment if it will stop this madness."

He refilled their glasses and stood, raising his again.

"To finding peace in what we must do."

Moments later, they stepped back into the blinding daylight and a wall of heat enveloped them, dust-laden and still. Maves moved as if in a dream. They rounded a corner and the tiny Chapel of St. Christopher appeared at the edge of a circular cobblestone plaza. Meant to welcome and protect travelers, the chapel served as the center of the rally. A concrete obelisk marking a war memorial stood nearby.

Men in straw hats gathered beside the marker, talking among themselves, their faces grim. Women tended children beneath the shade of a towering pecan. The border bridge stood fifty yards beyond.

Zak moved into the crowd, greeting people and offering support. Maves followed and then paused to survey the scene. Two police cruisers flanked the bridge, blocking traffic. Beyond the customs booth, another crowd stood waiting. A chartreuse sedan idled just across the border. Blue exhaust poured from its tailpipe, rising opaque and specter-like in the windless heat.

A dim memory tugged at the back of his mind. He brushed it aside as a young man emerged from the chapel, followed by several others all with red bandanas tied across their foreheads. They walked among the crowd, handing out placards and bottled water. One of the men moved up

254

the chapel steps and lifted a bullhorn, introducing the organizers. The scattered groups of protesters moved into the brilliant sunlight of the plaza.

Maves only half-listened. For reasons he could not explain a growing sense of unease had settled over him. He stepped next to a panel truck and let his gaze drift past the plaza and on to the bridge itself, where two decorative cement columns flanked the crossing. Beside the nearest post the shadow of a figure spread across the sidewalk like spilled ink. Cigarette smoke drifted from behind the post in a rising cloud.

A man's face leaned past the corner, peering into the crowded plaza. Maves recognized him at once as Blas, the man in the boat. He ducked behind the truck, watching the man through the windows. Seconds later, Mata, his companion, scrambled up the riverbank and joined him.

Maves followed their line of sight to the opposite side of the plaza. Nothing obvious stood out. He squinted into the deep shade cast by the chapel. There in the shadows, surrounded by a shoulder-high hedge of oleander, stood Blanca. A purple scarf covered her head. His throat tightened at the sight of her.

She stared intently into the crowd, following the movement of a young man with a crimson goatee, the same man he had seen at the clinic. He strained to explain her connection to the man, or to Blas and Mata. A sense of dread gripped him.

All at once he felt a need to find Zak. He stepped from behind the truck and scanned the protesters, spotting him in the middle of the crowd. The group began to move toward the rally's starting point alongside the river. Zak paused beside a small girl and bent to tie her shoe. Maves started toward him then stopped at the sight of the chartreuse car turning onto the bridge, creeping along the railing.

In a sudden flood of images he recognized it as the sedan he and Abel had avoided after escaping Harlan and his men, the car belonging to one of the cartels. Blas' angular face shone behind the windshield. Maves turned his eyes back to the rally.

Blanca appeared at the edge of the plaza. Spotting him, she turned and scrambled behind a wall of protestors. The man with the red goatee was nowhere in sight. Maves started moving toward where he had last seen her, casting worried glances at the bridge. The police appeared oblivious to the car.

Zak emerged at the head of the rally and the crowd began moving toward the bridge. Maves pushed his way through the milling protesters, straining to catch a glimpse of Blanca while angling toward Zak. He wanted to warn him, though of what exactly he could not say.

The crowd parted before him and the man with the red goatee appeared in the middle of the street, Blanca next to him. The man held a leather valise. Maves froze, watching as Blanca handed him a thick envelope in exchange for the case. He vanished in one direction, Blanca in the opposite.

Maves started after her, stumbling through the shifting group. Seconds later he burst though the wall of people. Zak stood twenty yards to his left, Blanca before him. He seemed to be pleading with her. She glanced at a black car idling alongside the riverbank.

Instinctively, Maves turned to where he had last seen the chartreuse sedan. Blas still slouched in the passenger seat. At a nod from the driver he sat up and jumped from the car, starting toward Blanca, one hand thrust inside his pants pocket.

Maves stood frozen, unable to move, his leg again burning with pain. An image of Riley's slumped form filled his mind, the blood spreading across his khaki shirt like a crimson flower. He blinked, for an instant blinded by the vision, and then he blinked again, forcing the memory from his thoughts. He called out but his voice scarcely rose above the restless crowd. Cupping his hands around his mouth he called again with even less effect. Yet the warning was enough. Zak turned toward him.

He pointed into the crowd. An instant later Blas burst through the wall of protesters, pulling a pistol from his pocket. Zak threw himself at Blanca, knocking her to the ground as gunfire echoed across the plaza. Maves stumbled backwards, the deafening blast ringing inside his head.

The protesters surged forward like a rising wave. Then the panicked crowd crashed into him, sweeping him away from the bridge and into the plaza memorial, pinning him to the obelisk. A young girl, her knees bloodied, fell at his feet. Lifting her onto the base, he dove back into the melee, clawing his way against the flow.

Suddenly the crowd thinned and he found himself alone on the plaza. He rushed to where Zak lay slumped in the street, his clerical coat soaked with blood, his scarred hands still clutching Blanca's purple scarf. Maves knelt and eased him onto his back.

Blanca lay crumpled next to him. Her face was unrecognizable behind a matt of bloodied hair. Maves started to reach for her but Zak grabbed his shirt, pulling him close. He tried but could not speak, and instead fell back onto the pavement.

Footsteps sounded behind him and he turned to find the crowd rushing back at him in a chaotic line. Realizing Zak had been shot they surrounded him, some stopping to help, others rushing past and onto the bridge. Within seconds a group had circled the chartreuse sedan. He watched as Blas slipped inside just ahead of them.

A protester's hand reached through the window, jerking the keys from the ignition and tossing them over the rail. The metal glinted in the crystalline air. Closing in on the sedan, the frenzied mob began rocking it one way and the other, tossing the men about.

A gunshot popped from within but the crowd raged on, lifting one side and tipping the sedan onto the rail. The car teetered, its roof straddling the metal guard, the men inside screaming. Then it slipped over the edge.

Time seemed to slow. The sedan pirouetted in midair, the men's arms outstretched, their hands reaching. The quiet air stood still. Then, in a flash of green and orange, the car struck the boulder-strewn river bottom and burst into flames. Screams of victory mixed with anguish erupted from the group.

Stunned by the spectacle, Maves rose from his knees and was immediately brushed aside by medics and law officers, some in uniform others in suits. Onlookers crowded in, pushing him further from the scene. Dazed, he turned from the melee and stumbled across the plaza.

The little girl he had pulled from the crowd appeared from behind the memorial. Without a word she took his hand, leading him away from the bridge and past the buildings of downtown. The streets seemed to move of their own accord, rising and falling as if the unrelenting heat had turned them liquid.

The road opened onto a shaded plaza wedged between a triangle of abandoned buildings. In the center was an artesian spring. Ringed by a low wall, travertine rose from the fountain in an irregular rectangle, its rippled sides gleaming like water captured in stone.

The girl led him across the cobblestones, pulling him down onto the fountain wall. She dipped her hand in the crystalline water, reaching up and tracing the side of his face. A stream of crimson droplets fell from her fingers, staining the surface. He leaned over the edge, spotting in the wavering reflection a deep gash across his right cheek.

Pulling a handkerchief from his jeans, he dipped it into the spring and held it to the cut. The burn he had felt earlier returned as a veil of white spread across his vision. He slumped over the water, realizing of how close the bullet had come to killing him.

He eased himself down onto the street, leaning his back against the wall. The tiny plaza vibrated before him, unfocused and translucent. The girl slipped from the wall and vanished down a dark alleyway. For a moment he watched after her. Then the veil returned, moving over the street and buildings as if the white-hot sky had descended onto the town, blotting out all time, all memory.

He dreamed of Blanca again. She faced him, her black hair floating about her head like smoke, her caramel-hued skin smooth and luminous. She ran her hand along his cheek. Her touch burned like molten metal. Seeing him wince in pain, she stepped away and pointed a finger at his chest.

"Over there," she shouted. "That's him."

She seemed at once both near and far away. He squinted at her, trying to decipher her meaning.

"Is he conscious?" a voice called from a distance.

"Please help him," she pleaded.

A shadow moved across her and she was gone. In her place the young girl stood over him, a man in uniform behind her, a stethoscope dangling from his neck. Maves tried to raise himself but the veil moved over him again and the scene faded, shifting from white to gray to black.

Chapter Twenty-nine

Maves paused in the kitchen doorway. Suddenly the floor tilted beneath him as if gravity had given way, the walls swirling by in a blur of motion. He grabbed a countertop to steady himself. After a moment the room settled back into place and he eased onto a chair. Frida peered across the table at him.

He reached up and ran his fingers across the stitches under his good eye, aware of how he must look, and how close he had come to total blindness, or worse. The force of the bullet had fractured his cheekbone. Though two days had passed, his head still ached from front to back.

She stood and took his chin in her hand, turning his face to the light and gently probing the wound. He leaned back and closed his eyes, relaxing at the warmth of her touch. For the first time since the protest he allowed himself to think of Zak.

A sudden wave of sadness and regret surged over him, taking his breath. He could scarcely believe his friend had died protecting Blanca. He wondered if any of what he felt was concern for her or merely self-pity. Try as he might, he had been unable to learn of her whereabouts or condition.

He opened his eyes to find Frida staring at him, her face lined with worry. Wanting no part of her pity, he pushed himself up out of the chair, moving to the counter and pouring a cup of coffee. She followed him with her gaze.

"Stop watching me like you think I'm going to collapse any second," he grumbled. "I'm forty-eight not eighty-eight."

"I can worry if I want to. You had a close call, Maves. Your injury is worse than it looks."

He sipped the coffee and studied her, the hint of a smile crossing his lips.

"I should've guessed you'd had medical training, the way you took to veterinary work. Why didn't you say so?"

"I wanted to tell you but I was ashamed of not finishing."

"Webb said you're hoping to get licensed to practice here."

"The waiting is hard for me. I try not to think about it."

"I know what you mean. I'm already itching to get back to work." He ran a hand across his face as an unexpected idea came to him. "Since we're both in a sort of limbo, come with me to Zak's funeral. It's day after tomorrow. To tell the truth, I could use the company."

"Yes," she nodded, her eyes filled with emotion, "I owe him much for his many kindnesses."

A late-summer storm, wall-like and ominous, loomed over the twin bell towers as they approached the small church. Beneath the sanctuary's stained-glass windows a narrow cemetery stretched to the street, the rows of gravestones crowded like buildings in a miniature city. Church officials milled about the markers while onlookers lined the wrought iron fence, overflowing into the street.

Maves followed Frida to the edge of the crowd. A group of nuns filed past in their gray habits, making their way to a row of folding chairs near the gravesite. He watched them talk among themselves, his mind filling with memories of Zak.

Moments later a young the priest stepped to the podium and began reading passages from a tattered leather Bible. The gilded pages flickered beneath the midday light. Maves watched them flash, the glittering gold reminding him of Blanca and the greed that Zak had fought against.

His gaze wandered over the crowd and on to the abandoned buildings beyond the churchyard. Their empty doorways stood deep in shadow. A sudden gust of wind swirled past as a cloud passed before the sun, paling the shade and offering a brief respite from the heat.

261

In the cloud-dimmed light a figure appeared beneath the arched entryway of a former bank. His blonde hair shone pale-white against the darkened windows. A man in a dark suit and sunglasses stood with him.

Maves grabbed Frida's arm and pointed her to the archway. That instant the cloud passed and the sunlight returned, throwing the entry back into shadow. She squinted at the building and then shook her head, putting a finger to her lips before turning back to the service.

Frustrated, he started across the street, reaching the abandoned building in seconds and slipping beneath the arch. The entryway stood empty. A pile of crushed cigarette butts littered the dingy tile floor. He pivoted and stepped back onto the sidewalk.

The cemetery went silent as a quartette of priests lowered Zak's walnut-hued coffin into the earth. Maves said a brief farewell beneath his breath. Seconds later footsteps sounded behind him, the unmistakable click of leather-soled shoes on pavement. He turned to find the man in the suit rounding the corner of the building. Maves looked past him but there was no sign of his blonde-haired companion.

He motioned toward the archway with a nod of his head and Maves followed him back inside. Singing drifted from the churchyard as if putting voice to his many questions. Lighting a cigarette, the man studied him through a cloud of blue smoke.

"His name is not actually Muntz, you know," he finally said, seeming to read Maves' thoughts. "He's an undercover agent that infiltrated the Guatemalan gang network before he started working on a cancer medication scam out of Mexico. As a goodwill gesture to Guatemala, he was assigned to protect an informant, the young woman with you now."

"He killed a man at my home."

"As I said, his job was to protect her." He removed his sunglasses. "I can assure you the incident has already been made to disappear."

"What else don't I know?"

He dropped the cigarette and crushed it with the toe of his shoe, then pulled a handkerchief from his coat pocket, bent and wiped away the telltale ash.

"I'd like to show you something." He waved the cloth at the street corner. "It's only a couple of blocks from here."

Maves pointed a finger in his face. "You need to tell me who you are."

"It's best to leave names out of this business."

"The last time I heard that," he grumbled, "things didn't turn out so well."

"Let's just say I work for the federal government." He replaced his sunglasses and pulled a badge from his coat pocket, flipping it open. "I can assure you there's no danger in taking a short stroll with me."

Maves considered telling him of Blanca's involvement in the medication theft but instead nodded his willingness to go along. Minutes later they stopped before the town cemetery. Scattered with hedgerows, the green expanse ended in a brush-choked creek. A gravel road stretched between the gravestones.

He led Maves along the narrow path in silence. A murmur of voices drifted over the bushes. Moments later a small crowd appeared midway down a row, a mound of fresh dirt before them.

The man slipped behind a nearby hedge. Maves moved next to him, wondering why he had brought him there. He studied the mourners. Except for a single gray-clad nun, all were young women.

"Who are they?" He said, facing the man.

"Refugees," he whispered, "mostly from Guatemala."

"They have some connection to Frida?"

263

He pointed his chin at gravesite. "Take a look at the marker."

Maves squinted into the midday light, blinked and looked again. Cast in shadow, Blanca's name reached across the smooth stone in deeply etched letters. He turned away, unable to face the reality of her death.

"She was helping in a sting operation that went bad," the man continued. "We caught her selling stolen cancer medication. As part of a plea bargain, she agreed to lure her contacts here for an exchange, cash for medication.

"What we didn't know was that the cartel planned to take over the cancer drug business by eliminating her. Their mistake was in killing the priest in the process. On the other hand, that exploding car was a beautiful sight."

"I suppose helping refugee women was just a smokescreen for the smuggling." Maves muttered, suddenly feeling exhausted.

"No, that was legit."

"She helped those women," he said in disbelief, "at the same time she was stealing medication from kids who would die without it?"

"I've seen stranger things in my business. People are complicated."

He lit another cigarette and pulled an envelope from his coat.

"These were in the package we confiscated. I'd appreciate it if you'd pass them on. They're the young woman's medical school transcripts."

Maves glanced at Blanca's gravestone. All at once he wanted to flee, to free himself from her memory, from the oppressive hope of gaining her favor that had so long followed him. He took the papers and without a word started for the gate.

Moments later he rounded a corner and the church came into view. Backlit by a slanting sun, the stained glass windows vibrated with color. Above them the bronze bell swung in a smooth arc, echoing along the street, the nearby buildings multiplying its resonant tone into a ringing choir.

The cemetery crowd had dwindled to a few small groups huddled between the gravestones. Frida stood at the fence watching as he crossed the street toward her. Even from a distance he could see the glisten of her red-rimmed eyes.

"Please forgive me," she called, blinking back tears. "I can't help crying when I hear church bells. They remind me of the father I never knew. Mother said he loved the sound."

He wondered if Zak had been right in keeping their kinship secret. In any event, he would honor his promise not to tell. He nodded toward the gate.

"Will you come with me?"

"I was so caught up in the service I didn't realize you had left," she said as they weaved among the gravestones. "Where did you go?"

"I went to see Blanca's grave."

She stopped with a gasp. "Oh Maves, she has died also?"

He managed a nod as he approached Zak's grave, its proximity somehow easing the reality of her death. Taking a breath, he told Frida all he had heard. She stood listening, her gaze distant.

"If not for Blanca I also might be in a grave somewhere," she said as if talking to herself. "It is difficult to think badly of her."

"You might think otherwise if you'd seen those dying children," he admitted with regret. "I confess I had trouble facing the truth about her. But that's over and done with now. We have to move on."

In a sudden moment the sun slipped behind a wall of clouds, casting the cemetery in shadow and dimming the stained glass windows to a dull gray. Thunder thumped in the distance. Her eyes grew dark with feeling.

"I too have a confession," she started. "I was less than truthful with you earlier."

She avoided his gaze as he waited for her to continue.

"I don't know if I can tell you," she whispered, putting a hand to her mouth, "without crying."

He moved nearer and reached out a tentative hand then dropped it. She looked up at him, taking a ragged breath.

"I passed my board exams, Maves."

"But that's good news…" he paused, realizing there was more, "isn't it?"

"And I have accepted a job in an El Paso hospital," she continued, blinking back tears. "They're badly in need a bilingual pediatrician. It all happened so fast. I start in less than a week. You understand, don't you, Maves?"

He could only nod, his throat clinched with emotion. A profound sadness settled over him as he watched her wander among the markers. His gaze drifted to the twin towers, the bronze bell shining dully in the fading light. Thunder rumbled overhead. Seconds later the first drops of rain began splattering the headstones in dark splotches. Facing Zak's grave, he made a silent promise to do his best to help her.

Chapter Thirty

Webb paused at the living room doorway and Frida's absence settled over him, sharp and unavoidable in the over-quiet stillness. Their parting had been tense and awkward, his renewed dream of winning her affection crashing up against the demands of her new life. Standing at the top of the stairs, she had turned to face him. A cab stood idling below the porch.

"Why won't you let me take you to the airport?" He gestured down the stairs to a faded red pickup. "It isn't much to look at but it gets the job done."

"Please try to understand, Webb. I need to handle things for myself now."

"But it's not too late to change your mind, Frida. You could find work here. I'm sure of it."

She touched his arm lightly.

"Please don't make this any harder than it is."

"I still don't understand why you have to go so far away," he muttered.

"But think of it, Webb," she continued, unable to contain her excitement. "After what happened with Zak and Blanca, there's a kind of poetry in working at a children's hospital, don't you think?"

"I just thought since your husband... I thought you might see things differently."

"Oh Webb, I..."

A car horn blared, cutting out her voice. He started to speak but the horn blared again, breaking the spell of his daydream. He blinked away the memory. The van sat idling in the driveway. With a tinge of satisfaction, he imagined Maves sitting behind the steering wheel muttering to himself. For reasons he could not explain, he had agreed to accompany him on a return trip to Quintero.

Two hours later the tan buildings marking the border town appeared above the highway like loaves of fresh-baked bread. Maves angled the van before the twin-towered church, the stucco walls blinding white beneath the crystalline light of early autumn. He climbed out and squinted up at the massive bell, recalling the first time he had stepped onto that walkway. The man he had been that day now seemed an apparition, no more known to him than a complete stranger.

The arched wooden doors to the chapel creaked open and a young priest stepped through. A starched clerical collar gripped his neck. He motioned them inside with a stiff wave.

Maves started up the walkway at a brisk pace. His memories of the shooting still raw, he wanted to complete the business and be on his way. Webb struggled to keep up.

"What is it we're here to see?" he said between breaths. Maves had been typically vague about the trip.

"The new priest found a letter with my name on it tucked away inside Zak's Bible."

"What would he write and not want to tell you himself? You were one of the last people to see him alive."

Maves winced at hearing the words. "Whatever it is, the priest felt he should deliver it in person."

They stepped into the dim light of the sanctuary. The young man waited in the foyer, an envelope in his hand. His pinched face held the false certainty of a zealot.

"Father Zakros was hardly a model priest," he stated flatly, "but we have managed to settle his affairs without additional scandal. We are passing this note along in the hope there will be nothing more to tarnish to the church's image."

"A man dies and you're thinking about your reputation?" Maves grumbled.

"Saint Paul tells us," he continued, his tone patronizing, "the wages of sin is death."

"So much for forgiveness," Webb quipped.

"Forgiveness comes through prayer." A forced smile crossed his lips as he held out the envelope. "The church fathers want to put the unfortunate business to rest as soon as possible. Whatever you choose to do with this, we trust you will be discreet."

Maves felt the burn of anger rush across his brow. He pointed a finger into the man's face.

"Your so-called unfortunate business was the death of my friend," he barked. "And I don't give a damn about the rest."

"There is no need for rudeness," he said, taking a step back.

"You and your fathers can go back to your praying or whatever it is you do." Maves snapped the letter from his hand. "Just leave me the hell out of it."

He slammed through the double doors and paused on the walkway, squinting into the brilliant sunlight. Not two blocks away the border bridge hummed with traffic. A blurred image of Blanca, her hair matted with blood, flashed through his thoughts.

He swayed in the fuming heat, dazed by the vision. The street stood silent and pale before him, as if the land had been drained of sound and color. Then Webb's hand landed on his shoulder, breaking the trance. He motioned at the envelope.

Following his gaze, Maves blinked and raised the letter to the light, pinching the coarse paper between his fingers, unsure whether to open it. A part of him wished he could go to the bridge, drop it over the edge and walk away. Knowing the contents will change nothing, he told himself.

Instead he took a breath, determined to finish the job, and slipped his thumb beneath the flap. The single sheet of paper within held the address of a Mexican bar. Beneath the address was a name in Zak's slanting scrawl, the name of Blanca's daughter.

He started for the border at once. Webb hurried alongside, saying nothing. He knew better than to ask questions when Maves had that look.

269

They rounded a corner and the plaza came into view. The bustling border stood just beyond. Maves crossed at a brisk pace, his eyes locked on the bridge. Moments later they passed into Mexico. He paused to survey the scene.

Winding away from them at a severe angle, a narrow street crowded with shops and cafés disappeared between a clutch of low-slung buildings, their pockmarked brick facades dusted with a fine layer of sand. A man squatted alongside an abandoned shop, a prosthetic leg propped next to him. His cloudy eyes rolled at their approach.

Spread before him, a woven blanket lay scattered with beaded necklaces, earrings and bracelets. Raising a half-completed rosary into the air, he shook the rose-hued beads into a light clatter of wood on wood. Maves paused and pulled a wad of dollar bills from his pocket, slipping three into the man's hand.

Webb watched with surprise. Eyes darting, the man patted the cloth with his palm, quickly locating a rosary and fingering the length before raising it. Maves took the necklace and slipped it into his shirt pocket, turned and started again.

Slit-eyed men glared at them from shop doorways. Otherwise, the streets stood quiet. The few passersby hurried along as if trying to avoid notice, their eyes to the ground. A sense of something amiss gathered in Maves' gut.

The street narrowed to a mere alleyway. Shuttered buildings loomed over the cramped space, dimming the air to a transparent indigo, a veil of blue haze. Outside a butcher shop's open door, bits of trash and blood-tinged chicken feathers swirled together in a gruesome ballet.

Opposite the shop a scattering of wrought iron tables and chairs fronted a low-roofed café crossed by a line of leaded windows. Neon lights glimmered behind the thick panes like dying stars. A sign above the entrance read 'Mercedes Bar' in ornate gold lettering.

Maves checked the letter again before crossing the street and stepping up to a roughhewn door painted the color of ripe plums. A web of iron bars crossed the door's single, high window. He pushed through and motioned Webb to follow.

Other than the two of them, the place appeared empty. Halfway across the dim interior he paused and turned a slow circle. Judging by the name, he had expected a rough, hard-drinking bar, with patrons to match. Instead, the paneled walls and ceiling gave the room a look and feel of a posh club. Leather booths and oak tables crowded the hardwood floor, their polished tops glowing with lighted candles in spite of the early hour.

Webb brushed past him and sat at the brass-topped bar. A tarnished mirror above the counter held a distorted view of the room behind him. Carved angels sat perched atop the wooden frame, their palms together as if praying for the lives of the sinners below. Maves climbed onto the stool beside him and squinted up at them.

"More angels," he grumbled. "I've had enough of saints, angels and praying to last a lifetime."

"Then why'd you buy that rosary?"

"I figured we could use the luck."

"The one-legged man who made it wasn't so lucky," he quipped.

"You just look for bad news, don't you?"

"You need a drink."

Webb pounded the counter with his palm and peered into the reflection. The room stood empty.

"Why is there no one here?" he mused. "It must be getting close to the lunch hour."

Still angry over the priest's words, Maves ignored him.

"That two-faced weasel of a priest got under my skin," he continued. "If there's one thing I can't stand it's talking down a man when he he's no longer around to defend himself. That's nothing more than cowardice."

271

"Now it's me who needs a drink. Besides, that's just politics as usual. Churches aren't exempt from shady maneuvering."

"Well, I've had enough of shady maneuvering to last two lifetimes." He sat up. "I'm about ready to take matters in my own hands."

He leaned across the counter, stretching to reach the beer cooler beyond. Webb glanced behind them.

"I don't like the sound of that, Maves."

"Since we can't seem to get noticed around here, I believe I'll help myself to some refreshment."

"Hold on, Maves," he whispered. "I'm not too keen on doing time in a Mexican jail."

He had just managed to slide open the beer cooler when a middle-aged woman with a mane of black hair emerged from an adjacent door, bottles of wine cradled in her arms. Seeing him stretched across the counter, she paused in mid-step. Webb grabbed his belt, jerking him back onto the stool.

She started again and slipped behind the counter without a word, storing bottles and stacking glasses as if she had seen nothing. Watching her Maves had a vague feeling of recognition, a troubling sense of intimacy where none should be. He pulled the letter from his pocket and spread the paper on the countertop, smoothing it flat as he tried to clear his mind of the distraction.

She looked up and then away, briefly locking eyes with him. In that instant, he thought he spotted a hint of fear in her dark eyes, eyes strange yet somehow familiar. She glanced at the exit and backed away from the counter.

"If it is payment you want," she announced, her accent thick, "I have no money. You can tell your bosses the killing of a priest so close to the border has ruined our cafe. There is nothing left for the cartels."

"We're just..." he started.

"No one will drink here for fear our town is under some curse, the spirit of the priest seeking revenge on the sinners among us, they say." She snorted in disgust. "The superstitions of people are matched only by the weakness of their minds. For myself, I believe in the living of life and nothing more. Well, that and a little tequila to ease the hardness of this world."

"Speaking of tequila," Webb jumped in, "any chance we can get a beer?"

"We need to stick to the matter at hand, Webb," Maves grumbled.

"I don't know about any matter," he replied dismissively, "since you never bothered to tell me what's in the letter."

"You never asked."

"I know better than to ask when you get that look."

"I was about to explain."

"Sure you were."

She set two beers before them and leaned her arms on the counter.

"You argue like family. Something tells me you are not of the cartel."

"We're just trying to find someone." Maves tapped a finger on the letter. "And we were given this address."

"Here, people are hard to find. Since the killing of the priest, the cartels have been fighting over territory, and now there is talk the government will close the border." She pointed her chin at the paper. "Who is it you look for?"

"She's a young girl of fifteen or so."

"A young girl, you say? How do you know this girl?"

"She's the daughter of a friend."

"Does this friend have a name?"

"Blanca Munoz."

Her eyes flickered with recognition.

"That is very strange," she said, pondering his answer. "And the girl's name?"

"Estela Munoz," he answered, troubled by her questioning.

"And you say this Estela Munoz is her daughter?"

"That's right. She's a girl of fourteen or fifteen with pale blue eyes."

"She told you this?"

He nodded.

"But I am Estela Munoz."

"I don't understand." He sat back, confounded by her reply.

"Blanca is my sister."

"She never mentioned a sister," he said to himself, realizing at once why she seemed familiar. He looked up at her. "Then you know where I can find her child?"

"She had no children."

"She told me she had a daughter."

"Children were always too messy for her."

"She said she had to return home in shame because she wasn't married when she got pregnant."

He tried to corral his racing thoughts. She studied him a moment.

"You know her well?"

"I used to think so."

"Then you know to believe nothing," she said, spitting the words, "nothing that comes from her mouth."

"Maybe she had a child and never told you."

"No, that is not possible." She motioned to the letter. "Who gave you this paper?"

"A priest, the one who was killed, left it for me."

"Ah, I see." She peered at him, her dark eyes softening. "You believed you were sent here to find a girl, Estela Munoz. Instead, you were sent here to find the truth."

An hour later they walked together along crooked streets now nearly empty, making their way back to the border bridge. The blinding midday sunlight had given way to a cloud-strewn sky split by distant lightning. Scattered raindrops slapped the pavement, steaming off the street into a low haze.

274

Maves absently watched as a man with no legs pushed toward them on a plywood cart fitted with roller skates. The hard wheels clattered along the pitted street like cheap castanets. Scraping the asphalt in a halting rhythm, the man's calloused knuckles reminded him of Zak's gnarled boxer's hands.

A figure appeared from between two buildings, a girl of no more than fifteen in platform heels and miniskirt. Her flimsy blouse covered nothing. Pursing her over-red lips, she whistled lightly, motioning them over with a quick jerk of her head.

He turned away, scarcely able to believe what he now knew as truth. The daughter Blanca claimed had been nothing more than a lie to gain his favor. Even Zak had fallen for the ruse. At least he could find some small comfort knowing he was not the lone victim of her manipulations.

They crossed the Mexican side of the bridge and into the crowded customs house. Tourists holding overfilled gift bags and bottles of liquor stood in restless lines. Young men in flopping sombreros, red-faced from cheap tequila, slurred a litany of offers to disinterested coeds.

Within minutes, they stood before a uniformed customs agent. A sharp nose jutted from his otherwise affable face like a ship's prow. He pointed his chin at the young men.

"Those kids are lucky to have had their fun. The cartels are in a turf war so the higher ups have ordered the border closed on both sides. No telling what'll happen before it's all over."

"We appreciate the heads up," Maves said distractedly, his mind still back at the bar.

"You men are wise to travel together. Going it alone is too risky. In any event, I'd steer clear of the river for awhile."

Maves thanked him again and they moved back into the cloud-dimmed daylight. He glanced at Webb, suddenly grateful for his companionship. He had put his life on hold, doing all he asked and more. And his easy way with Ewan, gentle yet firm, had been a pleasant surprise. Yet he had never told him so.

"Well, I guess it's just the two of us again," he said in his cryptic manner.

Webb paused and eyed him, guessing at his meaning.

"Not quite," he replied in a hopeful tone. "You still have Ewan around the office."

"Nope, he's gone to work for the judge."

"Can you blame him?"

"I'll admit she's better looking."

"And he won't be sewing up bovine privates."

Maves took a breath, determined to speak his mind.

"What I mean to say, Webb, is that I'm glad you were with me today, today and all throughout these last months, but especially today."

Webb stood speechless, surprised by his father's openness.

"She had lied to you before, Maves," he finally said. "Why was this any different?"

"I suppose hearing her own sister talk about her that way made it real. From the very beginning Blanca used my guilt over Riley's death to hide what she was really up to. And like a fool, I was blind to it."

"You loved her?"

"I believed so," he admitted, the words bitter in his throat, "and you and your mother paid for my mistake."

"A wise man once said a man is more than the sum of his mistakes."

"Who was that, Aristotle?"

"No, some old horse doctor by the name of Van Horn."

"I was probably just making excuses," he muttered.

They started along the bridge again. Ahead of them the young men circled the coeds, flinging their sombreros into the air in a fruitless attempt to impress. A gathering stream of workers filled the opposite sidewalk, hurrying to cross back into Mexico before the border closing. Maves paid them little notice, his thoughts elsewhere.

In a blur of movement Webb moved past him, grabbing his arm and jerking him around to face the street. Before them the mass of people surged forward. He pointed a finger into the crowd, first to one spot then the other. Maves squinted into melee.

An immense man in a loose-fitting suit stumbled over the curb, jostling the nearby walkers and scattering them into the street. In the open space a figure appeared, a small woman in a tight dress and oversized sunglasses, black hair framing her clay-colored face with a mass of curls. Unable to speak Maves watched her pass, the curve of her hips, the shape of her mouth hauntingly familiar.

Webb dragged him across the bridge and into the fast-moving flow, dodging bicycles and mopeds. The woman appeared and disappeared before them like fish in a stream. With the mass of people squeezing into the smaller and smaller space of the customs entrance, they could make little headway. Maves fought his way forward.

In a sudden shift the crowd parted again and the woman appeared to his right, the space between them only yards wide. She turned, startled by the sudden change, and stood facing him. Even with sunglasses on, the surprise on her face was clear.

As quickly as it opened the space closed again. He clawed through the mass of bodies, struggling to keep her in view. Ahead of him a whistle rattled in three short bursts. Seconds later the khaki uniform of the federal police flashed between the moving figures, scattering the crowd.

The officer raised a hand, stopping him. The man's broad face held no welcome.

"The border, it is closed," he announced with an official air. He waved a finger through the air. "We have much trouble from the cartel."

"But I saw someone…"

He could feel Webb's panting breath on his shoulder. The officer stepped nearer.

"The border is closed," he repeated, his voice rising above the clamoring crowd.

"I just need to…"

"You are not of Mexico," he barked. He thrust a hand over Maves' head, pointing him down the bridge. "You must go."

Maves ignored him, craning his neck and searching the crowd, finally glimpsing her near the customs house exit. She seemed to hesitate, half-turning and casting a quick glance over her shoulder. Then she slipped through the doorway and into the jostling throng. Unable to move, he stood with his eyes fixed to the spot.

Thunder rolled overhead. He blinked, slowly coming out of his trance. The officer's rancid breath burned his nostrils. He glared at Maves and spit into the street, moving a hand to his holster. Maves glared back.

Suddenly Webb's hand was on his shoulder and he found himself moving backwards through the dwindling passersby. Uncaring, he stumbled along. The officer and customs house receded from view. The bridge stood nearly empty.

Webb dropped his hand and Maves turned to face the town. A sudden wind coursed over the bridge, flinging a wall of sand into the air. Seconds later a paint horse emerged from the river. Clambering up the grass-covered slope, the mare paused, wild-eyed and panting. Thunder rumbled past again.

She hesitated, quivering and dark with sweat. Her eyes rolled at the swirling gusts. Tossing her head back, she jumped the curb in a blur of tan and white.

In seconds, she had reached the plaza, scattering sightseers as she raced across the cobblestones and past the obelisk. Then as suddenly as she had appeared she vanished down a narrow alley, leaving only the fading echo of clattering hooves.

Maves watched after her, thinking of the strange and unexpected turns a life can take. A smattering of raindrops peppered the sidewalk. Beyond the plaza the twin bell towers rose above the rooftops, pearl-like against the angry sky. A shaft of sunlight split the clouds, falling across the rooftops in a jagged line. The church's bronze bell glimmered briefly.

Oblivious of the coming rain, the young men gathered about the coeds. Their awkward laughter drifted on the restless breeze, coming and going like a seabird's call. Maves watched them cut their eyes at each other, shifting from foot to foot, unsure yet hopeful. Then he nodded to Webb and they started homeward again, walking together, saying nothing, the sound of their own footsteps enough.

www.ingramcontent.com/pod-product-compliance
Lightning Source LLC
Chambersburg PA
CBHW020243180626
46810CB00006B/2336